Dashiki

Dashiki

A Cozy Mystery

Florence Wetzel

© 2025 Florence Wetzel

All rights reserved.

Second edition. Originally published in 2011 by Writer's Club Press as *Dashiki*.

Any resemblance to actual people and events is purely coincidental. This is a work of fiction.

No part of this book may be reproduced or transmitted in any form or by any means, graphic, electronic, or mechanical, including photocopying, recording, taping, or by any information storage retrieval system, without permission in writing from the author.

Cover design and artwork by Henry Chen.

Feel free to contact the author at florencewetzel@yahoo.com.

ISBN: 9798328135238

Dedicated to my mother,
Marion Daisy Wetzel,
who passed on to me
her love of reading mysteries

"Murder, I have often noticed,
is a great matchmaker."

Hercule Poirot,
The A.B.C. Murders by Agatha Christie

Contents

Tuesday August 5, 2003 11

Wednesday August 6, 2003 87

Thursday August 7, 2003 143

Friday August 8, 2003 213

Monday August 11, 2003 251

Afterword 301

Acknowledgments 303

Stay in Touch 305

Tuesday
August 5, 2003

What am I supposed to do with this information?

That was the question Virginia Farrell asked herself as the door to 1305 Bloomfield shut behind her. She stood in the building's bare concrete courtyard, facing Bloomfield Street in the mile-square city of Hoboken, New Jersey.

Due to half-Irish, half-Spanish genetics, Virginia had shoulder-length auburn hair and light-olive skin. Her coloring tended to show her emotions for all to see, and that moment she could feel her cheeks flushing deeply.

Virginia pressed a hand to her chest. She needed to calm down and think logically.

"OK," she said aloud to herself. "You were given two pieces of information. One can wait until later, but you need to deal with the other one right now."

A wave of happiness surged through her. She thought again of what she had just seen. Tapes. From the historic 1957 Thelonious Monk–John Coltrane gig at the Five Spot in New York City. Recorded by Naima Coltrane and thought to be lost forever. Certainly the greatest discovery in jazz since—well, since Henry Grimes was found living in a hotel in Los Angeles after he'd been presumed dead for the past thirty years.

These tapes were not only a great discovery for jazz, but for music and people everywhere. Virginia's mission was to bring the news to the world.

But she couldn't do it alone, and she knew exactly who she needed to contact: Nathan Garrideb and John Upgrove. Nathan first, since he was a closer friend and worked right here in Hoboken.

"Excuse me," she called out to a passing woman. "Do you have the time?"

"Three on the dot."

"Thanks."

Virginia adjusted the straps on her knapsack. She could just make her 5 p.m. bus if she walked fast. This was news she wanted to give in person.

Virginia hurried past stately brownstones and turned left onto Frank Sinatra Drive, a scenic road near the old Maxwell House Coffee factory. She continued down to the Hudson River, eventually passing Frank Sinatra Park as she moved quickly along the waterfront.

The pleasant path was lined with trees and dotted with benches, the breeze off the river drifting softly through the air. The early August day was comfortably hot, and the waterfront was full of people relaxing in the sunshine, exercising their dogs, or taking a walk like Virginia.

Although no one else matched Virginia's purposeful stride. She was on a mission, and heaven help anyone who got in the way of the five-foot redhead propelling herself down the shady pathway.

Nathan worked at 111 River Street, one of the swank office buildings constructed in the late nineties as part of Hoboken's waterfront redevelopment. When Virginia entered the cavernous marble lobby and presented herself at the security desk, she saw the guard's watch: 3:25. She hastily signed her name and the time in a black logbook, then headed for the elevators.

Impatience rushed through her every time the elevator stopped to let out her fellow passengers. Finally the doors opened onto the seventh floor. She hurried out and ran toward the glass doors that announced *Jazz Now* in jaunty black letters.

She waved at Maggie the receptionist, then made a right and headed to Nathan's office. Previously located in dingy quarters in Manhattan's Chelsea neighborhood, *Jazz Now* had relocated to Hoboken six months previously. The carpets were mint green, the cream walls decorated with laminated album covers, and Louis Armstrong's "Cornet Chop Suey" wafted through the hallways. In fact, music was everywhere: each employee had a CD player in their office, and as Virginia barreled down the hall she heard bits of Jaco Pastorius, Billie Holiday, and Gary Peacock coming through the open doors.

Virginia was about to round the corner when Byron Ffowlkes came out of his office. He was the last person she wanted to see! Byron had bought *Jazz Now* a year before and installed himself as publisher, editor-in-chief, and resident know-it-all. Tall, dark, handsome, and English though he was, Virginia always thought he was rather cold, and nosy to boot.

Byron also had an affectation. Actually he had several, but the most glaring—literally—was his penchant for dressing all in one color, often in eye-popping hues like bright salmon or canary yellow. Today he was decked out in a turquoise suit, with an elegant little matching earring.

"Virginia!" he declared in his posh accent. "You look healthy. How are you?"

"Good," she answered breathlessly.

"On your way to see Nathan?"

"Yep."

"Very well. You know of course about the Rex Royal show at the Blue Note?"

"I do."

"Mortimer and I will be attending on Thursday. Late set of course. Shall we see you there?"

"I'm not sure of my plans yet. Maybe!"

Virginia gave a little wave and hurried off. Hopefully she had sounded casual, but that was unlikely considering she was panting and her cheeks were bright red.

But who cared about that when she was on the verge of making jazz history?

Nathan's door was open, and he was sitting at his desk marking up an article while Wardell Gray wailed from the stereo.

The office was a cozy disarray of jazz magazines, CDs, cassettes, and albums. Behind Nathan was a glorious view of the Hudson River and the Manhattan skyline. The wall on his left was nearly covered by a poster of the famous *A Great Day in Harlem* photograph, a 1958 group shot of dozens of jazz musicians gathered on the stoop of a Harlem brownstone.

"Nathan!" she exclaimed, shutting the door behind her.

"Virginia!" he replied with a laugh.

Nathan was tall with a ski-slope nose and long blond hair pulled back into a ponytail. He had a friendly, open face that radiated warmth and kindness. Virginia had met him about ten years before when he and his girlfriend moved to New York. She and Nathan kept bumping into each other at concerts, and it wasn't long before they recognized each other as fellow jazz geeks and became fast friends.

When *Jazz Now* offered Nathan a job, he immediately got Virginia work as a freelancer. As he rose up the magazine's ranks to his current position as managing editor, he remained the same: calm, trustworthy, and eminently sane.

"I have news," Virginia announced, dropping into a chair and setting her knapsack on the floor. "The biggest news ever."

Nathan leaned back in his chair. "Shoot."

She took a deep breath. "This afternoon, as you know, I had my interview with Betty Brown."

"Right. How'd it go?"

"Great, we really hit it off." Virginia leaned forward. "As you also know, Betty Brown used to babysit John Coltrane's stepdaughter in the 1950s. That's when Betty Brown was dating one of our favorite trumpeters, Shinwell Johnson."

"Right."

"But what you don't know is that one day while Betty Brown was babysitting at the Coltranes, Shinwell came by and stole something out of spite. A shoebox."

"OK. What was inside?"

"Tapes," Virginia said, her eyes sparkling. "From the Five Spot gig."

He sat up straight. "Go on."

"Betty Brown broke up with Shinwell because of that," Virginia continued. "She got back with him some years later, and when he died in 1969, Betty Brown took the tapes. And guess what? She still has them."

Nathan's mouth dropped open. "You're sure?"

Virginia beamed. "I saw them."

He pulled over a pad of yellow paper and started writing furiously. "Tell me exactly what you saw."

"Tapes. The old ones, the little mini reel-to-reels. Most in flat white boxes, a few not. Some were labeled. Dates, not names."

"The dates match the six months of the Five Spot gig?"

"I read the labels on about three of them, and yes, they did."

"How many tapes in total?"

Virginia wrinkled her nose. "It was a pretty big box. Like for a man's shoes." Her eyes lit up. "Maybe Coltrane's!"

Nathan bit his lip. "John Coltrane's shoebox," he said reverentially.

"The tapes were a bit haphazard. I don't think Betty Brown ever even touched them. I'd guess there were about a dozen tapes, maybe more."

"Seemed to be in good shape?"

"They looked fine to me."

Nathan stared at her. "This is not a joke. You're telling me the truth."

Virginia was so happy she was ready to cry. "I saw them with my own two eyes."

"My God!" he said. "This is huge! What happens now?"

"Here's the thing. Betty Brown feels horrible that she didn't say anything to the Coltranes at the time, or anyone else all these years. But it's different now because—well, Betty Brown has cancer. She told me she's dying."

Nathan grimaced. "I'm sorry."

"Me too. She wants to set things right before she passes and asked me to help her."

"So what are you going to do?"

Virginia raised her eyebrows. "Talk to you."

Nathan laughed. "That's a good start."

"And contact John over at the Institute of Jazz Studies and ask him to keep the tapes safe for us. We also need to get in touch with Monk's and Coltrane's closest relatives."

"That would be Monk's son T. S. Monk and Coltrane's second wife Alice."

"You can get their numbers?"

Nathan patted his Rolodex. "I have them right here. So tell me, where are the tapes now?"

"Still at Betty Brown's."

His eyes flashed with panic. "The apartment building could burn down tonight!"

Virginia shook her head. "That is not going to happen. Betty Brown has held on to those tapes for over thirty years. Another day won't make a difference."

Nathan drew a long breath. "It's hard to know what to do."

"We don't have to do anything right now. Just think about it. Talk things over with Melissa tonight if you want, but no one else. I'll call you tomorrow morning, then I'll phone John to see what he thinks."

"OK. You're 100 percent sure Betty Brown said we can take the tapes?"

"Definitely. She wants to clear this up before she dies. I'm supposed to call her tomorrow morning with a plan, so how about I tell her you'll come by to pick up the tapes?"

"That would make me feel better."

"But I still think we should sleep on it. This is a sensitive matter."

"You're right." Nathan ran a hand over his hair. "I need to go on a walk and get some fresh air."

Virginia glanced at the clock on the bookshelves: a few minutes to four. "And I have to get my bus." She grabbed her knapsack from the floor. "I'll call you first thing tomorrow. Remember, mum's the word."

"Alrightee. Thanks for including me on this."

She waved a hand. "Don't be ridiculous! Who else would I tell?"

Virginia rushed out of *Jazz Now* and hopped into the elevator. After signing out at the security desk, she hurried to the PATH station just a block away, where a bus for New York was about to leave. She paid the fare and settled into a seat.

By the time Virginia arrived at her gate in Port Authority, it was ten minutes to five. Bill, her favorite bus driver, was standing by the door taking tickets.

"Hey there!" he called out in his booming voice. "Going home?"

"Yep," Virginia answered. "It's been a long day."

Bill tore a ticket from her commuter pack and gallantly waved her onto the bus. She sank into a seat, and at exactly five o'clock, the bus roared off to the Catskill Mountains.

Detective Robert Smith sat at his desk in the bullpen of the Hoboken police station, catching up on paperwork.

Or at least trying to, because Detective Tony Oliveto was sitting at the desk next to him, munching on a doughnut while flicking paper clips into an empty coffee mug. Tony was all caught up on his paperwork. So he claimed.

"You know what your trouble is?" Tony said suddenly. "When it comes to women?"

Robert looked up. He was tall and thin with angular features, dark-brown eyes, and light-brown hair receding at the temples. "Do I have a choice about hearing this?"

"Nope. You need some advice." Tony, a short, plump man with heavy features and thick black hair, leaned toward Robert's desk. "Your trouble is you don't talk."

Robert frowned. "I talk."

"You think? Take that nice lady at my ma's on Sunday. You didn't say two words to her."

Sunday dinner at Mama Oliveto's apartment at 327 Grand Street had been a tradition for Robert ever since he and Tony joined the force five years ago. Also traditional were the single females who suddenly turned up and were always seated next to Robert.

Including this latest young woman. She had been nice, Robert supposed, and rather pretty. Plus she mentioned several times how exciting it must be to work as a cop. Most women found Robert's job sufficient reason to reject him, so he had been intrigued. But when she asked to play with his gun, that crossed the line.

"I talked to her," Robert said.

"But not the kind of talk ladies like. They love hard-luck stories. They go wild for guys with a sensitive heart."

Robert thought a moment. He had heard the sort of stories Tony told women. "Doesn't pretending to have a sensitive heart mean you don't actually have one?"

"That's why you never get the ladies. You're too old-fashioned." Tony regarded him with pity. "When's the last time you had a girlfriend?"

Robert stared at him.

"OK," Tony said. "Here's an easier question. When did you last go on a date?"

"I don't know. Three years ago?"

"What?! Jeez, this is an emergency."

"I haven't met the right person."

"Looking for Miss Right, Boberino? Allow me to pass on a little advice: there's Miss Right, and there's Miss Right Now. Know what I'm sayin'?"

Robert winced. I really am old-fashioned, he thought. He turned back to his paperwork, hoping Tony would take the hint.

Not that Robert disliked Tony. In fact, Tony was his closest friend in Hoboken. They had a great deal in common, particularly the fact that they both became Hoboken policemen rather late in life.

Robert had first worked on the force in New York City. He joined immediately after college and quickly reached his goal as homicide detective. Robert developed a reputation as the solver of unsolvable murders, and was often loaned out to other precincts. His nickname in the department was Sherlock, which gave him untold secret pleasure.

In his midthirties, Robert got tired of murders. He had yearned for excitement during his childhood in a small town in Kansas, but after fifteen years as a cop in New York City, he'd experienced enough adventure to last a lifetime.

He started eyeing Hoboken and wondering how he could transfer. The little city was just across the river from Manhattan, but it was so tame it was practically bucolic. Hoboken averaged about one murder a year, and they weren't the sort of deaths Robert was used to. More like a guy had a heart attack during a mugging and died three days later, which barely counted as a murder.

So at age thirty-five, Robert retook the civil service exam. Sitting next to him was Tony, a Hoboken fireman who also wanted a change. They were side by side at the exam, side by side while getting sworn in, side by side at the Police Academy in Sea Girt. They helped each other through their first year of training and subsequent years on their respective walking beats. Robert knew how to be a policeman, and Tony knew Hoboken, so they helped one another learn their jobs.

When Robert was appointed detective, Tony followed him a few months later. Now after five years on the force, they were practically brothers. If a tall, thin WASP could be related to a short, rotund Italian.

Nevertheless, certain of Tony's habits grated on Robert's nerves. When Robert decided to become a policeman, he made a solemn vow: no doughnuts. Whereas Tony had never met a doughnut he didn't like. Robert's other solemn vow occurred when he joined the Hoboken force: no Frank Sinatra. But that vow was not so easily kept.

"Say what you want about Hoboken," Tony often proclaimed, "but this city produced Mr. Francis Albert Sinatra, and you cannot make that claim about any other place on earth."

Robert watched himself sink helplessly into the stereotype of a Sinatra-loving Hoboken cop. Tony and a few other officers liked to play the music in the bullpen, which meant Sinatra began seeping into Robert's subconscious. One day he found himself humming Sinatra in the shower, a few weeks later he rented *From Here to Eternity*, and soon after he visited Sinatra's birthplace at 415 Monroe Street.

The final straw came one day as Robert and Tony were cruising merrily along Frank Sinatra Drive singing "Me and My Shadow." That's when Robert understood that it was too late. His fate was sealed, and to mark the occasion he bought his first Sinatra CD. Oh well, Robert thought. If he and Tony had to share a stereotype, better Sinatra than doughnuts.

So working with Tony was fine. Except for the advice.

"You know," Tony said, giving Robert the once-over. "Wouldn't hurt to do a bit more with your appearance. Take your hair. Little mousse might not be a bad thing."

"I never think about my hair."

"It kinda shows. But if you want a beautiful lady, you gotta be a beautiful guy."

Tony ran a hand over his own hair, which was thick, black, and astonishingly vertical. Robert had to admit that Tony did date quite a number of attractive women. Often simultaneously.

"Beautiful women make me nervous," Robert said.

"You gotta know how to approach them. And believe me, beautiful ladies want to be approached. It just takes some style. A little finesse. And you, my friend—" He shook his head.

It never boded well when Tony called Robert "my friend."

"Don't get me wrong," Tony went on. "You're a good-lookin' guy. You got that tall, lanky thing, and the ladies like that. I myself do fine, but I wouldn't say no to bein' a few inches taller."

Robert looked at the clock. Five-thirty. Only half an hour more, and then he could go home.

"Furthermore," Tony said. "Your clothes. You oughta—"

"Smith, Oliveto!"

They looked up and saw Captain Kelly rushing over to their desks.

"Sir?" Robert said.

"Homicide at 1305 Bloomfield. Uniform's there now, get going."

Tony took a camera and fingerprinting set from his desk. As the two men grabbed their jackets, they exchanged a puzzled glance. Homicide—in Hoboken?

"**N**ame's Baseema Baheera," an officer said as Robert and Tony rushed up to the door of 1305 Bloomfield, after double-parking behind an ambulance and a squad car. "Dead from a hit to the head. The kid in there found her."

He nodded toward a frightened-looking Black boy visible through the building's glass doors. A woman stood behind the boy with her hands resting on his shoulders, tears streaking her worried face.

Robert took in the scene outside the building. Neighbors and passers-by had gathered in the courtyard, chattering excitedly.

"Disperse the crowd," Robert instructed the officer. "Or at least get them on the sidewalk. And set up cones to redirect traffic. Where's the apartment?"

"First floor. Around the corner to the right, next to the elevator."

Robert and Tony entered the building and found the apartment. An officer had just finished securing yellow crime-scene tape across the door.

"I went in to check the body," the officer told Robert. "Otherwise nobody's touched anything."

"Good. Wait here for now."

"You want we should go in?" Tony asked.

Robert paused. He and Tony were the same rank, but since Robert had so much homicide experience, it made sense for him to take the lead. Although just for now: the procedure for violent crimes was that Hoboken uniform and detectives did the initial footwork, then turned everything over to the Hudson County Prosecutor's Office.

"Hold on," Robert said. "Let's talk to the witness first."

As they approached, the boy's eyes widened with fear. Robert smiled to reassure him.

"It's all right, son," he said, kneeling in front of the boy. "You've done nothing wrong. What's your name?"

"Alex."

"All right, Alex. Why don't you tell us what you saw?"

The boy looked up at the woman, who inclined her head. He cleared his throat and said, "My mom, she asked me to check on Miss Baheera. 'Cause she's been sick, and we bring her food most days. I went over to see if she wanted some dinner."

"Go on," Robert said.

"I knocked, but no one answered. Miss Baheera sometimes didn't hear so good, so I tried the door. It was unlocked and I went in. I saw her on the floor. There was blood."

"Did you touch anything?"

Alex shook his head vehemently. "No, sir. I went right back and told my mom."

"And your apartment is—?"

"Next door," the mother said. She had a round, attractive face with liquid brown eyes. "We've been neighbors for years. We looked after Baseema, as much as she'd let us, especially when she got the cancer."

"You're the one who called 911?"

"Yes."

Robert turned back to the boy. "Alex, did you see anyone in the hallway or going into the elevator?"

He shook his head. "No, sir."

"Did you, ma'am?"

"No. It was quiet. At least then it was."

"How do you mean?"

"The walls here are thin. I had the radio playing, but throughout the afternoon I heard Baseema talking with someone, laughing now and then. That was unusual; she didn't get many visitors."

"No raised voices or sound of a struggle?"

"Not that I noticed. Like I said, I had the radio on. If the song was on the quiet side, I could pick up a bit from next door, but mostly I didn't hear too much."

"OK. Why don't you two go back to your apartment, and an officer will take your statements." Robert smiled encouragingly at the boy. "You did a good job, Alex."

"Officer?" the mother said. "I want you to know that Baseema was the most harmless creature on earth. I can't imagine why anyone would want to kill her."

"We're going to try to figure that out," Robert replied.

Together with Tony, he walked back to the apartment.

"Ready?" Tony said.

Robert gave a brief nod. "Ready."

Robert lifted the yellow tape. They ducked under it, and Tony pushed the door open with one hand. Robert took a deep breath and stepped into the apartment.

A short entry hall led into a small, square living room. To the left was a compact kitchen and an open door leading to a bathroom. On the right was a closed door, most likely the bedroom.

The living room had two windows, bookshelves, and framed pictures on the walls. A beige couch, a black-leather armchair, and a coffee table sat on light-blue carpeting. Near the front door, a small table held a black purse and a dish with keys.

And on the floor, a thin Black woman in a light-green dress and dark-blue headscarf lay face down. A wound on the back of her head had seeped blood onto the carpet.

Tony and Robert moved forward and knelt by the body. Robert reached out a hand and placed it gingerly on the woman's back.

"Still warm," he commented. "This happened less than an hour ago."

Tony nodded, not taking his eyes off the prone woman.

Robert eyed a thick glass vase on the coffee table. Blood stained the outside of the vase, and a crumpled napkin lay next to it.

"Looks like our weapon," Tony remarked.

Robert nodded. "And that napkin was probably used to wipe off the prints."

He looked around the apartment. It had been a hot, sunny day, and beams of light still shone through the two windows.

"OK," Robert said. "Go ahead with the photos and prints."

As Tony clicked away, Robert examined the room. The coffee table drew his attention a long time. The table held two teacups with spoons on the saucers, a white sugar bowl, a creamer of milk with a layer of film on top, and a stack of napkins. The vase, which judging by the layout of the cups had originally been the centerpiece, was near a corner.

There was also a piece of paper torn from a notebook with a name and number written in big letters:

VIRGINIA FARRELL
845-435-3191

Virginia said good night to Bill and stepped off the bus near her home. It wasn't an official stop, but Bill always did her a favor by pulling over next to the stream.

She walked over a small wooden bridge, breathing deeply and inhaling the clean, sweet air. The countryside was quiet, with colored strips of sunset nestled around the rounded green mountains.

Virginia's plan to think on the bus had not materialized. She had fallen asleep almost at once, a mix of waking up early and nervous exhaustion. Never mind. She would have a quick dinner, then go to her room, get under the covers, and mull everything over.

But as Virginia walked up the dirt path to her house, she saw a red pickup truck in the driveway. Which meant her roommate Socks had company. Oh well. As much as Virginia wanted to collapse into bed and ponder her day, part of her was thankful for the distraction.

Virginia and Socks lived in a roomy log cabin surrounded by trees, with a large meadow in back. They had met in the now-ancient 1980s when Socks was an actress and performance artist, and Virginia had interviewed her for an alternative newspaper. They had become fast friends, which was unusual for Virginia: never before and never since had she befriended someone she interviewed. But Socks was special.

She opened the door and heard Socks' lilting voice: "Not that being a beekeeper is without its problems. Buzz buzz!"

Virginia slipped off her shoes and hung up her knapsack. She loved coming home. The cozy living room had dark wooden paneling, a low-beamed ceiling, and a wood-burning stove. A quilt in rose, mauve, and ivory covered the main wall, with the other walls displaying Virginia's jazz memorabilia, alongside Socks' collection of framed dried flowers.

The room was dominated by two oversized dark-purple couches, piled with pillows and throws. The large oak coffee table held a colorful mix of teacups, knickknacks, and bowls of peanuts and popcorn. *Avalon* by Roxy Music played on the stereo, and the low lighting and lit candles gave the room a snug, soothing feeling.

Socks was curled up in a corner of one of the couches. Next to her at a polite distance was her friend Dr. Bundle. Socks wore a gold satin kimono, and her hair was piled into a large topknot held in place by chopsticks.

"Hi, Socks," Virginia said, flopping onto a couch. "Hey, Dr. Bundle."

Socks was perhaps the most physically perfect human Virginia had ever seen. Close to six feet, she had long, thick blonde hair framing strikingly symmetrical features, with large eyes in a most unusual charcoal gray. Virginia lived vicariously through Socks' height; it must be wonderful to be so tall.

Although only forty, Socks was already retired. She had left her acting career to marry a wildly successful Wall Street trader, but she tired of being married to a man who was married to his job, and they divorced several years later. Socks' ex-husband gave her an extremely generous settlement, and as a result Socks never had to work. So she didn't.

Socks moved upstate after her divorce and spent years trying to convince Virginia to join her. In early 2002, Virginia took the plunge and left Hoboken for the country. But although Socks had long ago turned her back on city life, Virginia still traveled down weekly. There was, after all, not much jazz in Little Mountain, New York.

"How did it go?" Socks asked eagerly.

"Really well," Virginia replied as she propped her feet on the coffee table.

"Did she like the honey?"

Although retired, Socks did take on the odd project now and then. Her good friend Hana was a beekeeper who sold jars of honey, and Socks decorated the labels with florid cursive writing and drawings of bees in bright Day-Glo colors.

"She loved it," Virginia smiled. "Did you know that 'Hana' means happiness in Arabic?"

"Ooh!" Socks exclaimed. "Hana will be thrilled."

"Who did you interview?" Dr. Bundle asked.

A few inches taller than Virginia, roly-poly with bright-red cheeks and a salt-and-pepper crew cut, Dr. Bundle was one of Socks' many admirers. Virginia thought he was the best of the lot: he had nice manners, a good sense of humor, and most importantly he loved jazz.

"Actually, V," Socks cut in. "Before you start—you had a mysterious male caller about an hour ago."

"Nathan?"

"I didn't recognize the voice, and he wouldn't give his name. Hence the mystery."

"What did you tell him?"

"I said you were probably on the bus home, and he should try again after eight-thirty."

A shiver ran down Virginia's neck. That was strange. Did the phone call have something to do with the tapes?

"So who did you interview?" Dr. Bundle asked again.

Virginia shook off the uneasy feeling. The phone call was surely nothing important. "That's her right there."

She pointed to an album cover on the wall. A beautiful Black woman with a huge Afro, wearing a brightly colored dashiki and black miniskirt, stood with hands on hips glaring at the camera. Multicolored bubbles floated around her, each containing a Black man with an equally huge Afro and a bright-blue trumpet raised to his lips.

Yellow letters near the top of the album proclaimed DASHIKI, and fuchsia letters along the bottom read SHINWELL JOHNSON AND THE FUNKY SENSATIONS.

Dr. Bundle's eyebrows went up in respect. "You're kidding!"

Virginia smiled. "It's true."

"Dang! How did you manage that?"

"I'd heard rumors for years that Betty Brown lived in Hoboken, and I always kept an eye out for her when I was living there. I even did a little research at City Hall, but I never found her. Then through a piece of luck, my editor Nathan found out where she lives. Turns out Betty Brown was in Hoboken all along, but she converted to Islam in the 1970s and had a different name."

"Like the saxophonist Gigi Gryce," Dr. Bundle mused. "He also converted to Islam and dropped out of sight."

"That's right!" Virginia said eagerly. "He became Basheer Qusim."

"Weren't there other musicians who did that?"

Socks, whose idea of hell was a conversation composed of obscure jazz facts, quickly changed the topic. "Betty Brown is the reason why Virginia and I became friends."

"How so?" Dr. Bundle asked.

"The first show Virginia saw me in had a whole homage to 'Dashiki.' But my Afro was bright red, and dancing around me were five men dressed only in trumpets. It was based on Betty Brown's performance on *The Mike Douglas Show* all those years ago. Did you ever see that episode?"

"Can't say I did," Dr. Bundle answered. "But of course I know the song. I heard it on the radio the other day, as a matter of fact."

"When I saw that show as a child," Socks said, "it blew my little suburban world apart. I said to myself, 'I want my life to be like that.'"

"I saw it too," Virginia chimed in. "My babysitter had it on, and I remember Betty Brown was so cool and funky. But I didn't want to be her, I just wanted to talk to her."

"So when did this interview come about?" Dr. Bundle asked.

"Very suddenly. Nathan called Betty Brown last week, and we booked a time today. I'm not doing too many articles nowadays since I'm working on my book, but I couldn't pass this up."

"How is the misty Miss Christy?"

"Wonderful," Virginia said. "As always."

Socks rolled her eyes. She was not fond of the subject of Virginia's book.

"I wish you could see her the way I do," Virginia sighed.

"You know I admire you," Socks said, "and I think the world of your writing. But sometimes I question your role models."

They both turned their heads to a framed photograph close to the stereo. A small woman wearing a black dress with a high neckline and full skirt stood in front of a microphone. She had blonde hair pulled back into a ponytail, with bangs that cut off abruptly in the middle of her forehead. Her face was twisted into a wry expression and she was—Virginia's favorite part—barefoot. June Christy, 1940s big band singer and 1950s hit solo artist.

"June is nothing but soul," Virginia said loyally.

"She looks like a Mouseketeer," Socks countered.

"The two things are not incompatible."

"It's not even so much how she looks, although that haircut has got to go. It's her songs; they're maudlin. What's that one line? About not drinking with strangers because she usually drinks alone?"

"That's from 'Something Cool.' It's her signature song."

Socks shook her head. "I'm not saying the music is good or bad. But if you listen to lyrics like that long enough, they're going to affect you. What do you want to be: forty and fabulous, or middle-aged and maudlin?"

Virginia looked at the ceiling. Dr. Bundle coughed.

"However," Socks said hurriedly, "I do love the song about mashed potatoes."

"Yes!" Virginia agreed eagerly. "That's 'Give Me the Simple Life.' I always sing that in the shower. Which reminds me, when are we going to the karaoke diner again?"

"The right time will reveal itself," Socks stated. "Until then—"

The CD whirred to a finish. Virginia looked at Socks expectantly; this was always a delicate moment.

"All right," Socks relented. "You may play jazz. But only Miles Davis."

Before Socks could change her mind, Virginia hurried to the stereo and put on *In a Silent Way*.

For all Socks' virtues, she had one horrible flaw: she did not like jazz. Hated it, even. Virginia worked hard to convert her, and in time Socks could bear a little Miles Davis and—if the mood was exactly right—early Louis Armstrong.

"My friend Hooper told me a story about Miles the other day," Dr. Bundle said, reaching out to grab a handful of popcorn.

Virginia's eyes lit up. "Tell us!"

"When Thelonious Monk died in 1982, Hooper went to the funeral in New York. It was crowded as all get-out, but he found an empty seat up front. Few minutes later, he feels a tap on his shoulder. He turns around, and it's Miles Davis."

"Ooh! What happened?"

"Miles says to him—" Dr. Bundle slipped into a low, gravelly voice— "'That's my seat.' So Hooper gets up and says, 'Mr. Davis, I'm sorry.' Miles looks at him and says, 'Don't be sorry. Be careful.'"

Virginia nodded. "Deep. Very deep."

"There has to be a perfect time and place to use that line," Socks remarked.

Virginia looked at her. "The right time will reveal itself."

The phone rang. Virginia looked at the clock: exactly 8:30.

"Must be the mystery man," Socks commented as she rose to answer. "At least he's punctual."

Dr. Bundle watched as Socks strolled into the kitchen. "Legs as long as a Michener novel," he murmured.

Virginia gave him a sympathetic look. "I think you need to take a number and get in line."

"No hope?"

"Her heart is a puzzle."

Dr. Bundle sighed wistfully.

"It's him," Socks declared as she walked back into the living room. "He'd like to speak to Miss Virginia Farrell, please."

"OK." Virginia got up and went into the kitchen. Painted a cheerful bright yellow, the room had jars of Hana's Honey lining the windowsills, their freshly drawn labels twinkling under the vintage ceiling lamp.

She picked up the landline receiver, which Socks had left resting on the table. "Hello?" she said cautiously.

"Virginia Farrell?" A man's voice, medium-deep. No one she knew.

"That's right."

"This is Detective Robert Smith from the Hoboken Police Department."

She frowned. "Can I help you?"

"I think you can. Did you by any chance see Baseema Baheera at 1305 Bloomfield Street today?"

"Baseema—oh, you mean Betty Brown! Yes, I did. I went to her apartment this afternoon. Is something wrong?"

"I'm afraid so. Miss Baheera has been murdered."

"What?!" Virginia gasped. "When?"

"Sometime this evening. I'd like to talk to you about your visit, if I may."

Virginia glanced up. Socks stood in the doorway, looking at her with concern. "I don't know what to say! Betty Brown was fine when I left. Are you sure she was murdered? I know she's been ill."

Pause. "We're sure she was murdered. Is there any way you can come to the Hoboken police station this evening?"

"I just got back from Hoboken! I'm home now in upstate New York. Can't we do this by phone?"

Another pause. "Give me your address, and I'll come to you."

"But it's 8:30, it'll take you at least two hours."

"I'll leave right now."

Virginia gave him directions, then hung up. She walked into her bedroom and collapsed onto the bed, utterly stunned.

Socks followed Virginia and sat on the edge of the bed. "Honey, what's going on?"

Virginia turned slightly. "It's Betty Brown. The man on the phone was from the police, and he told me she's dead. Murdered."

Socks placed a hand on her chest. "My God! I'm so sorry."

"He wants to ask me about my interview with Betty Brown. Here, tonight."

"A cop?" Socks' eyebrows shot up. "Coming to our house?"

"He's leaving Hoboken right now."

"I'm going to clean up. First I'll make you a cup of tea."

"OK," Virginia whispered.

Socks turned on the small bedside lamp. "If you're going to be sad, at least do it in style. Get under the quilt. And here's Louis." She handed Virginia her lone stuffed toy, a replica of Louis Armstrong that Nathan had bought for her in New Orleans.

"Thanks."

"I'll put on some music for you. What would you like?"

No question: *Sunday at the Village Vanguard* by the Bill Evans Trio.

Socks left the room and shut the door. As Evans' gentle piano filled the air, Virginia turned restlessly. Murder! What sort of murder? The detective hadn't said.

And when on earth did it happen? Virginia knew Joe Pascoe was supposed to come at three o'clock to take photos for the article. Joe was not her favorite person, but he would never murder anyone. Would he?

Socks returned and put a cup of tea on the bedside table.

"Dr. Bundle's gone," she announced, sitting once more on the edge of the bed. "I told him we had a family emergency."

"He didn't have to leave."

"Dr. Bundle is a man with a woman's nervous system. He understands."

"Socks?"

"Yes, dear?"

"I'm scared."

"Don't be," Socks replied firmly. "You don't have enough information to be frightened. Just rest a bit."

"All right."

"Can I get you anything else?"

Virginia shook her head. "No. But—"

A small crash. While crossing her legs, Socks had accidentally brushed a knee against the teacup.

"Oh dear," she said. "So much for tea."

"That's OK," Virginia said, turning on her side. "I didn't really want any."

She heard Socks leave the room, then come back and clean up the mess. Afterward Socks clicked off the bedside lamp, leaving the room in darkness.

Virginia began to cry, chest heaving. Why would anyone kill Betty Brown?

And now a policeman was on his way to question her. Virginia had never had any run-ins with the law before, and the very idea made her anxious.

And the tapes! What would happen with them now that Betty Brown was dead?

Virginia clutched Louis Armstrong tighter, her tears dampening the doll's smiling face.

The next thing Virginia knew, someone was calling her name. She opened her eyes and saw Socks standing in the doorway.

"Time to get up," Socks said softly. "The cop's here."

Virginia rubbed her eyes. "OK."

Socks started to leave the room, then poked her head back in. "By the way, he's rather handsome."

"Can you please just—"

"I'll tell him you'll be right out."

When the tall blonde woman with chopsticks in her hair opened the door, Robert assumed she was Virginia Farrell. But no, the woman told him to take a seat while she got Virginia.

Robert sat on a big purple couch, folding his hands around one knee. He was not particularly happy. Not because of the long drive, which he hadn't minded. It was a nice night, and in the privacy of the car he had listened to his *Classic Sinatra* CD over and over.

No, Robert was unhappy because when Captain Kelly came by 1305 Bloomfield to check up on Hoboken's first homicide in years, he said that the Hudson County Prosecutor's Office was understaffed due to summer vacations. Knowing Robert's background, they suggested he take over the case. So now Robert was investigating a murder, exactly what he never wanted to do again.

The tall blonde walked back into the room. "She'll be right out."

"Thank you."

Not a simple murder, either. Baseema Baheera's purse contained $65 and was sitting on the table next to the door. So it was doubtful this was a robbery, particularly in broad daylight in the home of an elderly woman who had nothing of value. And now Robert was about to talk to Virginia Farrell, who hadn't been particularly cooperative on the phone, and—

"Hello."

Robert looked up. He felt a reaction the likes of which he hadn't experienced in years, a sharp snap followed by a hum coursing through him. The woman standing in front of him had unusual coloring, dark-red hair and olive-toned skin. Her brows and lashes were dark, and her big green eyes were arresting. And she was petite. Pretty and petite.

"Hello," he said, standing up. "I'm Robert Smith. Detective."

"I'm Virginia." She sat on the other couch, smoothing a lock of straight shoulder-length hair behind one ear. He could tell she had been crying, which did nothing to diminish her charm.

Robert took his seat again. For a moment he had no idea what to say; all he wanted to do was look at her. He remembered his chiropractor telling him that whenever he was working on an attractive female patient, he distracted himself by thinking about politics. But who needed politics? This was a murder investigation.

The blonde woman emerged again. "Anyone like some tea?"

"Yes," they both replied.

"Back in a flash," she said, sailing out of the room.

Focus, Robert told himself. He pulled a pen and a small notebook from his jacket and turned toward Virginia Farrell.

"That's her," Virginia Farrell said, pointing to the wall.

"I beg your pardon?" Robert asked.

"On the album cover. That's Betty Brown."

Robert got up to examine the artwork. "Shinwell Johnson—I know that name. He's the jazz musician whose body was found in a cornfield in Pennsylvania. It's a famous unsolved murder."

"That's right," she said softly. "In 1969."

"There was another jazz musician who also died under mysterious circumstances around that time. His body was found in the East River."

"Albert Ayler. In 1970."

Robert sat down again. She really was distractingly pretty. "Miss Farrell—"

"Virginia."

"Why don't you start from the beginning and tell me why you visited Baseema Baheera today?"

She took a deep breath. "I'm a journalist. And I—" She stopped and looked at him with her large green eyes. "I'm not sure how much detail you want."

"Just tell me at your own pace."

"OK. I'm a journalist who writes about jazz—articles, reviews, a little bit of everything. Although lately I haven't done many articles, because I'm writing a book on June Christy."

Robert looked at her blankly.

She pointed toward the wall close to the stereo. "That's her, the blonde woman in the black dress. She was a big band singer in the forties, then she had a successful solo career in the fifties. She's considered obscure, although she absolutely shouldn't be, since she's one of the most amazing singers of the last century."

He nodded. Too much information, but he didn't need to cut her off yet.

"Anyway," Virginia went on. "About a year ago, I published an article on June Christy in the magazine *Jazz Now*. A Japanese man named Mr. Togasaki read it and told me he'd bankroll me if I wrote a book on her." Virginia lifted a shoulder. "So I have a patron."

Robert raised his eyebrows. "Mr. Togasaki—do you mean Toshiro Togasaki, the industrialist?"

"I don't know what he does. I just know he loves jazz, and he has a lot of money."

"OK," Robert said, making a note. Her remark struck him as rather naive.

The blonde woman came in and put a tea tray on the coffee table. Robert inclined his head, encouraging Virginia to continue.

She took a deep breath. "So as I was saying, I haven't been writing articles lately. But then Nathan—he's my editor at *Jazz Now*—he told me last week he'd managed to track down Betty Brown. Right in Hoboken."

"What do you mean, 'track down'?"

"Jazz is full of people who have dropped out of sight. It could be anything—personal problems, moving out of the country, just leaving the scene for whatever reason. Nathan and I both have a passion for finding missing musicians."

"Go on," Robert said.

"I always loved the song 'Dashiki,' and I'm a big fan of Betty Brown. She's someone we've talked about for years, wondering where she was and how we could get in touch with her."

"Is 'Dashiki' a famous song?"

Virginia knit her brows. Now she was looking at him as if he were naive. "You'd know 'Dashiki' if you heard it. It's one of the few jazz songs to become a Top 40 hit."

"I see."

"The song came out in 1969. I was only a child, but I remember hearing it everywhere. It was on a car commercial a few years ago, and you still hear it on the radio now and then. It's a classic."

"So this impelled you to find Betty Brown. Was she a musician?"

"Not exactly. She used to dance with the band, and she's the one at the end of the song who shouts out 'Dashiki!' She was also on *The Mike Douglas Show* with them. It's a famous episode."

"All right," Robert said.

"But Betty Brown's connection to jazz goes deeper than 'Dashiki.' She grew up in Philadelphia, and she used to babysit John Coltrane's daughter."

"I think I know the name. He's a musician?"

Virginia looked at him as if he'd insulted her mother. And her grandmother. She pointed to the wall at a framed photograph of a pensive-looking Black man. "The saxophonist. One of the most brilliant musicians ever. One of the most inspiring human beings of all time."

Robert blinked and stayed silent.

"The point is," she continued, "Betty Brown knew him, as well as a lot of other musicians on the jazz scene. I wanted to interview her because I thought she'd have some good stories. Also I really wanted to meet her."

"So your editor found her?"

"Yes. We'd both heard rumors that Betty Brown was living in Hoboken, and when I lived there—"

Robert looked up. "You lived in Hoboken?"

Virginia glanced at him curiously. "Yes, for about fifteen years. Then I moved up here. Anyway, I always kept a lookout for Betty Brown, but I never had any luck. Then last week, Nathan was talking to Rex Royal and—"

"Who?"

Again that pained look. "The drummer, Rex Royal. One of the greatest living jazz musicians. A legend."

Robert made a note and nodded for her to continue.

"Nathan was arranging an interview with Rex, and when Nathan told Rex that *Jazz Now* had moved to Hoboken, Rex said, 'In that case, I'll look up my old friend Betty Brown.'"

"I see."

"Turns out Betty Brown had converted to Islam and changed her name. That's why she wasn't in any public records."

"What happened when your editor Nathan called her?"

"At first she was reluctant to be interviewed, but when Nathan offered to send a female reporter, she liked the idea better. He set up the appointment for today, and I met Betty Brown at noon."

Virginia looked at her hands.

"Are you all right?" Robert asked.

She shook her head. "I still can't believe Betty Brown is dead."

"Tell me what happened," he said patiently. "Try to remember as much detail as possible. You never know what might help."

Virginia took a deep breath.

"I was early, so I walked around the block. Exactly at twelve, I pushed the buzzer, and Betty Brown let me in. I got confused about where her apartment was, but then I found it next to the elevator."

"Did you see anyone else in the building?" Robert asked.

"Let me think . . . There was an old woman with a bag of groceries, but I doubt she noticed me. I knocked on the apartment door and there she was, Betty Brown."

"What was she wearing?"

Virginia thought a moment. "Simple clothes. Plain colors. A pale-green dress and a dark scarf on her head. What struck me was how thin she was. You can tell from the album cover that Betty Brown was a big, strong woman. She was still tall, of course, but she was much thinner."

"Go on."

"She invited me in. I sat on the couch, and she asked if I wanted tea. I said yes and she went into the kitchen, and while she was gone I set up my tape recorder."

"What kind of recorder?"

"A small handheld one. For regular-sized cassettes, not the micro ones."

"Where exactly did you put it?"

"On the edge of the coffee table, close to me so I could keep an eye on it. The tape was already in, all I had to do was press record. Then Betty Brown came out with the tea—"

"Did she use a tray?"

Virginia gave him a quizzical look. "Yes, but she put everything on the table and took the tray back to the kitchen."

"What did she bring out?"

"Tea things. Two cups, sugar, milk, spoons. Napkins."

"Do you recall seeing a vase on the table?"

Virginia thought a moment. "Yes, a glass vase. It was empty, and I remember wishing I had brought her some flowers." She paused. "Should I go on?"

"Please."

"We each fixed our cup of tea, then we made small talk. I knew Betty Brown had been reluctant about being interviewed, so I didn't want to jump right in with lots of questions."

"What did you talk about?"

"The weather, did I drive there, how impossible it is to find a parking spot in Hoboken—the usual. Oh, and I gave her Socks' honey."

"Socks?"

Virginia gestured toward the kitchen, which had been producing a constant clatter of pots and pans. "My roommate. She's also a fan of Betty Brown, so she asked me to bring a gift."

"Which honey?"

"This one." Virginia handed Robert the glass jar on the tea tray. The eight-ounce container had an oval label: *Hana's Honey—100% Organic from Little Mountain, NY*. The label was decorated with whimsical drawings of smiling bees in bowties.

"OK," he said.

"Socks draws the labels. It's top-quality honey."

Robert put the jar back on the tray without further comment.

"So Betty Brown and I chatted a bit," Virginia continued, "and eventually I asked if it was OK to begin. She said yes, and I pushed the record button."

"What did you talk about?"

"I asked her about growing up in Philadelphia, and I had a lot of questions about John Coltrane and his family. Then we talked about her moving to New York and the musicians she met there. And of course I wanted to know about Shinwell Johnson and 'Dashiki.'"

"How did she seem while you two were talking?"

"I think she enjoyed herself. She was happy telling me about Philadelphia and the old neighborhood, and she only had good things to say about everyone. Mostly."

Virginia hesitated.

"But—?" Robert prompted her.

"When it seemed like the interview was over, Betty Brown told me something I wasn't expecting to hear."

"Which was?"

Virginia took a deep breath. "She said she was sick. And she needed my help."

Robert looked at Virginia intently.

She picked up a napkin and started shredding it. "Betty Brown has cancer. Had cancer. She told me she didn't have much longer to live. There was something she wanted to set right, and she was hoping I could help her with it."

Robert remained silent. Virginia's face twisted a little, in pain or confusion he wasn't sure. "I guess it won't mean much to you because you're clearly not into jazz, but she had some extremely rare tapes. Her boyfriend Shinwell Johnson stole them from John Coltrane in 1958, and after Shinwell died in 1969, she kept them."

"What kind of tapes?"

"Recordings from a 1957 gig at the Five Spot—that's an old club in New York—with Thelonious Monk and John Coltrane. I don't know how I can emphasize their value. It's like someone finding a collection of Picasso paintings from his blue period."

"What did she tell you about these tapes?"

"Betty Brown wanted help returning them to the Coltranes and the Monks, but she felt ashamed because the tapes were stolen so long ago. She figured that since I'm in the jazz world, I could help her. Tell me," Virginia burst out, "were the tapes still there?"

"Where were they?"

"In an old brown shoebox, a bit oversized with a dark-brown lid. There were about a dozen tapes inside, all old reel-to-reels. The last I saw the box, it was still on the coffee table. Tell me, did you see them?"

Virginia's green eyes widened, imploring him to give her the answer she needed.

Robert hesitated. It was a delicate moment. The detective part of him wanted to reveal nothing. For all he knew, Virginia Farrell killed Baseema Baheera, and this was part of an elaborate ploy.

The nondetective part of him felt that Virginia was sincere. And Robert's natural inclination to help a woman—particularly this beautiful woman—was quite strong.

He decided to split the difference. Robert hadn't seen the shoebox, but they hadn't yet done a thorough search of the apartment. "We're still gathering evidence. Nothing's finalized yet."

Virginia's shoulders sagged. "If those tapes are missing—"

Then I have a motive, Robert thought. "Go on."

"They were my responsibility. I promised Betty Brown I'd take care of them. And now they're gone before I even started."

"We don't know that for sure," Robert replied. "Tell me, what happened after you promised to help out?"

"Betty Brown was visibly relieved. We talked a bit more, then I left. I gave her my number in case she needed to contact me, and I told her I'd call her tomorrow morning."

"What time did you leave?"

"The photographer—his name's Joe Pascoe—was coming at three, and I wanted to go before he showed up. I left at three exactly; I know because I asked someone on the street outside Betty Brown's building."

"Did you see the photographer?" Robert asked.

"No. I rushed off to *Jazz Now* to talk to Nathan. I wanted to tell him about the tapes and get his advice."

"What time did you arrive at *Jazz Now*?"

"Around three-thirty. I went straight to Nathan's office."

"What did he say when you told him about the tapes?"

"Nathan was thrilled, just like me. I told him to sleep on it, and then we could talk in the morning. Our tentative plan was to get the tapes to the IJS for safekeeping, then contact Coltrane's and Monk's families."

Robert looked up. "The IJS?"

"The Institute of Jazz Studies. It's part of Rutgers University in Newark."

"Did you see or speak to anyone else at *Jazz Now*?"

"I waved at Maggie, the receptionist, and I spoke briefly with Byron Ffowlkes. He's the publisher and editor-in-chief." She looked over at Robert's notebook. "Two Fs. He's English."

"Did you tell him about the tapes?"

She wrinkled her nose. "Byron? Definitely not! He just asked me if I was going to the Rex Royal show this week. The only person I told about the tapes was Nathan." She shrugged. "And now you."

"Did Byron Ffowlkes know you were going to see Betty Brown?"

"I imagine Nathan must have told him about the interview, but I can't say for sure."

"Did anyone else know?"

"Socks did. And my friend Mortimer Burns. He's a writer at *Jazz Now*."

"Did you see him at the magazine today?" Robert asked.

"No. I saw Mortimer last Friday, and that's when I told him about the interview. We haven't spoken since."

"What time did you leave *Jazz Now*?"

"Just about four," Virginia replied. "I was in a hurry to catch my bus at five. I walked over to the PATH station to get a bus into the city, then I caught my bus at Port Authority with a few minutes to spare."

"How did you pay for the buses?"

"I used cash on the Hoboken bus, and I had a ticket for my bus ride upstate."

Robert glanced up from his notebook. "May I see your tape recorder?"

"Well—OK."

Virginia walked over to the door and unhooked her knapsack. After a brief search, she pulled out a portable gray recorder. Robert examined the device before setting it on the coffee table.

"And the tape?"

After another search, Virginia pulled out a plastic cassette box, neatly labeled with the date and *Betty Brown Interview*. Robert opened the box and looked at the cassette, which was also labeled on both sides.

He put the cassette back in the box and placed it on the table. "Is your conversation about the tapes on this?"

"Yes. The cassette ran out just as we finished."

Robert looked at his notebook. "You say you arrived at noon and left at three. This is a ninety-minute cassette, so assuming you spent about fifteen minutes talking in the beginning, the tape would have finished about 1:45 p.m. What happened during that final hour and fifteen minutes?"

Color rose to Virginia's cheeks. "We talked. Off the record."

"About what?"

"Nothing relevant to this case."

"You'd be surprised what might be relevant."

"Betty Brown spoke to me about her old boyfriend, Shinwell Johnson."

"What did she say about him?"

"She said—" Virginia hesitated. "She told me he treated her poorly."

"How?"

"Verbal abuse, mostly. Weird psychological stuff."

"Anything connected with the tapes?"

Virginia wrung her hands. "Just what I told you, that Shinwell stole them. I guess that was pretty typical of his behavior. She even broke up with him because of it."

"When was that?"

"In 1958. Then Betty Brown was with another guy for a long time, but he died in Vietnam in the midsixties. After that she got back together with Shinwell, and in 1969 they made 'Dashiki.'"

"And Shinwell Johnson disappeared that same year?"

"That's right. A few days after his band was on *The Mike Douglas Show*." Virginia sat up a little straighter and looked Robert in the eye. "The thing is, Betty Brown didn't want any of this in the article. She just needed to get some things off her chest."

Robert jotted a few meaningless phrases in his notebook. During the past few minutes, Virginia's entire demeanor had shifted. Her color had deepened, her eye contact was not as strong, and she was pressing her hands together nervously.

She was lying. Why?

Virginia watched the detective as he jotted in his notebook. Good job, she told herself. You acted perfectly normal. There's no way he knows you were lying.

The smell of brownies wafted in from the kitchen. Socks always made desserts when she was nervous, and by the almost constant rattle—and occasional fall—of pots and pans, she was ready to open a bakery.

Virginia shifted restlessly on the couch. If only this Robert Smith Detective would leave! She had so much to think about . . .

He stopped writing and picked up the cassette. "May I borrow this?"

Her eyes flashed. "No, you may not! You can't ask a journalist to hand over tapes."

The detective eyed her steadily. He was a tall, thin man, handsome in a plain way, with even features, dark brown eyes, and elegantly receding hair. But handsome men never distracted Virginia, and she met his gaze without flinching.

"This is a murder investigation," he said quietly. "Your cassette might have important evidence—a background sound, maybe something she muttered. It could help a great deal."

"Journalists never surrender their material! I won't do it."

"I'm not asking you to reveal a source. I'm asking you to help me find Betty Brown's killer." Again that measured look. "I believe we're on the same side."

She softened. "We are. Just it's my only copy."

He looked over at the elaborate stereo system, part of the bounty from Socks' divorce. "Could you make one for me?"

Virginia hesitated. For all her bluster, she wasn't certain of her rights. It had never come up before; after all, Virginia interviewed jazz musicians. She had a vague idea that the detective could subpoena her for the tape, and it wasn't worth the bother.

"I suppose," she answered huffily.

"Thank you," he replied.

Virginia went over to the stereo, put in her cassette as well as a blank one, and pushed a few buttons. She sat back down and busied herself with the tea, avoiding the detective's gaze.

Suddenly he asked, "Do you miss Hoboken?"

Virginia looked at him sharply. "Is your interrogation over?"

The detective almost smiled. "I prefer to think of it as questioning. And yes, for the moment it is."

She shrugged. "It's great living up here, but I still love Hoboken and New York. I go down every week to hear music or do research on my book."

"Do you still have an apartment there?"

"A musician friend lets me stay at his place. He's mostly on the road, so it works out pretty well."

"Where does he live?"

The interrogation—the questioning—might be over, but it certainly didn't feel like it. "Jackson between First and Second. Do you live in Hoboken?"

"Policemen in Hoboken are required to live there. Not that I mind, it's a great city."

"Where do you live?"

"A studio on Garden between Ninth and Tenth. It's a nice block, very quiet."

She picked up her teacup and said nothing.

A few moments later, the stereo clicked to a halt. Virginia rose and took out the two cassettes, then sat down and labeled the copy and its case. Unidentified tapes made her crazy.

"Here," she said, handing the duplicate to the detective.

"Thank you. That's a big help."

He rose to leave, and suddenly Virginia felt a wave of fear. "Detective Smith?" she asked uncertainly.

"Yes?" he said, looking down at her.

"I—I don't know if this is against police procedure or what, but could you tell me if you find the tapes? I know they're not mine, but I promised Betty Brown I'd help her with them, and I still need to do that."

The detective stared at her impassively. It was impossible to read his expression.

"All right," he said finally. "I'm planning on going to the apartment first thing tomorrow morning. I'll call you when I'm done."

"I really appreciate that." She took a deep breath. "And if you don't find them?"

"I'll call you as well."

"OK. Thanks."

Virginia rose and walked him to the door. Policeman or not, she felt bad that he had to drive back to Hoboken so late. "It's a long ride," she commented.

"I don't mind. I play music."

"What do you listen to?"

"Oh—classic rock."

She raised an eyebrow. Typical.

The moment the door shut behind Detective Smith, Socks emerged from the kitchen. Her fuchsia apron was dusted with flour, and one of the chopsticks in her hair was askew.

"He's gone?" she asked.

"Yep," Virginia said, flopping onto the couch.

"How was it? Did he shine a flashlight in your eyes and try to intimidate you?"

"He was actually very polite."

Socks sat down as well. "Why were you yelling at him?"

"What do you mean?"

"You were in a shemozzle about something."

"I wasn't happy when he asked for the interview tape. Journalists never hand over their material!"

"Virginia," Socks said calmly. "Someone's been murdered."

"Since when are you such a law-abiding citizen?"

"He's just trying to find Betty Brown's killer."

Virginia twisted her lips. "I guess I did yell a little. But I finally made him a copy." She looked at Socks. "I need to fill you in. I planned on telling you earlier, but Dr. Bundle was here."

She told Socks about the Five Spot tapes. Socks' jazz knowledge was minimal because that's how she preferred it, but even she could appreciate the tapes' significance.

"My, my," Socks said, giving a low whistle. "And where are these tapes now?"

Virginia folded her arms, frowning. "I'm not sure. Detective Smith is going to call me tomorrow and let me know if he finds them."

"That's mighty organic of him." Socks paused. "Handsome, no?"

"As if that matters!" Virginia snorted. "It's not like he was here to take me on a date."

"Perhaps not, but he's the only man who's visited you since you moved in. It's something of a milestone."

"I guess." Virginia sighed. "I still can't believe Betty Brown was murdered."

"By the way, V, do you know how she—?" Socks stuck out her bottom lip.

"Died? I didn't ask."

"Let's hope it was quick and painless."

"Yes, let's." Virginia looked at the clock. "I should go to bed, but I feel so sad and bejiggety."

"Tell you what," Socks said, patting Virginia's hand. "I have three trays of brownies cooling in the kitchen. Why don't I pile a bunch on a plate, pour two enormous glasses of milk, and we can watch *The Universal Mind of Bill Evans*?"

Virginia's eyes lit up with surprise. It was her favorite video, but she was only allowed to watch it when Socks was asleep. "Really? You'd do that for me?"

"I would. I feel sad too, you know," Socks said, wiping away a tear. "Poor Betty Brown."

Virginia rested her head on Socks' shoulder and closed her eyes.

Robert sat at the counter of a diner about fifteen minutes from Virginia's house. He ordered a black coffee, then eyed a plate of glazed doughnuts sitting under a glass dome.

No, he told himself sternly. You are not allowed.

"Anything else?" the waitress asked.

"A slice of chocolate cake, please."

Robert took out his notebook and reread his notes. At least now he had a possible motive, as well as a list of people to interview: photographer Joe Pascoe, managing editor Nathan Garrideb, editor-in-chief Byron Ffowlkes, and journalist Mortimer Burns.

He also wrote a reminder to go to Baseema Baheera's apartment first thing tomorrow and look for those tapes. And call a friend from his former precinct and ask him to dig up the file on Shinwell Johnson.

Robert checked his watch. It was almost midnight, which meant he would probably get about four hours of sleep.

His jaw tightened with displeasure. The long hours were one of the reasons Robert stopped being a New York City homicide detective. He much preferred working in Hoboken, where he usually investigated robberies and called it a day by six.

Robert had also hoped his lighter schedule would help him meet women. As it turned out, women minded his job no matter how many hours he put in. Another problem was that after years of nonstop work, Robert's already minimal dating skills had atrophied. Badly.

Which brought him to Virginia Farrell. What good fortune to meet a woman who affected him so strongly, and what bad fortune to meet her on the job!

Not that he had made a good impression. Robert cringed as he recalled that clunky "Robert Smith. Detective." Then of course she yelled at him. And she was a suspect.

But Robert didn't think Virginia Farrell killed Baseema Baheera, for two reasons.

First, at the time of the murder, Virginia had been on the bus to New York, and then she was on another bus to Little Mountain. Assuming she was telling the truth. Robert could verify her movements through security at 111 River Street and the bus companies, and he was confident her alibi would check out.

Robert's second reason for doubting her guilt was because she wasn't the type. During his years as a psychology major at Hunter College, Robert had read extensively on criminal behavior. His thesis concerned a theory he'd developed, namely that murderers fall into two distinct categories: psychological and conditional.

In Robert's view, psychological murderers were predisposed to killing due to genetics and upbringing. These individuals often lacked empathy and placed little value on human life. They might never commit murder during their lifetime, but their psychology made it a possibility.

In contrast, conditional murderers killed due to specific circumstances, often driven by strong emotions such as fear or anger. If they found a burglar in their house, let's say, or if someone they loved was being attacked.

Robert's theory also included the concept of the tragic flaw, which he had gleaned from a Shakespeare course. Few people were burdened by something truly tragic; usually their flaw was petty, or simply embarrassing. But everyone had at least one weakness, and particular traits made crime more likely. For instance, a person prone to greed might steal, and under the right conditions this could lead to murder. It all fit together.

It always amazed Robert how quickly people revealed their shortcomings. Take Virginia Farrell. Her blind spot was being naive. Not knowing about Toshiro Togasaki indicated Virginia was out of touch with the world at large. No surprise there, given her obsession with jazz. But not knowing about him when he was her main source of income was naive.

Virginia's protest about giving over her tapes also revealed her vulnerability. Journalism had been her profession for years, yet she didn't know her basic rights.

As character flaws went, being naive wasn't a bad one. And it wasn't the type that led to crime, particularly murder.

But something was off with Virginia Farrell. She wasn't telling him everything that happened between her and Baseema Baheera.

Robert took a last sip of coffee and motioned for his check. Maybe the tape would give him a clue.

Robert started playing Virginia's tape as soon as he got into the car. By the time he was on the New York State Thruway and halfway home, he had learned plenty about Baseema Baheera. And Virginia Farrell.

Virginia was clearly good at her job. Her warm, professional manner put Baseema Baheera at ease, which allowed Baseema to open up considerably over the course of the interview. True to the neighbor's statement, there was a great deal of laughter. Virginia's extensive jazz knowledge also shone through as she effortlessly cited names and dates.

Robert learned that Baseema Baheera was born in 1940 and grew up in the Strawberry Mansion neighborhood of Philadelphia. In the early 1950s, John Coltrane moved two doors down with his mother and cousin. Baseema's mother and Coltrane's mother went to the same Methodist church, and the two families became close.

In 1955 Coltrane married Juanita Austin, who went by her Muslim name Naima. Coltrane's new wife had a daughter named Syeeda, and Baseema became the girl's babysitter.

Here Virginia probed delicately but firmly about Coltrane's family life. Baseema said she was fond of Naima, who taught her how to sew and talked to her about religion. She also loved Syeeda, who was six years old and full of energy.

As for Coltrane, Baseema said he was a kind man with a gentle voice. She remembered that he was constantly practicing the saxophone, and he also ate a lot of sweets, including a weekly outing with Baseema and Syeeda to get ice cream cones.

Baseema babysat for Syeeda for about a year, then Coltrane and his immediate family moved to New York City. Around that time, Baseema's mother remarried, but her new husband wasn't interested in being a stepfather. As soon as Baseema graduated from high school in 1957, she left home and moved in with an aunt in Harlem.

The Coltranes also lived in Harlem, and once again Baseema started babysitting for Syeeda. Baseema's connection to the Coltranes placed her in the heart of the vibrant Harlem jazz scene, and she attended shows most evenings.

Which is how she met Shinwell Johnson.

The moment Baseema said his name, her voice grew softer and slower. She seemed hesitant to talk about Johnson, and only with gentle prompting from Virginia did she open up. Baseema revealed that she first met him at a Sonny Rollins gig at Minton's Playhouse. They dated for about a year before she broke up with him, although she didn't offer a reason why.

In the early 1960s, Baseema met Joseph Jackson. Not a musician, she emphasized, but a nice fellow who worked at his father's dry-cleaning store in Harlem. They were happy together and planned to get married. But he was drafted in 1965, and a year later he died in Vietnam.

In 1968, Shinwell Johnson came back into Baseema's life, and they quickly moved in together. Virginia asked about the origins of "Dashiki," and Baseema said that one afternoon while she was in the living room mending clothes, Johnson was taking a bath, taking his trumpet with him as usual. He played a riff over and over, and when he emerged from the tub, he announced he had a hit song. When Baseema asked what it was called, Johnson glanced at the clothes she was mending. He looked up and cried out, "Dashiki!"

Johnson worked on the song furiously for the next few days until it was just right. His Blue Note contract had run out several years before, so he contacted Milestone. Everyone there loved "Dashiki" and they decided to put out an album right away.

Both Johnson and Milestone agreed that if the new song was going to make it in the mainstream, they needed a woman in the group, even if all she did was dance and look pretty. That's where Baseema came in. The album *Dashiki* was released a few months later, and the rest was history.

Virginia asked a few more questions about that period, then she probed delicately about Shinwell Johnson's death.

Baseema's voice became so low it was almost inaudible. She said that a few days after *The Mike Douglas Show*, Johnson left the apartment and never came back. He had other girls on the side, particularly a blonde named Christine, and Baseema assumed he had gone off with one of them. That was something he did now and then, usually for a weekend or so, but he always came back. The only difference this time was that he didn't take his horn. He never went anywhere without it, and it struck Baseema as odd.

She grew concerned when Johnson missed a few gigs, and soon all his friends started calling and asking where he was. But Johnson never came home.

Things stayed in limbo for a few months, then one day the police called. A farmer in Kutztown, Pennsylvania, had run over Johnson's body in a cornfield. It was impossible to detect the cause of death: the body was badly decayed, plus the tractor did a lot of damage.

Virginia gently asked if she had any theories. Baseema replied that when Johnson disappeared, Christine vanished as well. She was probably involved somehow, but why he ended up on a farm in Pennsylvania was anybody's guess.

The tape had been running about an hour. Robert listened carefully as Virginia thanked Baseema and said she would be sure to send her a copy of the interview when it came out.

Baseema spoke again, her voice shaky:

"Do you have time to sit a bit longer? I want to ask you somethin'."

Robert turned up the volume. He heard Virginia say, slightly surprised: "Sure."

"I got a situation. And I was hopin' you might be able to help me out."

"What do you need?"

"I'm a dyin' woman. I got the cancer. Won't be long now, two months at most. There's somethin' I need to clear up before I pass."

"OK."

Silence. Robert rewound and leaned forward, straining to hear better. He caught the faint thud of a door opening and shutting, followed by a slight thump.

Virginia's voice: "What are those?"

"Tapes from the Coltranes' house. Shinwell took 'em."

"These are—"

"I know what they are. At the time it didn't matter so much, but I realize what they would mean for folks today."

Now it was Virginia's turn to sound shaky. "How did you get them?"

"When I first met Shinwell, he was doin' pretty well. He was puttin' out records and gettin' steady gigs. But he was always wantin' to break through, always lookin' for the big time. Shinwell was willin' to do anythin' to get there, and he thought maybe he could hitch onto someone else's star.

"Everyone knew John Coltrane was on his way up. No one knew how high he'd go, not then, but it was for sure he was one of the best. When Shinwell found out I knew the Coltranes, he begged me to introduce him to John, so I said he could pick me up from babysittin'. Which he did, but then he did somethin' dumb. Before I could stop him, Shinwell bust into the room where John was practicin'.

"Now, I never saw John get mad at nobody, but that wasn't good manners. I couldn't hear much of what they was sayin', but Shinwell was talkin' all high and excited like he got. When he finally walked out, he seemed pretty angry.

"Naima came home then, she paid me and we left. I asked Shinwell what happened to make him so mad. Apparently he had asked John to join his group, but John said no.

"A few evenings later, when I was sittin' for the Coltranes, Shinwell dropped by. It was just me and Syeeda, and she was in bed. I musta left Shinwell alone when I checked on Syeeda or somethin', 'cause the next time I was at Shinwell's apartment, he showed me a shoebox full of tapes. He said he'd stolen them from the Coltranes.

"I begged Shinwell to return 'em. I even offered to sneak the box back myself. But he was mad at Coltrane and wouldn't budge. He was childish like that, mean and spiteful.

"The whole thing tore me up inside. I broke up with Shinwell, and I never did sit for Syeeda again. Naima kept callin' me, but I always made excuses, till finally she didn't call no more.

"Later when I was back with Shinwell, he still had the tapes. Then when he died, I got 'em along with all his other stuff."

Virginia's voice, very soft: "Did you think about giving them back?"

"All the time. John passed in 1967, but Naima was still alive. So was John's second wife, Alice, who I also knew. Problem was, I was too a-shamed to tell anyone what happened. Sometimes I thought about mailin' the tapes to Naima or Alice, but I was scared they'd get lost." Baseema exhaled loudly. "I didn't know what to do, and as time went on, it got harder to do anythin'."

"That happens sometimes," Virginia said kindly.

"It sure happened to me. And now I don't got much time at all. So like I said, I want to make this right. Will you help me?"

"Of course. What would you like me to do?"

"Can you promise me to get these tapes to the Coltranes? The Monks too, I suppose. You can tell 'em what happened. I don't care anymore what anyone thinks about me, I just want to fix this."

"I'll do that for you. I promise."

"Then they can put out this music, right? That would sure make folks happy."

"It certainly would," Virginia said softly.

"All right then." Baseema's voice was notably relieved. "You seem like a nice girl. I'm gonna trust you."

"Miss Brown, if it's OK, I'd like to think everything over tonight and give you a call tomorrow. I need to get in touch with a couple of people who can help me with this. Here—" Sound of a pen scratching, a piece of paper being ripped from a notebook. "If you'd like to contact me, this is my number. But I'll definitely call you first thing tomorrow morning with a plan."

"All right." Pause. "Would you like to—?"

The tape clicked off. Suddenly Robert became aware of his surroundings: he was on Route 17, about half an hour from Hoboken.

Everything went exactly as Virginia had said. She was an admirable woman, Robert thought. She handled Baseema Baheera's surprise with discipline, and he was impressed by her composure. Not only pretty, he mused, but smart and accomplished as well. Also naive—but that wasn't important, not really.

Enough, Robert scolded himself. You need to think about all the people you have to question tomorrow.

As for Virginia Farrell—why, he would have to talk to her again, right? He had promised to call her about the tapes, and he also needed to ask her what Baseema Baheera was saying when the tape cut off. "Would you like to—?"

Would you like to what?

"Would you like to promise me somethin' else?"

Betty Brown's words echoed in Virginia's head as she tossed and twisted in bed. She checked the clock: almost two. After milk, brownies, and Bill Evans, she and Socks had said good night and adjourned to their rooms.

Socks' operatic snores were now filling the cabin, but Virginia was too keyed-up to sleep. She couldn't avoid her thoughts any longer. It was time to face what happened in the last part of the interview.

Virginia shut her eyes.

"**W**ould you like to promise me somethin' else?"

Virginia glanced at the tape recorder, which had just clicked off. "One moment," she replied. "I need to put in a new tape."

Betty Brown shook her head. "We don't need no recorder for this one."

Virginia tilted her head and looked at Betty Brown. She was a beautiful woman, with alert eyes and smooth skin stretched over strong cheekbones. Her thin frame and careful movements betrayed her illness, but otherwise she had the regal bearing of a queen.

The clock on the wall read one forty-five. Virginia definitely wanted to leave before Joe Pascoe arrived at three for the photo shoot, but that still gave her plenty of time. Poor Betty Brown—she clearly needed to talk, and she seemed so alone.

"What would you like me to promise?" Virginia asked.

"I guess just to listen. And then not tell nobody what I said."

"Sure, I can do that."

Betty Brown smiled. "You're a journalist, but I'm askin' you not to be one right now. I guess I'm hopin' you'll be a friend. Or just humor a dyin' woman."

"All right," Virginia answered. "I promise."

Betty Brown looked out the window. She drew in a deep breath and released it shakily. "It's about me and Shinwell."

"OK," Virginia said.

"Shinwell was not a good man." Betty Brown waved a hand. "Oh, I know, he was a great musician, and 'Dashiki' was a big hit. But I'm talkin' about the person. I'm talkin' about who he was when he put down that horn.

"See, the first time around with Shinwell, I was only eighteen. But I had good sense, and even before he took those tapes, I knew somethin' was off. Shinwell had a need to dominate. He could never let a person breathe, to just let 'em take up the space they took.

"At first, I thought Shinwell was real excitin.' He was always playin' music and readin' me poetry, and it felt like I was gettin' a free education. Plus he was such a fine musician, with his own group and lots of albums out. I'd been pretty sheltered, and he seemed like the most amazin' man in the world.

"But I saw pretty quick that there was only room for him. Shinwell would play opera or classical records, actin' like he was doin' it for me, but I wasn't allowed to have no opinion. Or if I did have one, he never liked it. Everythin' I said was wrong, and everythin' he said was right. That was real confusin' for me. I was a young girl, didn't know much about these things, so I was never sure what was good and what was bad.

"But when Shinwell stole the tapes, I knew in my bones that was wrong. John and Naima were fine people, and they hadn't done nothin' to nobody. So I left him.

"At first, Shinwell got real angry. Then he tried winnin' me back, callin' all the time, showin' up at my aunt's. But I never phoned back, and my aunt, she hated Shinwell, she wouldn't even let him in the door. Finally he found someone else and let me be.

"I dated other fellows, but then I got lucky and met Joseph." She turned around and pointed to a picture of a handsome Black man in an army uniform. "He was a good man. Hard workin', clean livin', helped out his dad at their dry-cleanin' store. Treated me like a queen. We had a nice long courtship—movies, walks in the park, goin' out dancin'. It was everythin' I ever dreamed of. He was savin' up so we could get married, but then he was drafted."

She looked out the window. Her light-brown skin glowed in the sunlight. "Joseph said we shouldn't get married before he left, 'cause if he didn't come back, I'd be a widow. In the end he didn't come back, and instead of bein' a widow, I was nothin'.

"Everythin' went numb. I wasn't feelin' a thing, and that went on some time. Then in early '68, Shinwell showed up again. By then my aunt had moved away, and I didn't have the strength to say no. Shinwell made all kinds of pretty promises, and next thing I knew, we was livin' together.

"In the beginning, before he really had me back, Shinwell was good to me. But once he knew I was his, he was twice as bad as before. There wasn't no hittin', or I guess you could say all the hittin' was on the inside. Mean stuff, like givin' me the silent treatment, or yellin' at me with his twisted logic that made my stomach hurt. Like I said, everythin' I did was wrong. Even how I looked."

Virginia raised her eyebrows. Betty Brown waved a hand. "I know. But that was part of it, him chippin' away at me so he could dominate me. I was like his slave, runnin' errands, makin' phone calls, doin' what he wanted when he wanted. He just got bigger and bigger, and me, I got smaller and smaller.

"Shinwell wasn't right in the head. He was a clean livin' guy, didn't drink or nothin', but he smoked and drank black coffee like they was goin' out of style. That kinda unhinged him, I think. Plus Shinwell didn't sleep much, couldn't waste time 'cause he always had to be learnin' somethin' new.

"He was craziest of all when he was practicin' the trumpet. I couldn't move a muscle when Shinwell practiced, he said the noise disturbed him even if I was in the next room. I told him I'd go out so he'd have some peace, but no, he wanted me there. But that wasn't no good neither, it was impossible to make no sound at all. Once when Shinwell was in the bedroom practicin', I dropped a spoon in the kitchen and he got hysterical angry. I'll never forget it."

She sighed wearily. "You're probably thinkin', 'Betty Brown, why didn't you up and leave that man?' I've thought about that a lot over the years. It's like Shinwell hypnotized me. He sucked out all my strength, and I stayed 'cause I wasn't strong enough to go. I knew I should, and I wanted to, but I was too weak.

"Plus you got to know somethin' else. Shinwell could be sweet as pie, the nicest, most affectionate man on earth. Every time he did somethin' crazy, he'd come back at me twice as nice: 'Baby, I'm sorry, let's put it behind us.' He'd buy me flowers, we'd get dressed up and go dancin', and for a while everythin' would be real good."

She shrugged. "But it never lasted. And as time went on, Shinwell just got angrier and angrier. He was bitter about the music world, bitter about Art Blakey pickin' Lee Morgan over him, bitter about not bein' the superstar he wanted to be.

"The bigger problem was that people weren't into jazz so much anymore, the young ones they liked rock-and-roll. Famous guys like Miles did OK, but middle guys like Shinwell didn't do so hot. He was in his midthirties then, so time was kinda runnin' out.

"Shinwell became obsessed with gettin' a hit. It was all he thought about, all he talked about. He started buyin' rock records and studyin' them, tryin' to figure out which way to go. Shinwell wanted to be like Sly and the Family Stone, and that's why he named his new group Shinwell Johnson and the Funky Sensations. Used to be the Shinwell Johnson Quartet, and I always thought they sounded real good, but that wasn't enough for Shinwell.

"Then he wrote 'Dashiki.' Everyone loved it, and that's where I came in. Shinwell decided he needed a dancin' girl. Me, I loved to sing, always had a real pretty voice, but Shinwell didn't care about that. The Black Power movement was happenin' then, and Shinwell wanted me to look like I should be carryin' a machine gun. 'Don't smile!' he'd yell. 'Look mean.' It made me scared the way Shinwell screamed, but turns out me lookin' frightened was the same to him as me lookin' mean, so it worked out.

"And the clothes Shinwell had me wear! I got nothin' against miniskirts, but I was a shy girl, and I didn't like standin' up in front of people wearin' barely nothin'. Shinwell bought all those clothes for me, they was part of the image he wanted. The guys in the band wore dashikis too, but at least they didn't have to freeze their legs off. And to justify me bein' up there, Shinwell made me yell out at the end." She smiled sadly. "Waste of a life."

"Oh, no!" Virginia broke in. "That's not true! You were cutting edge. I thought you were inspiring."

"Inspirin'?" Betty Brown put a hand to her chest and laughed. "Child, you are too much."

"It's true. Socks and I—that's my roommate, the one who gave me the honey for you—we both saw you on *The Mike Douglas Show*. You danced so well, and you seemed so strong."

Betty Brown shook her head sadly. "That's sure funny to hear, 'cause I never felt weaker. Shinwell had me dancin' up a storm at all his gigs, and I hated just about every minute. But 'Dashiki' had become a huge hit, so it wasn't like I had no choice." She looked out the window. "A few days after *The Mike Douglas Show*, that's when I did it."

Virginia frowned. "Did what?"

"That's when I killed Shinwell."

Betty Brown picked up her tea and took a long sip. She set down the cup and looked down at her hands.

"It was a Thursday afternoon," she said quietly. "Me and Shinwell were in our apartment on Morton Street in Greenwich Village. He said somethin' to me, I don't even recall what it was. Not one of his big fits, just some small criticism he laid on me.

"Don't know why it was then and never before, but me, I snapped. Shinwell turned his back, and I picked up a lamp and hit him on the head, hard as I could."

Betty Brown stared out the window. "Shinwell went down like a broken doll. I kept waitin' for him to get up, but when I leaned over and got up close, he wasn't breathin'.

"Somethin' happened to my mind then; I suddenly felt all cold and logical. There was a dead man in my apartment, and I needed to get him out of there. I took a moment to think, then I decided to put Shinwell in a trunk. He was tall but super skinny, nothin' but a bitty thing, so I had no problem pickin' him up and fittin' him in.

"I took the trunk outside on a dolly, thinkin' I'd put it in the car and dump it somewhere. We was always movin' out equipment for gigs, so I knew no one would think nothin' if they saw me haulin' out stuff. But no one did see me.

"Then I got lucky. A few doors down, a couple hippie kids were movin' out, they had a big truck with Pennsylvania plates. When they went inside again to get more stuff, I rolled the dolly up a ramp into the truck and slid the trunk off. Threw one of them moving blankets around it so no one would notice. It was kinda risky, but I felt in my gut it was gonna work.

"After that, I brought the dolly back home. I went over to Washington Square Park and sat on a bench till it was dark. When I got home, the truck was gone.

"Then I got luckier still. Shinwell had other women, but that one girl Christine showed up at his gigs a lot, and I think they was gettin' serious. She roomed with Rex Royal's girl at the time, and a few days after I put Shinwell in the truck, I found out Christine was also missin'. No note, no nothin'. Never did find out why she left or what happened to her, but everyone figured Christine had somethin' to do with Shinwell disappearin'.

"And my luck held out. When those kids opened that trunk and saw a dead Black man, they musta freaked out and dumped him in a field. Then that farmer found him, but since he ran over Shinwell with his tractor, no one could say for sure how Shinwell died. The police they questioned me, but no one thought I had anythin' to do with it. I got off scot-free. Or at least I did on the outside."

Betty Brown looked down at her hands again. "'Cause you don't forget. On the one hand, I wasn't sorry at all. Shinwell being dead meant I never had to listen to that man again, and sometimes that alone made it seem worthwhile. But I was raised by God-fearin' folk, and I knew what I did was wrong.

"It haunted me. Always. I moved out of Manhattan, stayed away from jazz clubs, never even listened to the music on the radio. But I still couldn't escape what was goin' on inside. Truth be told, some days got pretty dark.

"Then I had some luck again. I was livin' in a little studio in Jersey City, and I became friendly with the woman next door. A Muslim woman. We had lots of long talks about religion, and finally I decided to convert. It was like bein' a baby again. I got a new name and a new way to be. Finally my strength came back."

Betty Brown placed a hand on the side of her face. "But you know, you can convert all you like, but it still don't take away the stain of murder. *The Quran* says, 'The recompense of an injury is an injury the like thereof.' That's why I'm at peace with this cancer, see, because I must needs pay for my actions. Only Allah can judge me now. That's comin' soon, and I'm ready."

She inhaled deeply. "It's been thirty-four years since Shinwell's gone, and thirty-two years since I converted. I pray for forgiveness every day. I say, 'Allah, don't let what I've done kill the beauty of my soul.' And I don't think it has. No, I don't believe it has at all."

Betty Brown turned and looked Virginia right in the eye.

Virginia sat frozen, barely comprehending what the melodious voice had just told her.

When she realized that Betty Brown had finished speaking, Virginia said haltingly, "I—I'm so sorry you had to go through all that. And I'm glad you found a way to—to get some peace."

Betty Brown gave a wry smile. "Guess I didn't find much peace, or I wouldn't be spillin' all this to a stranger."

Virginia blushed. "Do you regret telling me?"

"Nope. Not that I planned to or nothin'. I was hopin' I'd be able to talk about the tapes, but I never dreamed all this would come out. Never told another livin' soul. For obvious reasons, I suppose."

"I won't say a word to anyone," Virginia said solemnly. "I promise."

Betty Brown tipped her head and stared at her. "I know you won't. You're a good girl, I can see it in your eyes." She glanced at the clock. "That photographer will be here soon."

Virginia looked up. Five minutes to three! She put the tape recorder in her bag and stood. "I need to go."

"It was a real pleasure to meet you," Betty Brown said, standing a bit unsteadily. "And you thank your friend for the honey. That was real sweet of her."

"Socks is a big fan of yours. She'll be thrilled to hear you liked it."

Betty Brown walked her to the door, and Virginia hesitated. After such an emotional encounter, she longed to hug Betty Brown or at least shake her hand. But Betty Brown just opened the door and offered a small bow, which Virginia returned.

As she walked down the hallway, she heard the apartment door shut behind her.

And now? Virginia thought, hugging her Louis Armstrong doll as she stared at the ceiling. Betty Brown was dead, the Five Spot tapes were in limbo, and the police had launched an investigation.

But surely Shinwell Johnson's death—his murder—had nothing to do with Betty Brown and the tapes! Virginia had made a promise, and she intended to keep it.

Don't worry, she reassured herself. What happened to Shinwell Johnson is totally unrelated to Betty Brown's death. That detective isn't going to start nosing around in the past.

Comforted by these thoughts, Virginia's eyes grew heavy. In the deep stillness of the quiet mountains, she finally fell asleep.

Wednesday
August 6, 2003

When Virginia emerged from her room at eleven, Socks was sitting at the kitchen table in her morning attire of white turban and burgundy silk pajamas. She was nursing a cup of tea and gazing pensively out the window at the deer grazing in the sunny meadow.

"Morning," Virginia greeted her, putting on the kettle. In contrast to Socks' glamour, she wore oversized white shorts and a faded and beloved Thelonious Monk T-shirt.

"Good morning," Socks answered, her voice unusually subdued.

Virginia looked at her suspiciously. "What's going on?"

"You need caffeine first."

"Tell me now."

Socks took a deep breath. "It appears you now have enough information to be scared."

"What do you mean?"

"Your detective friend left a message early this morning. The tapes are gone."

Virginia's stomach flipped.

Socks looked at her sympathetically. "I saved the message, of course. You might want to give it a listen."

Virginia picked up the landline and dialed into voicemail. A recording from 8:15 that morning started to play.

"Hello, this is a message for Virginia Farrell. This is Robert Smith, the detective from last night. I'm sorry to tell you, but another officer and I just did a thorough search of Baseema Baheera's apartment, and we found no sign of a shoebox or any tapes."

Pause. "I know this is bad news for you, but we're going to do everything in our power to get the tapes back."

Another pause. "I have some follow-up questions, so I'll be in touch."

An even longer pause. "I hope that your day is good."

Virginia hung up and sat down at the kitchen table. She put her head in her hands. "They're gone," she moaned. "And it's all my fault."

"Now, now, none of that," Socks said briskly. The kettle, which was designed to resemble a cow, started whistling. "English Breakfast?"

Virginia nodded miserably.

"It's not your fault that someone killed poor Betty Brown," Socks went on. "Nor that they stole the tapes." She set a teacup on the table and sat down. "Blaming yourself isn't going to help."

"I hope that your day is good!" Virginia fumed. "What kind of dumb thing is that to say? My day just started, and it's definitely not good."

The two women drank their tea in silence. As the caffeine set Virginia's mind in motion, she decided Socks was right: there was no use blaming herself about the missing tapes. And even though Virginia felt terribly sad about both the murder and the music, it was pointless to sit around and wallow.

Sip by sip, Virginia's feistiness returned. She had promised Betty Brown to get the tapes to their rightful owners, and she could still try to keep that promise.

When Virginia's teacup was empty, she put it down decisively and announced, "We have to find Betty Brown's killer."

Socks blinked. "Aren't the police going to do that?"

Virginia waved a hand dismissively. "You saw that detective, he was clueless! How could anyone not know who John Coltrane was?"

"Actually . . ."

"Besides," Virginia went on, "the killer must be someone I know."

"An even better reason to let the police handle it."

"I'm not talking about anything extreme. Just a little quiet sleuthing. And I need your help."

Socks looked alarmed. "You do?"

"Every sleuth has assistants. Nancy Drew had Bess and George, and I have you."

Socks bit her lip.

"Think of Betty Brown," Virginia pleaded. "Remember how much you love 'Dashiki.'"

Socks stared at Virginia. One could always sway Socks by issuing a moral imperative.

"All right," she declared. "You're on. How do we start?"

"With our brains. We need to analyze the situation, then develop a plan of action."

"A yellow notepad is essential." Socks turned around and took one out from the drawer of the antique cupboard sitting behind her. "And a pen. My favorite purple one will do."

Virginia straightened up. "First of all, should we presume that the person who killed Betty Brown is the same one who took the tapes?"

"We have to assume that," Socks replied. "Anything else will give me a headache."

"Let's list everyone who either knew about the tapes, or knew I was seeing Betty Brown."

"Very well." On the top line, Socks wrote in capital letters SUSPECTS. "Who knew about the tapes?"

"Me," Virginia said.

Socks put pen to paper.

"Don't!" Virginia cried out. "I'm not a suspect."

"Who else?"

"Nathan."

Socks began to write.

"No!" Virginia protested. "He didn't do it either."

Socks looked at her dryly. "Everyone is guilty until proven innocent."

"All right, put him down. But with an asterisk, because it couldn't possibly be him."

"What's his last name again?"

"Garrideb." Virginia reached for the pad. "Here, I'll write it."

"Who else?"

"Joe Pascoe was at the apartment right after me. Betty Brown might have confided in him as well, or maybe Joe saw the tapes on the coffee table."

"Write him down," Socks instructed. "Now tell me, who knew you were going to interview Betty Brown?"

"You did."

"I think it's safe to exclude me. Who else?"

"I'm almost certain Nathan told Byron Ffowlkes. He's the editor-in-chief, after all."

"Let's put him down."

Virginia wrote his name, and Socks frowned. "You have an extra f."

"That's how it's spelled. He's English."

"Good Lord. Who else?"

"I told Mortimer."

"Your eccentric little friend with the bright-red hair?"

"Yes. But he wouldn't hurt a fly. Write his name, but give him an asterisk too."

"That's it?" Socks asked.

"As far as I know."

"Very well. Now we need a brainstorming session." Socks looked at the clock, which had little chickens instead of numbers. "For the next fifteen minutes, only silence and deep thoughts. Then we'll confer."

"Good idea," Virginia agreed.

"First we need fresh cups of tea."

"But of course."

Settled at the table with their steaming cups of tea, the two women started to think. Virginia doodled aimlessly on the yellow pad, and Socks stared out the window with a frown.

If Virginia were to judge strictly on personality, Byron Ffowlkes would be her number-one suspect. Hands down.

Virginia had distrusted Byron since their initial meeting a year earlier. Not merely because he asked, "How's the air down there, little lady?" Rather it was because he was cold. The first time Byron looked at her, he stared right through her, as if she were invisible. So cold!

As time went on, Virginia liked Byron even less. Partly because he often referred to her using the horrific appellation "short stuff," but mostly because he was an intellectual bully. He knew a great deal about jazz, but he used his knowledge to belittle others. For Virginia, jazz was about joy, but it was clear Byron never had any fun.

A few months ago, Byron's attitude toward her changed. Virginia was in *Jazz Now* on her way to see Nathan, and Byron stopped her in the reception area. He inquired most politely about her health, and asked if she was getting enough promotional CDs. Byron went so far as to invite Virginia into his office to browse his collection, in case she wanted something new to listen to.

When she finally extracted herself, she walked into Nathan's office. "Byron was nice to me just now," she said in bewilderment.

Nathan grinned. "Someone told him that Mr. Togasaki is your patron. Byron asked me about it right before you came."

After that, Virginia was one of the elect. No more short stuff. Whenever she ran into Byron, he fawned over her and invited her to a show. But Virginia was not fooled. Byron hadn't really changed, he just thought she might be useful.

Then there was the incident with Mortimer. Oh dear.

Every Tuesday afternoon at 4.30, Byron ran a mandatory listening session. He claimed to be appalled at his staff's ignorance, or as he once announced pompously at a staff meeting, "You have no *spine of knowledge*." So now every week, the staff piled into *Jazz Now*'s conference room and listened to early jazz for ninety minutes. Which no one minded, but they also had to listen to Byron drone on and on about it. No one else was allowed to speak. And Byron never served refreshments.

As a freelancer, Virginia was not required to attend. Also, prior to becoming one of the elect, she was not deemed worthy because she was female. "Women," Byron once proclaimed in her presence, "are not interested in music. They're only interested in musicians." Virginia's eyebrows had shot straight up, and they remained that way for quite some time.

But although Virginia didn't attend the listening sessions, she certainly heard enough about them from disgruntled staff members, particularly after the incident with Mortimer.

Mortimer Burns was a special person. He was completely obsessed with John Coltrane. That was the only music he listened to, and the sole topic of his conversations. Fortunately Mortimer was able to make a living from his passion; he was currently hard at work on his third book about Coltrane, and he wrote one of the magazine's most popular columns, "Coltrane's Corner."

Mortimer's singlemindedness was enough to alienate anyone, and his peculiar appearance didn't help. Slightly taller than Virginia, he had fiery red hair, thin and parted neatly in the middle, like someone from a 1920s barbershop quartet. His complexion was ghastly pale, and his big blue eyes were tremulous and unfocused. He also wore the same outfit every single day: khakis and a button-down shirt with thick blue-and-white vertical stripes.

Certainly most people thought Mortimer strange. Yet he was a gentle soul, and there were definitely worse obsessions than John Coltrane. In fact, as fixations went, Virginia thought Coltrane was rather a good one. She was obsessed with him as well, and it was nice to have someone to share that with. And despite Mortimer's quirks, he had a wife and a kind one at that, so he clearly had something going for him.

However, requiring someone like Mortimer to listen to Bix Beiderbecke, Bunny Berigan, and the like was simply counterproductive. It showed Byron's complete ignorance of his staff, and this lack of understanding backfired on him in an unexpected way.

It happened one day when Byron was playing an extremely rare Hot Five record from his personal collection. Since it wasn't Coltrane, Mortimer fell asleep. Unfortunately, he had been sitting tipped back in his chair, and when he fell backward his foot kicked the table, which jostled the turntable and put a deep scratch in the record.

From what Virginia heard, Byron turned bright red and called Mortimer every foul name he could think of for five minutes nonstop. During the verbal assault, Mortimer sat stunned on the floor. When Byron was done, Mortimer ran to his office, locked the door, and played *A Love Supreme* five times straight. He came out only when Nathan called to say that Byron had left for the day.

Byron's reaction was completely unnecessary, Virginia mused. Mortimer was a highly sensitive person, anyone could see that, and he certainly hadn't meant to scratch the record. As far as Virginia was concerned, people mattered more than a piece of vinyl. But not so for Byron, which made him her number-one suspect.

Nevertheless, the listening session took place every Tuesday, so that's where Byron was yesterday afternoon. He couldn't have murdered Betty Brown even if he had known about the tapes. Which he hadn't.

Virginia sighed. Back to square one. If only—

"**T**ime's up!" Socks called out. "What have you got?"

Virginia frowned. "Not much."

"Do tell."

Virginia shared her suspicions about Byron Ffowlkes. Socks knew about Byron because Virginia had been bemoaning his existence since the day he bought *Jazz Now*. Socks also knew about his meltdown over the scratched record.

"But no one informed him about the tapes?" Socks asked.

Virginia shook her head. "I didn't tell him, and I can guarantee Nathan didn't either. First because I asked Nathan not to tell anyone, and second because Byron is the last person Nathan trusts."

"Is there a chance Byron listened through Nathan's office door?"

"The door was closed, Nathan had music playing in his office, and there's music piped into the hallways. That's a lot of white noise. Plus Nathan's pretty soft-spoken, and we weren't talking loud."

"What about the adjacent offices? Maybe Byron was listening from there."

"That wouldn't work either. On one side is Dimitris' office, but he has a padlock on his door."

Dimitris Petrakis, the magazine's art director, had taken a two-month leave of absence to travel to Greece. Officially he was visiting his sick grandmother, but unofficially he needed a break from Byron, whom he loathed.

"And on the other side?" Socks asked.

"Mortimer's office."

"Hmmm. How are Byron and Mortimer getting along since the big blowup?"

"The whole thing shook Mortimer's confidence, and now he's terrified of losing his job. He and Byron have morphed into a weird master-slave duo. Mortimer wants to make up for ruining Byron's record, and Byron is milking his guilt."

"Creepy," Socks remarked.

"I know! Mortimer runs errands for Byron all the time now, and they go out to clubs together practically every night."

"So if Byron asked to come into Mortimer's office and eavesdrop, would Mortimer let him?"

"Probably, but it wouldn't do him much good. The wall he'd be trying to hear through has floor-to-ceiling bookcases on both sides." Virginia paused to think. "And why would Byron want to listen to us anyway? I visit Nathan all the time, it was nothing out of the ordinary."

"So no eavesdropping."

"I'm also pretty sure Byron has an airtight alibi," Virginia went on. "He always holds his listening session on Tuesday afternoon."

"What about Mortimer? Why didn't you mention the tapes to him?"

"I needed a cool head. Telling Mortimer about the recordings would have sent him into hysterics." Virginia sighed. "I'm glad I stayed quiet. Otherwise I'd have to explain that they were missing, and we'd be dragging him off the Brooklyn Bridge right now."

"Where was Mortimer yesterday afternoon?" Socks asked.

"I'm sure he was at the listening session."

"So when you said you didn't have much, you meant it."

"What about you?"

Socks smiled widely. "I thought you'd never ask."

Socks set her palms on the table. "I have two theories."

"Go on," Virginia said eagerly.

"First is the asterisk theory. Look at the list and tell me who has an asterisk."

"Nathan and Mortimer."

"So it's one of them. Based on the fact," Socks said, holding up a hand to silence Virginia, "that it's always the person you least suspect."

"Socks! That's only in books. We're not in an Agatha Christie mystery, this is real life."

"I admit my theory has flaws. But it's worth considering."

"I'm almost 100 percent sure Mortimer was at the listening session. And Nathan said he went for a walk."

"A walk? Hmmm."

"Don't 'hmmm' me. What's your second theory?"

"The photographer Joe Pascoe. He's a crucial link in all this."

"You're right," Virginia agreed. "We have no idea what happened when he was at Betty Brown's apartment."

"We need to find out."

"He lives in Kingston, you know."

"Would it be weird if you went to see him?"

"No. But I need a bodyguard."

"Ah, yes," Socks said. "I do recall you mentioning that Mr. Pascoe is fond of female company. Ideally we could speak to him before our handsome detective does. Catch him off guard, if you get my drift."

Virginia looked at the clock. "There's a bus to Kingston in half an hour."

"Forget the bus! Dr. Bundle's on vacation this week, he'd be delighted to drive us."

"You mean to drive you. You're the love of his life."

Socks shrugged. "I haven't made up my mind about him yet. So for the time being, we're just friends."

Virginia stayed quiet. Socks had many friends.

While Socks spoke to Dr. Bundle on the landline, a plan took shape in Virginia's mind. She drummed her fingers, waiting impatiently for the meandering conversation to end.

At last Socks set down the receiver. "Dr. Bundle will be here in a half hour." She sat down and picked up her teacup. "Your eyes are twitching. Got an idea?"

"I do." Virginia leaned forward. "Let's say Joe killed Betty Brown and took the tapes. What would he do afterward?"

"Drive home and hide them in his apartment."

"Exactly. Joe lives on North Front Street in Kingston. It's a railroad apartment with a photography studio in the front room, a small kitchen in the middle, and a bedroom and bathroom in the back. Assuming Joe has the tapes, where would he hide them?"

"In the bedroom."

"Exactly again. What if someone distracts Joe while another person searches his bedroom?"

"Go on."

"And what better distraction than an attractive woman? One who he's never met before?"

Socks gave Virginia a level stare. "I don't like where this is going."

"I need you, Socks! Joe already knows I'm not interested in him. But you!"

"Fresh blood."

"Precisely."

Socks twisted her lips.

"Betty Brown," Virginia reminded her. "Bess and George."

"Oh, all right. How do we do this?"

"I can call Joe right now. I'll tell him I'm coming to Kingston to do errands, and I'll ask to stop by to see the Betty Brown photos. While I'm busy looking at the pictures, you just wait for Joe to make his move. Trust me, he always does."

"What's his modus operandi?" Socks asked.

"He'll compare you to an instrument."

"Did he do that to you?"

"Yes."

"Which instrument?"

Virginia blushed. "A pocket trumpet. Little and cute. I was never so insulted in my life."

"At least it wasn't a kazoo."

"When it's obvious Joe is interested in you, I'll excuse myself to go to the bathroom. Then I'll sneak into the bedroom. How's that for a plan?"

"Most excellent." Socks stood up and clapped her hands. "Let's get started."

Robert entered the lobby of 111 River Street at 9:30 a.m. He showed his identification at the security desk and asked to speak to the person in charge.

"Steve Dooney," the guard replied, pointing to a door behind the desk. "Right in there."

Robert knocked on a door marked PRIVATE in big gold letters.

"Come in," a voice called.

Inside was a medium-sized room filled with television screens and computers. A genial-looking man in his forties, chubby with curly gray-black hair, was leaning back in his chair and blithely eating a Danish.

"Steve Dooney?" Robert asked.

"That's me."

"Detective Robert Smith. I'm here on police business."

Dooney put down his Danish and wiped his hands on his pants. "Police business!" he said in a thick Jersey accent. "I thought all you Hoboken cops did was get kittens out of trees and peel drunk kids off the sidewalk. How can I help you?"

"It's in connection with a murder."

"Murder! Where? Not here in Hoboken."

Robert pointed to a copy of *The Jersey Journal*, still folded up and unread. "There's a story on the front page. We didn't release much information, but I can tell you it was an older woman who lived uptown. As part of our investigation, I need to know the whereabouts of several people who work in this building."

"Sure. I can find out when they came in, when they left, and whether they had mayo on their roast beef sandwich. Ha ha—that's a joke! But these cameras do the trick, you'd be surprised what we pick up."

"I need the arrivals and departures for the following people yesterday." Robert handed Dooney a list. "They all work here, except the woman at the bottom, who visited late afternoon."

Dooney looked at the names and read aloud, "Nathan Garrideb, Byron Ffowlkes—" He squinted at the paper. "You spelled it wrong."

"That's actually correct. He's English."

"—Mortimer Burns, and Virginia Farrell. Where do they work?"

"At *Jazz Now*."

"No problem. See, anytime someone comes in or goes out, they swipe their ID on the red panel on the turnstiles in front of the elevators. Just give me a little time, and I can pull up the info. Plus get the reception book from yesterday and tell you about the woman. Wanna wait?"

Robert stood. "I'm going up to *Jazz Now*. I'll stop by on my way out."

Dooney's eyes widened. "You think one of them murdered this lady?"

"That's what I plan to find out."

Robert pushed open the glass doors and entered *Jazz Now*'s reception area. A tall Black woman with a slender build was sitting behind a sleek white desk. She told him that Nathan Garrideb and Mortimer Burns were in, but Mr. Ffowlkes probably wouldn't arrive until eleven.

"I'll see Mr. Garrideb then."

"And your name is—?"

"Detective Robert Smith."

"Is Nathan expecting you?"

Robert noticed there were no newspapers on her desk, only a copy of a Miles Davis biography facedown. "No. Tell him it's about Virginia Farrell."

The woman picked up the phone and punched a button. "Nathan? A Detective Robert Smith is here to see you . . . About Virginia . . . All right." She put down the phone and pointed to her left. "Go down that hallway and make a right. He's in the second office."

"Thank you."

Robert walked slowly down the hall, taking in the atmosphere. There was music everywhere, piped into the hallways and coming out of each office. The carpeting was new and the paint job still fresh; it was clear *Jazz Now* had not been here long.

As Robert passed the corner office, he saw the nameplate BYRON FFOWLKES. Then a curious thing, a padlocked door. Stranger still was a row of empty secretary stations along the right.

Next to the locked door was the nameplate NATHAN GARRIDEB. Robert stood in the doorway and saw an intelligent-looking man with a blond ponytail, about thirty-five years old, sitting at his desk with a worried expression. The big windows behind him revealed a magnificent view of Manhattan and the Hudson River.

Garrideb looked up when he heard Robert. "Is Virginia all right?" he asked quickly.

"She's fine." Robert walked in and held out a hand. "I'm Detective Robert Smith. From the Hoboken Police Department."

Garrideb stood and shook Robert's hand, his grip dry and firm. He motioned Robert to sit, then sank into his chair. "And I'm Nathan. But I don't understand. This is about Virginia, and she's all right?"

"Actually," Robert said, sitting on the edge of a green-cushioned chair in front of the desk, "it's more about Baseema Baheera. Betty Brown."

Garrideb looked puzzled. "Betty Brown?"

"Have you spoken to Virginia Farrell today?"

"Not yet. She promised to call me first thing, but so far she hasn't."

"I'm afraid Betty Brown was murdered yesterday afternoon."

Garrideb gripped the edge of his desk. "She what? How?"

"In her apartment."

"Oh my God." He shook his head slowly. "I'm so sorry to hear that. But—have you spoken to Virginia? Do you know about the tapes?"

"We do. They're missing."

Garrideb closed his eyes and let out a long sigh. "Oh no. I can't believe this." He looked at Robert ruefully. "Please don't get me wrong. I'm really sorry about Betty Brown, but those tapes—they're priceless."

"We're going to do our best to find them. You can help us out by answering a few questions."

Garrideb echoed Virginia's account, confirming how he had tracked down Betty Brown's whereabouts, as well as their telephone conversation to set up the interview.

"So," Robert said, "you knew that Virginia was at Betty Brown's apartment yesterday afternoon?"

"Yes."

"Did you expect to see Virginia after the interview?"

"We didn't have an appointment, but I thought she might stop by. Virginia does that frequently," Garrideb added. "Less now, though, since she moved upstate."

"When did she arrive?" Robert asked.

"About three-thirty, I think."

"How did she seem to you?"

"Excited. Agitated, but not upset, if that makes sense. She couldn't wait to tell me about the tapes."

"Were you surprised by the news?"

"Oh, yes!" Garrideb declared. "I was thrilled. Finding a stash of recordings like that is every jazz lover's dream."

"So when you spoke on the phone with Betty Brown, she gave no hint about the tapes?"

"Absolutely not. It was a straightforward conversation about the interview. From what Virginia said, Betty Brown never told anyone about them."

"How did your conversation with Virginia yesterday wind up?"

"We both agreed we needed to get the tapes to a safe place. The Institute of Jazz Studies in Newark was the obvious choice. Plus we wanted to contact Monk's and Coltrane's heirs."

"OK."

"But we decided to deal with it this morning, just to give us time to digest the news. Virginia was supposed to call me first thing today, then I was going to phone Betty Brown and hopefully go to her place for the tapes."

"What time did Virginia leave yesterday afternoon?"

Garrideb thought a moment. "Around four. I remember because she was in a hurry to get her bus."

"What did you do then?" Robert asked.

"I went out a few minutes later for a walk. I needed to clear my head and sort everything out, so I went to my thinking spot."

Robert looked up from his notebook. "Where's that?"

"A bench on the Fourteenth Street Pier. It's beautiful, I go there a lot."

"How long did you stay?"

"I'm not sure. Maybe a half hour?"

"Did you speak to anyone, or see anyone you know?"

"No. I was just sitting and reading my notes, thinking things over."

"Your notes?"

"I made notes when I was talking with Virginia. Whenever a conversation is important, I make sure to document it. I plan to write a book one day about my experiences in the jazz world."

"Where do you keep your notes?"

"They're in a file at my apartment."

"Did you put yesterday's notes there as well?"

"Yes," Garrideb confirmed. "I brought them home last night."

Robert nodded. "After your walk, what did you do?"

"I came back to the office. Oh, wait! I made a stop at Carlo's Bakery. I was passing by on Washington Street when I decided to buy an Oreo cookie cake for my girlfriend."

"What time did you return to *Jazz Now*?"

"About five-thirty. I left for home a little while after that."

"Did you talk to anyone when you came back?"

Garrideb shook his head no. "I said hello to Maggie, our receptionist, but nothing more. Everyone else was at the editor's listening session."

"What's that?"

"Our editor-in-chief, Byron Ffowlkes, plays music for the staff every Tuesday afternoon at 4.30. He feels they don't know enough about early jazz."

"But you're not required to go?"

"No. I know all that music."

Robert looked up. Something in Garrideb's voice had changed. He sounded angry.

"Do you and Byron Ffowlkes get along?" Robert asked.

"Well enough."

"Is Mr. Ffowlkes popular with his staff?"

Garrideb hesitated. "Not exactly. I don't want to badmouth anyone, but Byron tends to expound a lot. Not everyone appreciates it."

"What can you tell me about Joe Pascoe?"

"Joe's a terrific guy," Garrideb said, clearly relieved to change the subject. "One of the best jazz photographers around. I needed some great shots, so I gave him the assignment."

"And you're sure he went to see Betty Brown?"

"I'm positive. Joe's a complete pro, I can always count on him."

"You didn't speak to him yesterday or this morning?"

"The last time we spoke was on Friday, when I called him to set up the shoot. Usually he drops by with the pictures a few days later."

Robert already knew that Joe Pascoe had been to Betty Brown's apartment, because they had spoken on the phone before Robert went to *Jazz Now*. Pascoe was going to meet Robert in Hoboken later that afternoon, and he was bringing the pictures with him.

"What about Mortimer Burns?" Robert asked.

"He's a special person," Garrideb grinned. "One of our best writers. Mortimer does a monthly column called 'Coltrane's Corner.'" His face clouded. "I couldn't wait to tell him about the tapes."

"But you didn't."

"Nope. Virginia swore me to secrecy. Except she said I could tell my girlfriend, which I did last night when I got home."

"Where's home?"

"Jersey City. A few blocks from the Grove Street PATH station."

Robert consulted his notebook. "About this listening session. Did it go on as usual yesterday?"

"Byron never cancels. When I left for my walk, I saw him in his office getting ready."

"Did he see you?"

"I waved at him."

"Did you say where you were going?"

"Oh no. He doesn't need to know my every move."

There it was again, that slight change in tone. "Mortimer Burns would have gone to the listening session as well?"

"Definitely."

"All right." Robert stood and put the notebook and pen in his jacket pocket. "Thank you for your help."

"I'm happy to do whatever I can. Like I said, I'm sorry about Betty Brown, and of course the tapes—"

"Actually, there is something you can do," Robert said. "I'd like to see your notes, the ones you took during your discussion with Virginia."

"No problem. Should I go home and get them now? It won't take long."

"That's not necessary. How about I come by tomorrow? Two o'clock, let's say."

"That's fine. I'll definitely be here."

"I'd appreciate that." Robert put his hand on the doorknob, then turned around. "One last thing—the padlocked door?"

Nathan grimaced. "That's Dimitris, our art director. He took a leave of absence to visit a sick relative and locked his door before he left."

"Isn't that a fire hazard?"

"I have a key, and so does building security."

"And he did this because—?"

Nathan looked Robert in the eye. "He doesn't trust Byron."

Virginia and Socks stood on the sidewalk in front of Joe Pascoe's building in uptown Kingston, a quaint area with nineteenth-century architecture and canopied sidewalks. They had just said goodbye to Dr. Bundle, who planned to browse in Alternative Books, then meet them for tea at Bread Alone.

Virginia looked at Socks. She stood long and lean in a navy-blue sleeveless top, white silk pants, and gold high-heeled sandals. Her thick blonde hair was straight and shiny, and she wore gold bracelets and enormous gold hoop earrings. Joe Pascoe didn't stand a chance.

"Ready?" Virginia asked.

"Always," Socks replied.

They pushed the door open and walked up to the second floor, the building's stairs creaking agreeably under their feet. At the top of the stairs, a door bore a sign in florid italics:

Joe Pascoe
Photographer

Virginia knocked loudly. A moment later, Joe pulled the door open.

"Hey there!" His face lit up as his gaze landed on Socks. "And hello to you!"

"Hi, Joe," Virginia greeted him. "This is my roommate, Socks."

"Pleased to meet you," Socks purred.

Joe stared at her in awe. "Oh no," he managed to sputter. "The pleasure is all mine. Come in, please!"

The studio was a spacious white room with a shiny wooden floor and large windows facing North Front Street. A red velvet couch, a matching chair, and a black kidney-shaped coffee table rested on a fuzzy white rug. The rest of the room was filled with equipment—lamps, umbrellas, backdrops, and neatly arranged cameras, tripods, and other gear.

A display of Joe's photographs of jazz musicians, in both color and black-and-white, covered almost every inch of wall space. A high-end stereo sat in one corner, beside shelves of meticulously arranged CDs, albums, and cassettes. An album spun slowly, filling the room with the languid sounds of Stan Getz's "Desafinado."

They moved toward the seating area. Virginia took a chair quickly so the others could sit together on the couch.

Joe's handsome, Virginia thought, watching him stare at Socks. He was tall and thin, mostly bald, with striking green eyes and sharp cheekbones. His passion for jazz and dedication to photography added to his appeal, and if his romantic style had been different, Virginia might have dated him. Unfortunately, Joe was stuck with the romantic style he had.

Virginia and Joe had collaborated on numerous articles over the years, and he was always professional on the job. But as soon as they were off-duty, he inevitably offered to buy Virginia a drink, an invitation she always declined. Even worse was when he tried to butter her up by saying she reminded him of a pocket trumpet, little and cute.

Joe's low point occurred about a year ago at an interview and photo shoot with trombonist Roswell Rudd. Afterward they all shared a late lunch at the Dietz Stadium Diner in Kingston. As Rudd reminisced about his days playing with Pee Wee Russell, Joe slid his hand up Virginia's calf. She responded by using her other foot to crush his fingers. Thankfully Joe's pained whimper was masked by the waitress asking if they wanted more coffee.

After the diner incident, Virginia asked Nathan to keep her interviews and Joe's photo shoots blessedly separate. She still ran into Joe occasionally at shows, but she was careful to keep him away from her ankles.

"Refreshments?" Joe asked. "Virginia, I know you don't drink, but perhaps your roommate would care to join me for a whiskey?"

"Delighted," Socks enthused.

"A woman who drinks in the middle of the day!" he said appreciatively, eyes fixed on Socks. "Straight up?"

"Is there any other way?"

Joe winked. He turned to Virginia. "And you?"

"Water's fine," she answered.

He headed into the kitchen, still talking through the open archway.

"I knew Virginia had a roommate," he called out, "but I had no idea you were so—photogenic. I'm glad you two came over."

Joe returned with a bottle of Jack Daniel's, two tumblers, and a glass of water for Virginia. He filled both tumblers halfway, then passed one to Socks. "Cheers," he proclaimed, raising his whiskey.

"*Skål.*" Socks clinked her glass against his.

Virginia wondered how Socks was going to wiggle out of drinking. But she needn't have worried. Socks raised the glass to her lips, then pointed across the room. "Who's that?"

"Where?" Joe said, turning his head.

Quick as a flash, Socks dabbed whiskey on her lips and emptied her glass into a nearby plant. "The Black man in a red shirt playing saxophone."

"That's David Murray," Joe said, turning back to face them.

"Such a powerful visual statement," Socks enthused.

"Thank you," Joe said, looking pleased. "I'm rather fond of that one myself." He glanced at Socks' empty glass. "Looks like you could use another."

"Desperately."

"I think I've found my partner in crime," Joe said, locking eyes with Socks as she handed him her glass.

Virginia hid a smile. Everything was going exactly as planned.

"So, Joe," Virginia began. "On the phone, you told me the detective called you. What did he say?"

"Not much. Just that someone killed Betty Brown." He shook his head. "It's so hard to believe! We only saw each other yesterday."

"I know," Virginia said somberly. "It feels strange."

"When I got there, Betty Brown told me you'd just left. I must have missed you by half a second."

"Did anything odd happen while you were there?"

"Nothing." Joe took a sip of whiskey. "I came in with my equipment, and Betty Brown asked if I wanted tea. I said no, then we chatted a bit. She seemed uncomfortable with being photographed, so I tried to put her at ease."

"What did you talk about?"

"Jazz mostly. Nothing earth-shattering. Then I set up my gear and began shooting. She seemed tired, but otherwise she was friendly."

"Betty Brown was ill. She told me she had cancer."

Joe nodded sadly. "That explains it. Still, the pictures came out great."

"I can't wait to see them. So tell me, what time did you leave?"

Joe thought a moment. "We chatted a bit more after the photo shoot, then I left around four-thirty. I figured she might want to rest before Nathan came over."

A shiver ran up Virginia's neck. "Nathan?"

"He called shortly before I headed out. From Betty Brown's end of the conversation, it sounded like he was on his way over to see her."

"You're sure it was Nathan?"

"I heard Betty Brown say his name, like she was repeating it after him. She said he could come by after four-thirty. I figured it had to do with the article."

"You don't think—" Socks ventured.

"Nathan?" Joe laughed. "No way! If Nathan were on the ground with someone kicking him, he'd be more worried about the guy's shoe. He's harmless as a kitten."

"I agree," Virginia said quickly.

Joe made a dismissive motion. "I figure Nathan didn't end up going over there after all, and some neighborhood kid killed Betty Brown during a robbery." He downed the rest of his drink and stood. "Would you like to see the photos now?"

Virginia rose as well. "Sure."

Joe led her over to a white counter with black stools. He picked up a manila envelope and slipped out a thick stack of 8-by-10 photos. "Normally I wouldn't print all my negatives, but the detective asked me to do it for their investigation. Gotta help the cops, right?"

"Gotta help Betty Brown," Virginia replied.

She flinched when she saw the first image: a close-up of Betty Brown's face, her expression calm and dignified. It made Virginia sad indeed to see Betty Brown alive and well, with no idea what lay ahead.

Joe peered over Virginia's shoulder. "That's a nice shot," he commented. "If I do say so myself."

"You didn't see anyone on your way out?" she asked, flipping to the next photo. "Someone lurking in the lobby maybe?"

"Nope. I hopped in my car and headed over to the Malibu Diner for dinner." He laughed. "I had a parking spot right in front of Betty Brown's building. In Hoboken, that's a miracle." He glanced eagerly over his shoulder at Socks. "Listen, Ginny, you keep looking, and I'll go hang out with your roommate."

Ginny, she thought scornfully. "Go right ahead. I'll need some time with these."

While Socks' laughter tinkled merrily in the background, Virginia focused on the photographs. Joe had several shots of Betty Brown sitting on the couch. He must have crouched near the apartment's front door, because the pictures gave a complete view of the coffee table. Everything was exactly as it had been when Virginia left, including the shoebox full of tapes. John Coltrane's shoebox, she reflected mournfully.

There were a number of shots of Betty Brown in profile, as well as images of her perched on the arm of a chair. Next came a series of stunning close-ups where light played on half of her face. Say what you wanted about Joe Pascoe, but he certainly appreciated women, and he knew how to bring out the best in them.

Speaking of which . . . Virginia turned slightly and looked over her shoulder. Socks and Joe were sitting knee to knee, Socks nodding eagerly while Joe explained a camera technique.

Virginia flipped back to the beginning of the photographs. About halfway through, she heard her cue:

" . . . remind me of a soprano saxophone," Joe was saying. "Have you ever seen one?"

"I'm not sure," Socks oozed. "Describe it to me. You describe things so well."

"Soprano saxophones are slim and elegant, and they make a unique sound. They're a bit of a rarity; not many musicians play them. When John Coltrane started using one, it opened new horizons for him." Joe lowered his voice. "That's the power of the soprano saxophone—it can change a man's life."

"That's so deep," Socks murmured.

"I knew you'd understand."

"Joe," Virginia called out, rising from the stool. "Do you mind if I use the bathroom?"

"Go right ahead," he said. "We'll be just fine here, take all the time you need."

Virginia walked through the tidy white kitchen into Joe's bedroom. After closing the door, she put her hands on her hips and carefully surveyed the room.

Luckily Joe was extremely neat, but unluckily he had a walk-in closet with shelves, some of them quite high. Virginia stepped into the closet, turned on a light, and brought over a chair. She saw to her great hope that Joe used shoeboxes for storage. In fact, the top shelf had a row of them. None looked like John Coltrane's, but perhaps Joe had thrown out the old box and transferred the tapes to a new one.

Virginia stood on the chair and quickly checked each shoebox. All she found were baseball cards, out-of-fashion belts, and ticket stubs. No tapes.

She checked the rest of the closet quickly. No tapes in Joe's black cowboy boots, none in the big pockets of his bathrobe, nothing in the canvas storage tote on the floor.

Virginia turned off the light and put the chair back where it belonged. She went through the drawers of a large white bureau, but there were no tapes among the clothes. The bureau itself sat flush on the floor, whereas the bed was about a foot-and-a-half off the ground. She knelt and peered underneath.

In the far corner, Virginia saw a shoebox.

Her heart leapt. That must be it!

Joe surely moved the bed to get to the box, but she didn't want to risk making noise. Thankful for her small size, Virginia wiggled under the bed frame and started inching toward the corner. A minute later, she grabbed the box and dragged it into the light of day.

It wasn't John Coltrane's shoebox, but it was about the same size. Holding her breath, she removed the lid.

Virginia's disappointment brought tears to her eyes, followed by a smile and a shake of her head. The shoebox was filled with pictures of women posing with instruments that matched their shape and clothes: a pear-shaped woman with a tuba, a tall skinny woman in a black dress with silver buttons cradling a clarinet, and a large woman in a tuxedo leaning against a piano. Virginia was oddly insulted to see a small woman in a gold pantsuit holding a pocket trumpet.

She was just pondering the meaning of her feelings when a thunderous crash rang out from the next room.

Virginia quickly replaced the pictures and maneuvered under the bed with the shoebox. She crawled back out, brushed dust bunnies from her T-shirt and jeans, then ran into the studio.

It was not a pretty scene. Joe stood tearing at his sparse hair, while Socks sat on a stool looking contrite. A formerly neat arrangement of tripods now lay strewn across the floor.

"You can't begin to imagine how expensive this equipment is!" Joe shouted. "I told you to be careful."

Socks glanced at Virginia and raised an eyebrow. Virginia shook her head.

"I'm frightfully sorry," Socks apologized as she stood up. "It certainly wasn't intentional. Does this mean the Newport Jazz Festival is off?"

"Please just leave," Joe said angrily. "I need to get this back in order. Virginia—"

"Thanks for letting me see the pictures," she said easily. "When Betty Brown's murder is cleared up, I'm sure *Jazz Now* will run some kind of article."

Joe walked them to the door and, throwing Socks one final glare, slammed it behind them.

"Did you find the tapes?" Socks asked at once as they hurried down the stairs.

Virginia shook her head. "Nope."

"Never mind. At least we know which instrument I resemble."

"Poor Joe. If you don't know how to play a soprano saxophone, it lets out the most awful squeal."

Robert stepped out of Nathan Garrideb's office into the hallway. He paused, then walked over to Byron Ffowlkes' office. Still empty.

He turned and went past the padlocked door and Garrideb's room. The next nameplate read: MORTIMER BURNS. The door was shut, but Robert could hear music playing.

He knocked. Something scurried inside, and a moment later the door opened to reveal one of the most peculiar-looking people Robert had ever seen. Barely over five feet tall, Burns had skin so white he looked like he had spent his entire life in a cave. His bright-red hair was parted in the middle, and his enormous eyes were pale blue and trembling.

"Mortimer Burns?" Robert asked.

"Yes," the man whispered.

"I'm Detective Robert Smith from the Hoboken Police Department. May I come in for a moment?"

Burns closed his eyes and opened the door wide, allowing Robert into his lair.

The blinds were closed, obscuring the same panoramic view that Garrideb had. On the left side of the room, floor-to-ceiling bookshelves held a stereo, albums, CDs, and books. The other wall was taken up with framed pictures. Music that Robert could not identify, except that it was jazz, poured out from the sound system.

Burns sat down at his desk, which was piled high with albums and papers. Robert eyed the room's lone chair and the precarious stack of albums teetering on the seat.

"I'll take those," Burns said, jumping to his feet. He scooped up the albums and put them on top of a stack of books on his desk.

Robert sat, shifting slightly to see Burns through the piles. "I'm here because—"

"What did I do?" Burns blurted out.

"Have you read *The Jersey Journal* today?"

"I never read the paper," Burns said in the same quivering whisper.

"There's been a murder."

"Murder?"

"Yes. Baseema Baheera. Also known as Betty Brown."

"Syeeda Coltrane's babysitter."

"That's right. Yesterday one of your magazine's writers had an interview with her and—"

"Virginia. Did she tell you to talk to me?"

"No. But I asked her who knew about the interview, and your name came up."

"Oh dear." Burns' forehead was now glistening with sweat, so Robert offered him a handkerchief. Burns dabbed his face with the cloth, then placed it in a desk drawer.

Clearly a different approach was needed. "Mr. Burns—can I call you Mortimer?"

"You may."

"I'm mostly trying to get some background. I don't know much about jazz, and I'm a bit over my head. I know that Betty Brown was part of a group—"

"Shinwell Johnson and the Funky Sensations."

"Exactly. Plus she had a connection with John Coltrane. I understand you write a column on Coltrane. Can you tell me a little about Betty Brown's relationship with his family?"

For the next fifteen minutes, Robert listened as Mortimer Burns poured out minutiae about the Coltranes. Everything from the address of the mosque Naima attended, Syeeda's grades at school, and even the lay-out of the Coltranes' house. One would have thought that Burns had spent his entire life as a fly on the Coltranes' wall.

The recitation worked. Burns relaxed, his pale face glowing with joy. Robert listened politely, aware that he was in the presence of a full-blown fanatic.

"Of course, the move to New York took time. First Coltrane stayed in Paul Chambers' apartment in Brooklyn. The address was—"

"That's great," Robert cut in firmly. "I feel much better informed now. So you must have been excited when you heard that Virginia was going to talk to Betty Brown."

"Oh, yes. I even planned to interview her myself soon. Not that Virginia isn't a good reporter, but she probably asked a lot of questions about 'Dashiki.' I don't care about that."

"When did Virginia tell you about the interview?"

"She was here on Friday to lend me an album. John Coltrane's *Live at the Village Vanguard Again!*" Burns peered at Robert. "Do you own a copy?"

"I can't say I do."

"That's a shame," Burns said. "I'm conducting an investigation. One of my readers insists there's a three-second gap in 'My Favorite Things.' I'm trying to find as many copies as I can and make a report. People need to know."

"Virginia was here to drop off her copy to you?"

"Yes. Which is when she told me about the interview with Betty Brown on Tuesday. She promised to tell me how it went."

"Did she?"

"I haven't talked to Virginia since Friday."

"She was here yesterday afternoon from about 3:30 to 4 p.m. You didn't see her then?"

"No. I don't wander around much. I stay in here."

"Wasn't yesterday afternoon your editor's listening session?" Robert asked.

"Yes. I went to the conference room at twenty after four. I'm always early. And I didn't see Virginia."

"Did you stay until the end?"

"Once I'm in there, I don't move a muscle."

"What about Nathan Garrideb? Did you speak to him yesterday afternoon?"

"Nathan didn't stop by my office, I didn't run into him on my way to the listening session, and I didn't see him when I came out."

"And this morning?"

"I waved at Nathan as I walked by his office. That's it. No words."

"What about Byron Ffowlkes?"

Burns' eyes widened. "Did Byron talk to you about me?"

"I haven't spoken to Mr. Ffowlkes yet. Have you discussed Virginia or her interview with him?"

"I don't speak to Byron. I listen to him."

Robert cleared his throat. "Did you listen to him yesterday about Virginia or her interview?"

"I did not."

Robert returned the notebook and pen to his jacket pocket and stood up. "I think that's all, Mortimer. As I said, I just needed a little background."

Burns swallowed loudly. "I tried to be helpful."

"I know you did."

"I've never been interrogated by the police before."

Robert bit his lip. "You did fine." He looked over at the wall full of pictures. "Those are—"

"John Coltrane. All of them."

"He was in a group with Thelonious Monk, right?"

"At the Five Spot. Here." Burns leapt up and pointed to a photo.

Robert squinted at the faded image. Four Black men were on a cramped stage, one wearing sunglasses and hunched over a piano, another absorbed in playing a saxophone.

"Are there any albums recorded from those shows?" Robert asked casually.

Burns shook his head. "None at all. Naima Coltrane made recordings on her personal tape recorder, but they got lost."

"Is that so."

"In 1993, a record label put out a CD claiming it was one of Naima Coltrane's recordings from the 1957 Five Spot gig, but it turns out it was a tape she made at a Coltrane–Monk gig a year later. All the music from the 1957 Five Spot gig is lost. Gone forever," Burns said wistfully, touching his fingers to the glass.

"That's a shame."

Burns stared at Robert with fluttering eyes. "It's a *tragedy*," he whispered.

"All right then. Thank you for your time."

"Goodbye, Mr. Detective," Burns said softly. He waited for Robert to step into the hallway, then slammed the door shut.

Robert shook his head a little. That was certainly interesting.

He looked down the hall and saw a light on in Byron Ffowlkes' office. Robert walked past Garrideb, past the padlocked room, and knocked on Ffowlkes' door.

"Come in," an English-accented voice commanded.

Robert entered the office. A man in his thirties, dressed in a garish rose-colored suit, was sitting behind a stately oak desk. Without rising, Ffowlkes pointed to one of the shiny leather chairs facing the desk. "Do have a seat."

Robert remained standing. "My name is Detective Robert Smith, and I'm—"

Ffowlkes waved a hand. "Our receptionist forewarned me about your visit, and I got the full story from Nathan while you were questioning Mortimer. I hope you glued him back together afterward."

Robert sat down and stared at Ffowlkes. He was a handsome man with a full head of black hair, strong features, high cheekbones, and piercing blue eyes. He oozed money, from his tailored suit to his luxurious furniture and elaborate stereo system, which was pouring out the sounds of— even Robert recognized him—Louis Armstrong.

Ffowlkes sat at his desk with a stiffly erect posture, staring at Robert as though he were a source of amusement. The hairs on the back of Robert's neck stood up: he did not like this man.

"Mr. Ffowlkes, I'm here about the murder of Betty Brown."

"Ah, yes. I read about it in *The Jersey Journal* this morning. How simply horrible."

"I understand two members of your staff were at Betty Brown's apartment yesterday?"

"Virginia Farrell and Joe Pascoe," Ffowlkes replied. "One of our best reporters, and one of our finest photographers."

"How long have you known about the interview?"

"Nathan told me last Thursday, if I recall correctly. He had a hot tip that Betty Brown was right here in humble Hoboken, and he wanted to assign Virginia and Joe to the story. I said go ahead by all means."

"Did you and Nathan Garrideb have any subsequent conversations about the interview?"

"Nathan, thank goodness, is one of my few employees whom I do not have to micromanage. So we did not discuss it further, except for him informing me—was it Friday?—that the interview would commence on Tuesday."

"Did you talk to Virginia Farrell or Joe Pascoe before the interview?"

"There was no need. Nathan sees to all the details."

"And yesterday, did you speak to Virginia Farrell?"

"I most certainly did," Ffowlkes answered. "Late afternoon, in the hallway."

"What did you talk about?"

"We exchanged pleasantries. I inquired as to whether she would be attending the Rex Royal show at the Blue Note. Virginia was uncertain about her plans, whereupon I informed her that I would be present, and she was welcome to join me."

"Did she agree?"

Ffowlkes raised an eyebrow. "Virginia gave her usual noncommittal answer. Don't misunderstand me, Detective. I was not asking her on a date. But it behooves my writers to stay current, and I thought it might be wise for her to attend."

"Did you ask about the interview with Betty Brown?"

"I did not. Frankly, I'd rather forgotten about it. As publisher and editor-in-chief, I have a great deal on my mind."

Robert glanced at his notebook. "After you spoke to Virginia Farrell, where did she go?"

"To see her great friend Nathan Garrideb. They're always having a natter about something."

"Did you speak to Virginia when she left?"

"No. I was preparing for my weekly listening session. You would be shocked, Detective, to learn that in a monthly journal devoted to jazz, my staff is woefully uninformed. They fall into their niches and lose all sense of the big picture. It's quite disheartening."

"Is that so," Robert said drily.

"Fortunately my jazz education is broad—" Ffowlkes gestured toward the shelves full of albums— "so I'm able to fill in their considerable gaps. I give a listening session each Tuesday afternoon at 4.30, and since I was busy gathering material, I did not see Virginia when she left."

"And Nathan Garrideb? Did you see him after he spoke to Virginia?"

"Nathan is the lone employee who is as well-informed as me, so he is not required to attend my sessions. I do recall Nathan waving at me from the hall shortly before I started, but that's all."

"And you didn't see him again yesterday afternoon?"

"No. After I left my listening session, I had no need to talk to Nathan, and he did not seek me out."

"Can you give me the names of the staff members who attended yesterday?"

"Certainly. Would you like their titles as well?"

"I'd appreciate that," Robert responded.

Ffowlkes gave the names one by one, his voice shy of condescension. All together there were twelve participants, including Mortimer Burns.

"And nobody left during the session?" Robert asked.

"Not a soul. We were all together in the conference room until 6 p.m."

Robert had no other questions, but he didn't want to leave just yet. "Mr. Ffowlkes, I noticed that all the secretarial stations are empty."

"Is this relevant to your investigation?"

"Yes."

"Your powers of observation are sadly incomplete," Ffowlkes said. "They are empty on this side of the office, but on the other side we have a room devoted solely to a secretarial pool. When I bought *Jazz Now* a year ago, we had too many secretaries doing too little work, so I fired most of them. The decision has had a tremendous impact on our overhead."

"Tell me about the padlocked door," Robert said.

Ffowlkes smiled, an unpleasant upward twist. "Once again, Detective Smith, I don't see how the inner workings of *Jazz Now* are relevant to the death of Betty Brown. But since I'm eager to help in any way I can, I'll humor you."

"Please do."

"Our art director, Dimitris Petrakis, has an active imagination, and he was under the delusion that his possessions would not be safe during his sojourn to Greece. Hence the padlock."

"Did you give him permission to do that?"

"I certainly did not. The work was carried out after I left one evening. Dimitris departed the following morning."

"Were you displeased?"

"What do you think, Detective Smith?"

"I don't know," Robert said innocently. "That's why I'm asking."

"I was most displeased. And I certainly plan on having a serious talk with Dimitris upon his return. Not only did he damage *Jazz Now* property, but he lowered staff morale."

"Were you in England before you came here?"

"Switzerland."

"In publishing?"

"Gemstones. But I've always had a passion for jazz, so this was a golden opportunity."

Robert made a note, then looked up and met Ffowlkes' stare. Ffowlkes reminded him of someone, but for the moment Robert couldn't recall who.

He shut his notebook. "That's all for now."

"Very well."

They both rose, and Ffowlkes walked Robert to the door. "Sorry I couldn't be of more help. But as you can see, *Jazz Now*'s relationship to this unfortunate event is tangential. Our business is music; we don't go around hitting people on the head."

Robert slowly turned to face him. They were the same height. "Pardon me?"

"I'm sorry. That sounded tasteless. My point is, we're professionals here, and we would never be mixed up in such a sordid business."

"Your tastelessness doesn't concern me, Mr. Ffowlkes. What does trouble me is that you seem to know how Betty Brown was murdered. That information hasn't been released to the public."

Ffowlkes blinked. "You yourself mentioned it."

"No, I didn't."

"Perhaps you're slipping, Detective," Ffowlkes said with a wink. "Maybe it's time for a vacation?"

Robert stared at him for a long moment. At last he said, "I'll see you again soon, Mr. Ffowlkes."

"I look forward to it." With that, Ffowlkes gave a small bow and shut his office door.

Robert stood in the hallway. Thinking.

Virginia and Socks walked into Bread Alone, a small café a few doors down from Joe Pascoe's apartment. The young woman behind the counter asked, "Are you two here to meet Dr. Bundle?"

"We are," Socks replied.

"He asked me to tell you that he ran into a friend, and they went to Snapper Magee's for a drink. He'll be back soon."

Virginia and Socks each bought tea and a chocolate hazelnut scone, then sat down at a small table in back.

"You first," Socks said. "What happened?"

Virginia shook her head. "I thought I found them, but it was a false alarm." She described the shoebox under the bed.

"Heavens!" Socks exclaimed. "How tawdry. With a bit less common sense, you and I would have ended up amongst those poor women."

"I was insulted when I saw the pocket trumpet. I don't know why."

"One does like to be unique, whatever the circumstances. So do we rule out Joe Pascoe Photographer?"

"He seemed awfully calm for someone who'd just committed murder and run off with a box of rare tapes," Virginia pondered. "And he didn't seem at all rattled about going to see that detective."

"It could be an act. Maybe right now Mr. Pascoe is pacing his apartment and wondering if he gave himself away."

"Or maybe he's busy cleaning up the mess you made. What happened?"

Socks gave a little shrug. "As predicted, the moment arrived when our photographer friend started moving his hand toward my ankle. So I got up and asked him about one of his photos. He waxed philosophic for some time, and eventually I sat on a stool to rest."

"Then what?" Virginia asked.

"I was crossing my legs in what I presumed was a fetching manner, and I accidentally knocked over his tripods. Sort of thing that might happen to anyone."

"Joe's very particular about his equipment."

"He didn't have to get into such a conflounder!" Socks protested. "It's not as if I broke anything."

"Did he really offer to take you to the Newport Jazz Festival?"

"Just before the fateful crash, Mr. Pascoe was envisioning us in the VIP tent, sipping champagne with the Marsalis brothers."

Virginia raised an eyebrow. "I never got an invitation like that."

"He was quite carried away."

"Tell me, did you like him? As in romantically?"

"Oh no!" Socks shuddered. "I could never date anyone so tidy."

"Do you think Joe murdered Betty Brown?"

"Perhaps. He says he went to the Malibu Diner after the photo shoot, but who's to say he didn't kill Betty Brown, then go eat dinner?"

"And the tapes?" Virginia prompted.

Socks cocked her head. "In his car. At a friend's." Her gray eyes widened. "The kitchen! I bet they're tucked inside the microwave."

"There's no way we can go back now and check," Virginia said woefully.

"So the upshot of our first sleuthing assignment is that I've entirely alienated one of our suspects. I'm sorry, V."

"Don't be. I wanted anyway to look at the photos of Betty Brown. Plus Joe never suspected we were sleuthing, so we didn't blow our cover."

"I like your positive spin. But you know," Socks said slowly, "he did say one interesting thing. About Nathan."

"What about him? Oh!" Virginia's hand flew to her mouth. "I should have called him this morning about the tapes! I can't believe I forgot."

"I'm sure our handsome detective has already informed him they're missing. But don't you remember? Joe said that Nathan called Betty Brown, and Nathan was on his way over to her apartment."

"But then Joe said that Nathan couldn't possibly have done it, and probably some neighborhood kid killed her."

"And stole a moldy old shoebox in the process?" Socks shook her head. "We agreed this morning that whoever killed Betty Brown knew about the tapes. And who knew about them? You and Nathan. And maybe Joe Pascoe."

Virginia knit her brows sternly. "Nathan did not kill her."

"Maybe it was an accident," Socks persisted. "Perhaps he couldn't bear to wait one more day, so he called Betty Brown and invited himself over. He went to her apartment, and they had some kind of scuffle."

"Absolutely not."

"We still don't know how she was killed. That's your assignment," Socks instructed, sipping her tea. "Next time you speak to your policeman friend, find out what sort of death we're dealing with."

"But Socks!" Virginia protested. "It doesn't make sense. Even if Betty Brown somehow died when Nathan was there—if he *was* even there—he wouldn't have taken the tapes and run. Nathan didn't want them for himself; he wanted to give them to the Coltranes and the Monks, and then make the music available to everyone."

"Who knows what lurks in the mind of a jazz collector?" Socks mused. "Maybe Nathan had an attack of greed."

"I don't think so. He's very level-headed."

"Don't get cross with me, V, but I do think your friendship with Nathan is blinding you a little."

Virginia's color rose. "On the contrary, I think it helps me to see things more clearly."

"Shall we move on to our other suspects? Namely Mr. Byron Ffowlkes and Mr. Part-in-the-Middle Burns."

Virginia pushed away her teacup and set her elbows on the table. "I think we can rule out Mortimer. He's not the murdering kind."

"But he's obsessed with John Coltrane, and he's just plain weird. Even you have to admit that."

"His wife is normal," Virginia said quickly.

"They must click on some unseen level, because that man is a handful. Anyway—you say Mortimer was at the listening session?"

"I believe so."

"We need to find out," Socks declared. "And the man with the two Fs?"

"Also there. Assuming it took place as usual."

"We'll find that out as well. How do we get to these fellows?"

"Let me think." Virginia bit her lip, then a smile lit up her face. "I know! Rex Royal is playing at the Blue Note this week, and Byron and Mortimer are going to the late show tomorrow night. Byron even asked me to come with them. So let's go! I'll call up and get us on the press list."

"The city," Socks winced. "You know I hate it. No trees."

"Please come! I'll deal with Mortimer, and you work on Byron."

"What exactly do you mean by 'work on'?"

"Exercise your considerable female charm. Get him talking. One thing about Byron, he loves to talk."

Socks raised an eyebrow. "Once again I'm being offered up as bait."

"No. Once again you're playing a crucial role in avenging a wrongful death, as well as recouping a national musical treasure."

"I like that!" Socks clapped her hands. "Very well. I'll do it."

"Great. Only thing is—well, Byron's nothing like Joe Pascoe. He's in a whole different league."

"Fear not. If I can handle my ex-husband, I can handle anyone. Speaking of Joe Pascoe," Socks added, "I feel sorry for his plant. I poured three shots of whiskey into the soil."

The door to Bread Alone opened, and Virginia looked up. "Here's Dr. Bundle."

"Hello!" he called out, rosy-cheeked and smiling as always.

Socks nodded toward the bag in his hand. "What did you buy?"

"I found something for each of you at Alternative Books."

He pulled out a book and handed it to Socks. Small with a soft ivory cover, it was full of exquisite prints of wildflowers. Socks turned the pages slowly, oohing and aahing over each image.

"Why, Dr. Bundle," she said at last. "It's just lovely. Exactly the sort of thing I adore."

He blushed, his blue eyes shining with the glow of the hopelessly smitten.

"And for Virginia?" Socks asked.

Virginia was prepared for a similar book and was ready to make insincere appreciative noises. So she was genuinely shocked when Dr. Bundle handed her a jazz treasure: *The Charles Mingus CAT-alog for Toilet Training Your Cat*, the great bassist's instruction manual on how he toilet trained his cat Nightlife.

"Dr. Bundle!" Virginia exclaimed, nearly in tears. "You can't imagine what a rarity this is!" She flipped through the pages, looking briefly at a shot of Nightlife perched on a toilet. "Would you mind terribly if I regift it to my friend Squid? He's a Mingus freak, and he's been looking for this book for years."

"Fine by me."

"That's really kind of you."

"Aww—" Dr. Bundle glanced quickly at Socks, who was looking at Virginia's book with her nose wrinkled in distaste. Other than that, it was impossible to read her thoughts.

After Robert met with Joe Pascoe, he returned to his desk a little before six and found Tony talking on the phone.

As Robert sat down, Tony put a hand over the receiver. "Personal call. I'll be done in a minute."

Robert leaned back in his chair. It had been a long day, and he was looking forward to sorting out his thoughts with Tony.

As usual, Robert's desk was neat as a pin, empty save for a phone, computer, desktop calendar, and an orderly stack of files. Right in the center of the leather desk pad was a thick manila envelope with his name on it.

He put Joe Pascoe's photographs on top of the files, then opened the envelope. It was the Shinwell Johnson file, with a note attached from his friend:

> Hey Sherlock! I dug this up without too much trouble.
> Hope they're keeping you busy in Sinatra-land! Geoff

Robert leafed through the file. It contained the usual reports, photos, and statements. After he spoke with Tony, he'd grab a quick dinner at La Isla, then go home and spend the evening reading the material.

He was surprised to realize how much he looked forward to it. Despite Robert's initial reluctance about taking the lead on Betty Brown's murder, he found himself more engaged the deeper he dug.

What fascinated Robert about investigating homicides was that the true story of the crime was already complete, and only his knowledge was fragmentary. Somewhere amid all the information he had gathered in the last twenty-four hours, the truth was waiting. It was a jigsaw puzzle, requiring patient and ongoing analysis of the facts, which would eventually come together and reveal the complete picture.

"Aw, baby!" Tony burst out. "I've been up to my neck all day. There's a murderer running loose, how could I find a second to call?"

Robert looked at Tony and raised his eyebrows.

"Look, I gotta go, someone wants to see me . . . Not another woman, for Chrissakes, another detective!" He put down the receiver. "She hung up on me."

"Debbie?"

"Cindy. Angry 'cause I didn't call her today, but who had time?" Tony shook his head. "Never mind her. Let's put our cards on the table and see what we got."

"You first."

Tony leaned back in his chair and flipped through his notebook. "After you and me searched Baseema Baheera's apartment this morning, I went door-to-door in her building, talking to neighbors. And I came up with zip, zilch, nada."

"Go on," Robert said evenly.

"People hardly remembered her name, just knew her as the quiet old lady next to the elevator. They'd see her in the laundry room, maybe hold the door open for her, but she only really spoke to the lady next door. Super says she was no trouble. He fixed a leaky faucet for her about two months ago, but he don't recall speakin' to her after that."

"What about her daily routine?"

"Got her groceries delivered from C-Town and her medicine from Tucker Drugs. Same story from them, nice lady but real quiet."

"OK. Anything else?"

"The coroner's report." Tony tossed a file onto Robert's desk. "It confirms what Virginia Farrell said about Baseema Baheera bein' sick. The lady had colon cancer, and the coroner says she had a few weeks left at most. Nothin' else in there is a surprise. She died from a knock to the head. Forensics confirms it was the vase, and all the prints were wiped clean."

"What about security cameras in the building?"

Tony shook his head. "Busted for the last six months."

"And nobody saw anything yesterday afternoon?"

"Nope. Everyone was at work. I did find one lady who remembers holdin' open the door for a guy with a bunch of photography equipment."

"Going in or going out?"

"He was goin' in, and he said thank you. And that's all I got, which as I said is a whole lotta nothin'. What about you?"

Robert told Tony about his interviews with Nathan Garrideb, Mortimer Burns, and Byron Ffowlkes. "And I just finished up with Joe Pascoe."

"What did he have to say?"

Robert looked at his notes. "Says he arrived at Betty Brown's a little after three. Parked right in front, brought his equipment in. Didn't see Virginia Farrell, exactly as she claimed. Pascoe told me Betty Brown seemed tired, but she was friendly and didn't act upset in any way."

"OK," Tony said.

"The photo shoot went well, they chatted a bit more, then Pascoe left around four-thirty. He drove to the Malibu Diner for dinner and afterward headed back upstate to Kingston."

"Zilch again," Tony commented.

"There's more. Joe Pascoe said that not long before he left, Betty Brown got a phone call. He only heard her side, but from what he could gather, the caller was Nathan Garrideb. Betty Brown told Garrideb that the shoot was almost over, and he could stop by after four-thirty."

"Did Garrideb mention making a call?"

"No."

"Interesting. Where do we go from here?"

"We need to check everyone's alibi. Before I went up to *Jazz Now*, I asked security to give me arrivals and departures for yesterday afternoon."

"Nice," Tony said. "What you got?"

Robert opened a file and took out a piece of paper. "Nathan Garrideb came to work at 9 a.m. sharp. He went for lunch between 12:04 and 1, then he went out again at 4:20 and returned at 5:38. Then he left for good at 6:09."

"And Ffowlkes?"

"Arrived at 11:05 and left at 7:12, had lunch delivered in and didn't go out all day."

"The others?"

"Burns arrived at 8:04 and left at 6:32, also with no break. And Virginia Farrell arrived at 3:25 and left at 4:02."

"So only Virginia Farrell and Garrideb were out and about at the right time," Tony speculated.

"Or so it seems. We need to nail down a few things. First, we have to verify that Virginia Farrell got on the bus at Port Authority at five, and we need to confirm that Joe Pascoe went to the Malibu Diner. Plus talk to a few more *Jazz Now* people to check that Ffowlkes and Burns were at the listening session the entire time."

"All right," Tony said. "I'll take care of everything tomorrow mornin'. Now can I tell you what I think?"

"Go ahead."

Tony smiled. "I think we got our murderer."

Robert tilted his head. "Who?"

"Garrideb!" Tony replied. "He stinks to high heaven. What's your take on him?"

"He seemed sincere. But he could be a good liar." Robert thought a moment. "Byron Ffowlkes is the one who raised a red flag for me. I didn't like him. He's the type who seems capable of anything."

"Including murdering a little old lady?"

"Even that." Robert snapped his fingers. "I just remembered who he reminded me of."

"Who?"

"A case I worked on in Manhattan in the early nineties. Handsome young guy with a Harvard degree. Married a rich older woman who died six months later."

"After—let me guess—changin' her will in his favor?"

Robert grinned. "Pretty good for a fireman. The point is, Ffowlkes is just like him. Bright, lots of superficial charm, but essentially an ice-cold sociopath."

"Ffowlkes is, however, a sociopath with an alibi. Sittin' in a room with a dozen people generally gets a guy off the hook."

"So how did he find out that Betty Brown was hit on the head?"

"Simple," Tony answered. "Garrideb or Pascoe did it, and they told Ffowlkes."

"I don't know. Garrideb doesn't like Ffowlkes. Virginia Farrell said that as well."

"Yeah, but if this Ffowlkes is such a slick guy, he's the one you'd run to if you had a box of tapes to unload. I'm sure there's some kind of black market for jazz collectors, and Ffowlkes is probably knee-deep in it." Tony shook his head. "We need more. It's time to shake these guys up a little."

"I agree," Robert said. "I've got an appointment with Garrideb tomorrow afternoon."

"I'll go with you. We'll do a little good cop–bad cop. Plus let's drop in on Mr. Ffowlkes, I'd like to look him over too."

"We also need to trace that phone call to Betty Brown's apartment yesterday afternoon."

"Consider it done," Tony said. "Now what about this Pascoe guy? What's your take on him?"

"Hard to say. He's the last one who saw Betty Brown alive, as far as we know."

"Did he mention the tapes?"

"No. And I didn't either. I wanted to see if he'd slip."

"And?"

"He didn't say a word about them." Robert picked up Pascoe's photographs and handed them to Tony. "These are from his shoot with Betty Brown."

Tony looked through the photos, then frowned. "Hang on a minute. You got the pictures I took yesterday, bring 'em out."

Robert handed him the file. Tony shuffled through the images and pulled out a photo, then selected one of Pascoe's.

"Boberino, take a look at this."

Robert stood and peered down at Tony's desk. On the left was Pascoe's shot of Betty Brown sitting behind her coffee table, and to the right was Tony's image, taken from almost the same angle.

"See this one," Tony said, pointing at Pascoe's photo. "There's the vase, the shoebox, the tea things, and a jar of honey. Now look at the other."

"There's the vase," Robert said slowly. "Only now it's shifted to the left, and a crumpled napkin is next to it. There's all the tea things. No shoebox."

"What else?"

Robert looked at Tony. "No honey."

"Did you see it in the kitchen this morning?"

"No, but Virginia Farrell had an identical jar in her house. She gave Betty Brown that honey as a present from her roommate. The label has odd little drawings on it, I would have recognized it immediately."

"I'll go back tomorrow and check again, but it looks like whoever pinched the tapes also took the honey."

Robert frowned. "Who would steal a box of priceless tapes, then decide to take a jar of honey?"

Tony shook his head. "Like I said, I'll check it out tomorrow. No need twistin' our brain cells till then. Hey, what's that file you got there?"

"A friend from my old precinct sent it over. It's the Shinwell Johnson case."

Tony looked skeptical. "You think that's relevant?"

"I'm not sure. It can't hurt to check."

"You're the pro. Me, all I know is how to track down burglars."

"Our murderer is also a burglar, so you'll be just fine."

Tony raised his hands. "I can see the headline now: HOBOKEN COPS ARREST HONEY-STEALER."

Robert laughed. But then he remembered Virginia Farrell, and he shook his head. "If only it was just a jar of honey. Quite a few people are counting on us to find those tapes."

"Now, if they was Sinatra tapes—"

Robert stood and picked up the Shinwell Johnson file. "If they were Sinatra tapes, you'd have Nathan Garrideb hanging by his toes in front of City Hall."

Tony put a hand on his heart. "Nobody hurts my Frankie."

"Good night, Tony. See you tomorrow."

Thursday
August 7, 2003

Another beautiful August day. The open window in Virginia's room carried in birdsong, a mild breeze, and the smell of pine needles.

Virginia was sitting in bed on top of the quilt, wearing her white shorts and Thelonious Monk T-shirt. A lap desk rested on her thighs, and she was writing on a pad of yellow lined paper. Surrounding her on the bed was a neat arrangement of books, albums, photos, index cards, and CDs, ready to be consulted at a moment's notice.

Virginia was concentrating deeply on a passage describing June Christy's January 1947 wedding to fellow Stan Kenton Orchestra member Bob Cooper. This was an important part of the book, and Virginia wanted to get it just right.

Someone cleared their throat from the end of the bed. Virginia looked up and saw Socks reclining on the quilt, attired in her white turban and burgundy silk pajamas.

"I'm terribly sorry to interrupt," Socks said, "but there's important business to discuss."

Virginia put down her pen. "What's up?"

"We need to decide what you're wearing tonight."

"Me?" she laughed. "You're the one who's supposed to be bait."

"This has no relation to our continual efforts to right the wrong of Betty Brown's death. This is about your social life."

"My what?" Virginia asked, wrinkling her nose.

"Just now over tea, I was pondering how it's possible that your field of expertise is dominated by the male gender, and yet you still don't have a boyfriend. You're constantly going out to clubs, but you've never come back with a single flirtatious anecdote. I've decided it's your wardrobe."

"Socks, I don't have a wardrobe. I have clothes."

"Yes, and for the most part they don't suit you. Frankly, V, you give off a Harriet the Spy vibe. Sans glasses."

Virginia was amazed. "I love that book! I must have read it a dozen times when I was in grammar school."

"Don't get me wrong. You're not shlubby, but a few items of your clothing are on the brink."

"I don't have time to think about those things."

"Which brings up another subject," Socks continued. "You would have time if you didn't think about j-a-z-z every second."

"That's what I like to think about."

"My dear, it's a big world out there."

Virginia questioned the wisdom of Sock's comment, given that it came from a woman whose only earned income came from drawing with colored markers. But since Virginia was being subsidized by a Japanese man with a June Christy fetish, it seemed best to keep quiet.

"What do you suggest?" she countered.

"I thought you'd never ask." Socks marched over to Virginia's closet and flung it open. "It's time for a fashion consultation. An in-depth wardrobe analysis."

"I don't think—"

"Why, you have clothes I've never seen before!" Socks rifled eagerly through the hangers. "What do we have here?" She brought out a dark-green silk dress with a scoop neck and three-quarter sleeves.

"Oh, that," Virginia said. "I wore it to a wedding once."

"Tonight you are wearing this dress," Socks declared.

"Not a chance! When I go out to clubs, I like to be comfortable."

"Which means jeans, T-shirt, hoodie, sneakers, and knapsack. Pure Harriet the Spy."

Virginia winced. "You say that like it's a bad thing."

"It won't do tonight, my dear. We're going to the Blue Note. My ex-husband took me there a few times, it's a fancy club."

"I never knew you'd been to the Blue Note."

"Oh, the places I've been," Socks said, waving a hand. "The point is, you're wearing this dress. It will look simply smashing with a string of pearls and matching earrings."

"Which I don't have."

"But I do," Socks beamed.

"I can't wear your expensive jewelry! What if I lose it?"

"Don't worry. I'll watch your neck."

There was no use opposing Socks once she got into this sort of mood. "OK," Virginia capitulated. "But I'm going to be uncomfortable on the bus."

"We're not taking the bus. Dr. Bundle is driving. And picking us up tomorrow as well."

"He's going to make the trip all the way down to the city, and then not even hang out with us?"

"I told him we're solving a problem of urgent cultural importance. That's true, is it not?"

"Ye-es," Virgina said slowly.

"So he's happy to help."

"Happy to help you."

"This dress needs ironing," Socks changed the subject. "Which I'm delighted to do. I'll give the pearls a shine as well. Shoes, however, are a concern."

"Somewhere in the closet is a pair dyed to match the dress."

"We'll dig them up later." Socks clapped her hands. "I'm so excited for you! Maybe tonight you'll meet a nice fellow."

"And maybe tonight Byron Ffowlkes will fall in love with you."

"As long as he hands over the tapes." Socks examined her ruby-red nails. "Any word from Nathan?"

"No."

"Don't you think that's—odd?"

"Why would it be? I plan to call him after I finish writing. I think we're both mourning the loss of the tapes."

"Perhaps," Socks mused.

"Don't you 'perhaps' me." Virginia raised her eyebrows. "I thought you were going to do some ironing."

"Indeed I was. Enjoy your writing."

Socks scooped up the dress and left the room.

With a sigh, Virginia folded her arms and looked out the window. Socks had only met Nathan a handful of times, so she didn't really know him. Otherwise she would never think such a thing.

Virginia reread her last paragraph:

> Still wearing their blue-black gabardine band uniforms, Christy and Cooper were married with the entire Kenton orchestra in attendance. The next morning, the newlyweds reported for work to play a 10 a.m. show.

Virginia selected a photo from the top of the pile. It was slightly faded, but still in good condition after almost sixty years. When the drummer Shelly Manne passed away in 1984, he left his papers and effects to the Institute of Jazz Studies, and this photo of Christy and Cooper posing with Stan Kenton at their wedding was among the treasures. Virginia's friend John had unearthed the photograph, and she planned to reprint it in her book, bringing the image to light for the first time ever.

Christy and Cooper were a handsome couple, although he was quite tall and she was rather short. Virginia kept a mental list called "Notable Short Women," and June Christy was at the top.

She gathered the stack of photos and glanced through them. Clearly June Christy had a wardrobe. In fact, one of Virginia's favorite images was Christy onstage in a satin dress with a flouncy skirt, bending over to shake a fan's hand.

Virginia put the photos aside and let loose another sigh. Harriet the Spy! Socks didn't understand. Virginia was writing a book, and finding a man was the last thing on her mind.

She picked up her pen and started writing.

"We're here to see Nathan Garrideb," Robert told the receptionist.

"He's expecting you," she said, pointing down the hall.

Robert walked slowly so Tony could take in the atmosphere. He also wanted a few moments to collect himself. The good cop–bad cop routine always made Robert feel uneasy, even if he never played the harsher role.

One reason Tony was always the bad cop was because Robert didn't get angry when suspects lied. He expected them to. Nobody wanted to go to jail, and if a lie might buy freedom or a little time, it was simply human nature to try.

Nevertheless, Tony's conclusion that Garrideb was their main suspect had proved correct. Right before Robert and Tony left for *Jazz Now*, the phone company confirmed that the call to Betty Brown's apartment on Tuesday at 4:15 p.m. came from Nathan Garrideb's office phone.

They found Garrideb writing at his desk, with soft piano music playing in the background. He was so engrossed in his work he didn't notice the detectives standing in the doorway.

"Hello?" Robert said.

Garrideb looked up. "Oh!" he grinned sheepishly. "I'm sorry. Please come in."

"This is Detective Oliveto."

"Nice to meet you." Garrideb reached out and shook Tony's hand. "Please sit down. Tell me, is there any progress with the tapes?"

"We have several leads," Robert said as they sat in the two chairs in front of the desk, "but nothing definite yet."

"Sorry to hear that. Here's my notes." Garrideb handed over a piece of lined yellow paper that had clearly been refolded several times. "I made a copy for my files, so you can hang on to the original."

Robert held out the paper so Tony could see as well. The notes were written in black ink in firm, slanted handwriting:

> tapes—5 spot—BB has cause Shinwell J stole—V saw—r to r—flat boxes—some labeled—dates match 5 spot gig—big shoebox—doz tapes maybe more—BB feels bad—dying—needs help—get to IJS—Alice C and TS Monk—call BB tomorrow and get tapes—wow!!!

Garrideb watched Robert read the notes. "That's just my chicken scratch," he said. "It's probably not much use."

"Any little bit helps." Robert folded the paper and put it in his jacket pocket.

"So, Nathan," Tony began. "And is it OK if I call you Nathan?"

"Sure."

"Detective Smith was fillin' me in on your conversation yesterday. But you know how it is, I always prefer to hear these things from the horse's mouth. Mind if we go over a few details?"

"Of course not. I only hope I can help."

"Great." Tony took a little notebook out of his jacket and flipped through it. "You say that Virginia Farrell got here about 3:30. Security downstairs says she signed in at 3:25, so what with the elevator ride, 3:30 is a good guess."

"OK," Garrideb said.

"They also say she signed out at 4:02, which again fits with what you said yesterday."

"Right."

"But see, it gets a little sticky when it comes to your movements. Hear me out." Tony moved forward in his seat and looked Garrideb in the eye, no longer consulting his notebook. "You say you left a few minutes after Virginia Farrell. Detective Smith, when someone says 'a few minutes,' how do you interpret that?"

"Five minutes," Robert replied. "Ten at most."

"And yet, Nathan, security has you leavin' at 4:20."

Garrideb grimaced. "I'm sorry. I should have been more precise. I was in such a whirlwind over the tapes, I guess I wasn't paying close attention to the time."

"None of this would matter so much, except accordin' to the phone company, there was a call from your office to Betty Brown's apartment at 4:15 that afternoon."

Garrideb looked stunned. "I didn't call her that day."

"Maybe you're still caught in that whirlwind, because the records show otherwise."

"I don't understand."

"Plus Joe Pascoe was at Betty Brown's apartment at 4:15. Pascoe says she got a phone call, and from what he could hear, it was clear she was talkin' to you."

Garrideb reddened. "That's not true. I didn't call her. I went for a walk."

"You didn't leave the building till 4:20."

"But I never called her!"

Garrideb looked at Robert, his eyes pleading.

Robert cleared his throat. "Why don't you tell us again exactly what you did from the moment Virginia Farrell left your office? Don't leave anything out. Even if you stopped at the water fountain, we want to know."

Garrideb frowned in concentration.

"Take your time," Tony declared. "We got all day."

"OK," Garrideb said slowly. "I decided to go on a walk to think over what Virginia had just told me. I left my CD Discman here because I didn't want any distractions. My wallet was in my back pocket as usual, and I slipped my notes in the other back pocket. I didn't take my knapsack."

"What happened when you left your office?" Robert asked.

Garrideb swallowed audibly. "Let me think . . . I didn't have a jacket because it was warm out like today. I walked toward the receptionist's desk. I passed Byron's office. He was inside looking through a stack of records, getting ready for his listening session. I waved at him, and he gave a little wave back."

"You didn't speak?" Tony asked.

"No."

"Not a word?"

"Nope. And then—right, I went to the men's room. No one else was there. I came out after a minute, and then—" Garrideb's face brightened. "I know where the time went! As I was passing by Ed Wilson's office—he's an assistant editor—he'd left his CD player on. I heard one of my favorite songs, 'The Promise' by John Coltrane. So I stopped to listen."

Tony raised an eyebrow. "How long is that song?"

"Hang on." Garrideb looked at the CDs in his bookshelves and plucked out one with a green cover and black lettering. "It's on *The Best of John Coltrane*. The song is six minutes and fifty-five seconds."

"You stood there lissenin' to the whole song?"

"Of course! I was lucky to catch it at the beginning."

Tony stared at Garrideb and said nothing.

"Then you went on a walk," Robert jumped in. "Tell us again about that."

"There's not much to say. I walked all the way uptown to the Fourteenth Street Pier. I guess I was going pretty fast, because I got there before I knew it. Then I sat on the bench at the end of the pier."

"Your thinking spot," Robert stated.

"Exactly."

"So when you was havin' all these deep thoughts," Tony asked, "did you speak to anyone?"

Garrideb shook his head. "No."

"Not at all? You didn't stop to pat some old lady's poodle?"

"I walked to the pier, then I sat on the bench and reread my notes."

Tony folded his arms. "You're aware that Betty Brown lived at Thirteenth and Bloomfield, a short walk from the pier?"

"I know." Garrideb's face reddened deeper. "But I didn't go there."

"You knew the address," Tony persisted. "And you knew the tapes were there."

Again Garrideb glanced at Robert. "That's true. But Virginia and I had agreed to call Betty Brown in the morning."

"How long did you sit there?" Robert asked.

"I'm not sure. A half hour maybe?"

"Then what?"

"I needed to get back to work. This time I walked on Washington Street, it's quicker than Frank Sinatra Drive. I didn't see anyone I knew, but I did stop at Carlo's Bakery. Wait a minute!" Garrideb reached into his back pocket. "I probably still have my receipt. I paid by credit card, and I haven't cleaned out my wallet for a while."

Garrideb pulled out a faded brown-leather billfold and took out a crumpled mess of credit card receipts.

"This is from dinner last night . . . One from Sam Goody . . . OK!" he exclaimed triumphantly, handing Robert a small piece of yellow paper. "Carlo's Bakery."

Tuesday at 5:32 p.m., Garrideb had purchased an Oreo cookie cake for $10.99.

"And afterward?" Tony pressed. "You came back here?"

"That's right," Garrideb said. "I stayed about a half hour, then I went home."

"Did you see anyone in the office?"

"Only Maggie, the receptionist. I said hello to her, but that was it. I took care of a few odds and ends in my office, then left at six as usual."

"And took your cake home?"

"Yes."

"You and your girlfriend enjoy it?"

Garrideb shook his head. "Actually, we didn't get a chance to eat it. I dropped the box outside the Grove Street PATH station. The cake broke into a million pieces, so I threw it away."

"All right," Robert said. "Anything else you need to tell us?"

Garrideb leaned back in his chair. He looked exhausted. "No," he said quietly. "That's it."

Robert didn't need to look at Tony to know what was coming next.

"Nathan," Tony said, letting out a heavy sigh. "That's sure a nice, neat story. But you gotta see it from our side."

"What do you mean?" Garrideb asked cautiously.

"You're one of two, maybe three people who knew about the tapes. You got no alibi for the time of the murder, and you admit to bein' in the vicinity of Betty Brown's apartment." Tony's hands flew up in exasperation. "Two plus two equals four, if you get my drift."

Garrideb's voice rose in frustration. "I didn't kill Betty Brown!"

"Fine. You didn't do it. So how about you help us find out who did?"

"I'd be happy to, if I can."

"All right. Let's say we eliminate you, puttin' aside the matter of the phone call for a moment. That would leave Virginia Farrell as our main suspect."

Garrideb shook his head. "Impossible. Virginia wouldn't harm a soul."

"Are you sure? What if she told you she was leavin' to catch her bus, but then decided not to? She hightailed it back to Betty Brown's, they had some kind of argument, and, boom, Betty Brown ended up dead. Miss Farrell called a car service, and she managed to get home with the tapes right at the moment when her bus was supposed to arrive."

"You don't know Virginia. She's one of the most honest people I've ever met."

"I'm no jazz expert, Nathan, but it seems like these tapes are pretty high stakes."

"The highest," Garrideb murmured.

"My point exactly. People act out of character when somethin' valuable is on the line."

"Not Virginia."

"All right, let's eliminate her. That leaves Joe Pascoe as our main suspect. He claims he left Betty Brown's apartment at four-thirty and went to the Malibu Diner. Waitress at the Malibu confirms Pascoe was there. But he still coulda killed Betty Brown and took the tapes, and afterward treated himself to dinner."

"Joe's not the type to kill anyone."

Tony threw up his hands. "So it wasn't you, wasn't Virginia Farrell, wasn't Joe Pascoe. Work with me here, 'cause somebody sure as hell killed Betty Brown." He paused. "Tell me, you like honey?"

Garrideb knit his brow. "Honey?"

"Yeah, honey. From bees."

"Sometimes I use it on oatmeal. Is that relevant?"

"Lemme ask you somethin' else," Tony pressed. "Yesterday when you were havin' your little talk with Detective Smith, you gave him the impression you didn't much like your boss, Mr. Byron Ffowlkes. Tell me, is that relevant?"

Garrideb's face tightened. "No. I mean—I don't think so."

"This is a murder investigation," Tony said in a steely voice. "If you got somethin' to say, I suggest you spit it out."

"I hate to talk badly about anyone. And besides, it's just rumors."

"We love rumors."

Garrideb sighed heavily. "It's our art director, Dimitris. Something was stolen from his office. Are you familiar with Eric Dolphy?"

"Nope."

"Dolphy was a great jazz musician, one of the real innovators. He died in Berlin in 1964, and Dimitris had an extremely rare bootleg from Dolphy's last tour, a recording made at a concert about a week before he died."

"Go on," Tony said. "I'm lissenin.'"

"Someone was doing an article on bootlegs, and Dimitris brought the tape in so we could take a photo. He left the tape in his office after the shoot, and when he came back from lunch, it was gone."

"And he thinks Ffowlkes took it?"

"Definitely," Garrideb said. "Byron was super excited about the recording. He said several times how valuable it was."

"Is that so," Tony commented.

"Dimitris was beside himself when he realized it was gone. He had a copy of course, but the original was priceless. A week after that, Dimitris left for Greece. He claimed his grandmother was ill, but it was really because of Byron. And also—"

"Yeah?"

"Ever since Byron started working here, little things have gone missing. CDs, mugs, cash taken out of people's coat pockets—that never happened before."

"Very interestin'. We appreciate you tellin' us all this. And you'll be happy to know," Tony continued, flipping through his notebook, "that while I was pokin' around here this mornin', your fellow employees had nothin' good to say about him either."

"That doesn't surprise me."

"But you won't be so glad to hear that everyone swears up, down, and sideways that Mr. Ffowlkes stepped into his lissenin' session at four-thirty, and he didn't budge for the next ninety minutes. So kleptomaniac or not, his alibi is tight as a drum."

Garrideb nodded miserably, his expression bleak.

"'Course, if Joe Pascoe did it, who cares about Ffowlkes? Or Virginia Farrell?"

Garrideb's expression tightened with anger. "Listen, Detective. I can see that things look bad for me. But I won't bad-mouth Joe or Virginia. They didn't do it, and I won't fall into your game of accusing them to save myself. They're my friends."

"All murderers have friends, Nathan. It still don't mean they're innocent."

Garrideb stared stonily out the window.

"Detective Smith," Tony said, turning to Robert. "You got any more questions for Nathan here?"

"No," Robert answered.

"Me either. At least not now." He stood. "We'll be continuin' our investigation, Nathan. May I suggest you don't go on any sudden vacations? Stick close to home in case we need you."

"Fine," Garrideb said shortly.

Robert and Tony stepped out into the hallway. Tony gave Robert a wink, a glimmer of satisfaction in his eyes. He pointed down the hall. "Ffowlkes' office?"

"Yep."

"Let's go."

When Virginia emerged from her room, she saw that Socks' door was shut. A large piece of paper was taped to the door, with electric-blue letters announcing NAP. Which Virginia would have figured out anyway from Socks' thunderous snoring.

The freshly ironed green dress hung from the closet door in the living room. Just above it, Socks had taped a playful drawing of a woman's face, with red hair, a big smile, and I LOVE JAZZ! written across her forehead.

Virginia shook her head and smiled. She went into the kitchen, which was spotlessly clean and bathed in mellow August sunlight. After helping herself to a glass of peppermint iced tea from a pitcher in the refrigerator, she uncovered the plate of brownies leftover from Socks' nervous bake-fest on Tuesday night.

Tuesday: interviewing Betty Brown, visiting Nathan at *Jazz Now*, Detective Smith's interrogation . . . It all seemed like a lifetime ago.

Virginia sat on the stool by the phone, setting her snack on the counter within reach. She dialed Nathan's number.

"Nathan Garrideb here."

"It's me."

"Virginia! Good to hear your voice. You won't believe what I've just been through."

"What? And don't mind if I eat while I talk to you."

"No worries." Nathan took a deep breath. "The police were here. Again."

"What!" Virginia burst out. "We really need to catch up. Although first I have to apologize for not calling yesterday."

"Don't worry about that. It was a crazy day."

"I'll say. A Hoboken detective drove all the way up here late Tuesday night, so I ended up sleeping in the next day. Then of course my original reason for calling you evaporated into thin air."

"You mean the tapes."

Virginia gulped down tears. "You were right, Nathan. We shouldn't have left those tapes at Betty Brown's apartment for a single night longer."

"Don't be hard on yourself. We couldn't just barge in on her. And if we had, we might have gotten killed as well." Nathan paused. "The police think I did it."

"You mean that Detective Smith?" she said angrily. "The man who didn't even know who John Coltrane was? He's not fit to investigate this case."

"Yesterday Smith was here by himself and he was pretty cool, but just now he showed up with a bulldog named Detective Oliveto. Boy, did he give me a hard time. He tried to get me to accuse you and Joe. I wouldn't do it."

"Don't let them intimidate you," Virginia urged. "The truth is on your side."

"The thing is, Detective Oliveto kept going on about a phone call. Apparently there's a record of a call from my office to Betty Brown's house. They say that Joe Pascoe overheard her talking to me. But I swear I didn't call her that day."

"Of course you didn't. It must be a mix-up."

"Plus I have no alibi," Nathan said, his voice tinged with worry. "I went on a walk to the Fourteenth Street Pier, and I didn't see or speak to anyone. It looks bad for me."

"Never fear," Virginia encouraged him. "We'll get to the bottom of this."

"We?"

"I don't want to reveal too much, but let's just say I'm doing a bit of detective work myself. With an accomplice."

"Have you come up with anything?"

"Not yet," she admitted. "Tell me, did Byron stay at the listening session the entire time?"

"Yes, the cops just said so. But even if Byron did leave the listening session, he didn't know about the tapes. You knew, and I knew. That's it."

"And maybe Joe Pascoe." She told Nathan about her visit to Pascoe's studio, leaving out the female instrumental photos so Joe could preserve a shred of dignity with his colleagues.

"In other words—" Nathan said.

"We proved nothing. But logically speaking, I was the only one who knew about the tapes. I told you, and you told no one. So it has to be Joe."

"I know you're not fond of Joe after what happened at the Roswell Rudd interview, but he's not a violent person."

Virginia pressed her lips together. "Maybe. By the way, do you know how Betty Brown was murdered?"

"I don't, actually. It wasn't in the papers, and I haven't asked."

"We need to find out. That'll give us a clue to the murderer's personality."

"I suppose so. I wish—" Nathan hesitated.

"Yes?"

"Out of everyone I know, the only person who I can actually imagine murdering someone is Byron."

"Me too," Virginia agreed. "But he has the best alibi of us all. My accomplice and I will be investigating Byron tonight, so who knows what might turn up."

"Where are you going?"

"The Rex Royal show at the Blue Note. I'd invite you along, but an extra person might upset our plans."

Nathan exhaled. "I can't go anyway."

"Another show?"

"Detective Oliveto told me to stay close to home."

"Surely you can go to New York!"

"I want to cooperate as much as possible. Like I said, things aren't looking good for me."

"Don't worry," Virginia assured him. "My assistant and I will clear your name."

"I hope so." He looked at her woefully. "And the tapes? Where are they?"

"Oh, Nathan. I don't know. But whoever took them knows their value, so they must be taking good care of them. Right?"

"I certainly hope so."

"Hang in there. Call me anytime. And give my love to Melissa."

Virginia hung up. She absentmindedly broke off a piece of brownie and put it in her mouth. So now in addition to finding Betty Brown's killer and recovering the tapes, she had to keep Nathan out of jail.

She looked out the window at the bucolic meadow, chewing and thinking.

"**D**etective Smith!" Byron Ffowlkes rose from his desk as Robert and Tony walked into the corner office. "A pleasure to see you again."

Robert gave a slight nod. "This is Detective Oliveto. If you don't mind, we have a few follow-up questions."

"But of course. Do have a seat."

They sat down in the leather chairs facing the desk. Ffowlkes, today dressed purely in cream, looked at them with amusement. "You must not be having much success if you're still sniffing around me."

"On the contrary," Robert replied. "Our investigation is going forward in several directions."

"Delighted to hear it. Ask away."

Tony eyed Ffowlkes with distaste and went straight for the jugular. "Tell me, you ever steal?"

Clearly Ffowlkes was not expecting this. He blinked rapidly. "What?"

"It's a simple question. The answer's either yes or no." He turned to Robert. "Detective Smith, you ever steal?"

"No," Robert answered.

"See? Simple. Yes or no. So which is it?"

Ffowlkes folded his well-manicured hands and took a deep breath. "I fail to see, gentlemen, what bearing such a query has on your murder investigation. Your question, in fact, smacks of harassment."

"Oh, cry me a river!" Tony said in disgust. "I'll take that as a yes. Next question. You told Detective Smith here you used to be in gemstones. Now, you gotta forgive me, but I'm just a Jersey boy so I don't know what that means."

"Precious stones. Diamonds, rubies, emeralds. Buying and selling."

"I see. Quite a ways from bein' a jazz editor."

"Jazz has always been my passion, Detective Oliveto. It's not so unusual for a man approaching midlife to make a career switch. Can I be arrested for that?"

"What was the name of your business?" Tony prodded.

"I worked on my own."

"But surely for tax purposes, there was a company name. Help me out here, Mr. Ffowlkes."

"It was in my own name."

"Located in Switzerland—where exactly?"

"Bern."

"Is that so!" Tony exclaimed. "I love a good coincidence. It so happens that a buddy of mine works in Bern as a private investigator. I'll give him a call, see what he can tell us about you and your gemstones."

"Go right ahead," Ffowlkes said coolly. "But once again, I fail to see the relevance to poor Betty Brown."

"Like you give a damn," Tony scoffed.

"Will there be anything else?" Ffowlkes looked at Tony as if he wanted to spit on him.

"Yes," Robert interjected, keeping his tone steady. "You said yesterday that *Jazz Now*'s involvement in Betty Brown's murder was only tangential. Nevertheless, two of your staff members were among the last people to see her alive. Can you give us any insight into Virginia Farrell and Joe Pascoe?"

"They're both excellent at their jobs, utterly professional in all circumstances. As I said yesterday, we're not in the habit of killing our interview subjects. And why would Virginia or Joe kill Betty Brown? It doesn't make any sense."

Robert wondered if Ffowlkes knew about the tapes. If he knew how Betty Brown was murdered, he probably did. But Ffowlkes was playing his cards close to his chest.

Tony must have been wondering the same thing, because he suddenly asked, "Mr. Ffowlkes, you like honey?"

"I beg your pardon?"

"Honey. From bees. You like it?"

Ffowlkes looked genuinely perplexed. "I take my tea with sugar. Once more, Detective Oliveto, I don't—"

"—see the relevance," Tony finished, waving his hand. "So you've said."

"See here, detectives," Ffowlkes declared, his color rising. "I am a busy man. I run a national monthly magazine, and I do so with a staff of fair-to-middling ability. An old woman has been killed and it's a truly sorry story, but I simply have no help to offer you. Now if you'll excuse me, I have work to do."

"We're leavin'," Tony announced, rising up from his chair. "But I got a funny feelin' we'll be meetin' again real soon."

"I can't imagine why," Ffowlkes snorted. "Good day, gentlemen."

Robert stood and nodded curtly, then followed Tony out the door.

They were halfway to the receptionist's desk when Robert said to Tony in a low voice, "I didn't know you had a friend in Bern."

"I don't," Tony said easily. "I was just bustin' him. Wait a minute." He looked at a nameplate, then poked his head into an office where a stout Black man was sitting at a desk writing. "Hey, Ed. We spoke this mornin'. Lissen, you got the CD *The Best of John Coltrane*?"

"I do," Ed said, surprised.

"Play it a lot?"

"Pretty often."

"Thanks."

Tony and Robert continued walking down the hall. They said goodbye to the receptionist, then went to the elevator banks.

"Now what?" Robert asked.

"We go to security. I need to confirm a hunch."

"About Ffowlkes?"

"I wish. This is about Garrideb."

It turned out Tony knew Steve Dooney. As a matter of fact, he had put out a fire in Dooney's mother's apartment.

"Saving her two toy poodles in the process," Dooney told Robert as he pumped Tony's hand up and down. "This is a great man you're workin' with, a great man!"

"Ahh, get outta here," Tony grinned, clearly pleased by the compliment.

"How can I help you guys?" Dooney asked eagerly. "Whatever you need, just ask."

"All this fancy equipment," Tony commented. "You got videos of who comes and goes?"

"Yep. Shows 'em exiting and entering from the elevator banks on the ground floor."

"Can you put your hands on Tuesday evening's tapes? Starting at 5:25 and then again at 6?"

"No problem. Give me a minute."

As Dooney pulled out a videocassette and fast-forwarded, Robert gave Tony a quizzical look. But Tony just raised his eyebrows and said nothing.

"OK," Dooney said. "I got it cued up at 5:25."

"Great," Tony replied. "Let it roll."

The three men sat around a small television screen, watching as people walked out of the elevators and into the lobby, on their way home. At last Nathan Garrideb appeared, moving in the opposite direction from the crowd.

"That's our guy," Tony exclaimed. "Can you slow it down?"

"Sure."

They watched Garrideb take out his wallet, press it on top of the turnstile, and walk toward the elevators.

"Give us a rewind, OK?" Tony asked Dooney. Then he turned to Robert. "Watch the bag."

Robert frowned in concentration. Garrideb held a bag from Carlo's Bakery tightly under his right arm.

"All right," Tony said. "Can you get us close to six? We need to see him leavin'."

Just after six o'clock, Garrideb came out of the elevator wearing a black knapsack. Headphones covered his ears, a CD Discman was clipped to his waist, and once again he was carrying the Carlo's Bakery bag.

Dooney asked, "You wanna see it again?"

"No need," Tony replied. "But lissen, can you make us a copy of those two parts? And keep the original in a real safe place."

Five minutes later, after enthusiastic goodbyes, Robert and Tony walked out with the tape.

"Let's get some fresh air," Tony suggested. "Then I'll tell you what's what."

After buying soft drinks from the hot dog vendor on the corner of First and River Street, they walked to Pier A Park. They crossed the length of the park and sat on a bench facing Manhattan, with the Hudson River meandering in front of them.

Robert snapped open his ginger ale. "What's going on?"

"Garrideb slipped up."

"How?"

"The Oreo cookie cake. Here's the thing," Tony said, turning to face Robert. "Those cakes are the best you can get in Hoboken, maybe the entire planet. You don't throw 'em out. One time I got one for my ma, and I dropped it when I got tangled up in a dog leash."

Robert bit his lip. "How did you—?"

"Don't ask. What I'm sayin' is, I dropped the cake and it broke into a million pieces. But I didn't toss it. I brought the box to my ma, and we ate every last bite."

"What's your point?"

"You don't throw out one of those cakes. It's like throwin' out gold—it's not logical."

"OK."

"But what if you had just stolen a shoebox full of tapes? And on your way back to the office, you realized you couldn't go sailin' in with a box that might get recognized down the line?"

Robert stared at Tony. "Go on."

"You'd need a bag. So here's my theory. Garrideb goes into Carlo's Bakery, buys an Oreo cookie cake. Leaves the bakery and steps into Court Street, which probably was empty 'cause it's just an alleyway with no real cars or foot traffic. Garrideb throws away the cake and sticks the shoebox inside the bag. Then he goes back to the office, and all you see comin' and goin' is Mr. Nice Boyfriend bringin' his girlfriend a cake."

Robert raised his eyebrows. "That's pretty good."

"It occurred to me as we were grillin' him. That's why I asked if his girlfriend liked the cake. As you heard, that cake never made it home."

Robert gazed at the river for a long moment. "So where are the tapes?"

"Might be at Garrideb's. But I doubt it. He probably met up with Ffowlkes and handed over the tapes to him. Which would explain why Ffowlkes knows how Betty Brown died."

"But Garrideb doesn't—"

"Like Ffowlkes? Lissen, Boberino, don't get taken in. That Ffowlkes is as slick as they come. That guy's capable of anything."

"You see that too."

"It reeks off him like rotten clams. I can imagine him strategizin' with Garrideb: 'Act like you can't stomach me, throw 'em off the trail.' Whadda they think, we're idiots?"

"And the honey? Neither of them reacted when you brought it up."

"The honey's one of those mishmash things. Maybe Pascoe pinched it on his way out, so it just seems like the murderer took it. Or that little kid who found the body grabbed it. I say we don't worry about the honey."

"Hmmm."

"Let's go see Cap now and get a warrant for Garrideb's arrest."

Robert shook his head. "I think it's better to sleep on this tonight, then talk to Cap in the morning. We'll lay it all out for him and see what he wants to do."

"Tomorrow morning! Garrideb could be in Hong Kong by then. I say we arrest him now."

"The problem is that most of our evidence is circumstantial." Robert held up a hand. "It's good circumstantial evidence, I know. But the fact is no one saw Garrideb at Betty Brown's building, and no one saw him with the tapes."

Tony huffed impatiently. "Is this how you people do things in New York?"

"The murder was Tuesday evening, and it's now Thursday afternoon. We've made quite a bit of progress, but this is exactly the point when we need to stay calm and not jump to conclusions."

"You're the Sherlock. I guess it'll keep till tomorrow, but don't come cryin' to me if Garrideb skips town."

"He won't."

"Say, what about all this Shinwell Johnson stuff? You find anything interestin'?"

"It's one of the most baffling cases I've ever seen. But there is someone I'd like to talk to about it, someone who knew both Shinwell Johnson and Betty Brown." Robert looked at Tony. "How would you like to go hear some jazz?"

"Next," the doorman said, nodding them in.

Virginia and Socks stepped into the Blue Note and stood before the hostess' podium.

"Farrell," Virginia declared. "I'm on the press list."

"Just a minute, let me see . . . Here you go." The hostess handed her a card that said PRESS: FARRELL PLUS ONE.

They stepped to the left of the podium, next to the bar. "I don't see Byron yet," Virginia said. "Let's wait a moment and get our bearings."

"Wise strategy," Socks agreed.

Virginia looked at Socks and smiled with pride. She wore a black miniskirt, black tights, flat black shoes, and a long-sleeved black T-shirt bearing the *Dashiki* album cover. Topped off by loose blonde hair and enormous gold earrings, Socks was simply gorgeous.

In contrast, Virginia felt like the world's biggest goofball. The green dress was all right, and the pearl earrings and necklace were pretty, plus Socks had brushed Virginia's hair behind her ears and put on, heaven help her, mascara. But Virginia wasn't used to wearing heels and stockings, and she longed for her usual clothes, which were sitting in a lonesome pile at her friend George's apartment in Hoboken.

Suddenly an imperious voice proclaimed loudly, "Two Fs. One big, one small."

Virginia looked over at the hostess' podium. There stood Byron, dressed from fedora to shoes in lemon-yellow, leaning on the podium and glaring at the hostess. Behind him lurked Mortimer, as always pale with his hair parted in the middle, wearing khakis and his usual striped shirt.

Virginia nudged Socks, tilting her head toward the podium. "That's him."

Socks gave Byron the once-over. "Goodness! He looks like the Man with the Yellow Hat from the Curious George books."

"Doesn't he just."

"When I was little, I asked my kindergarten teacher what the Man with the Yellow Hat did when he had to go to a funeral. She told me I had an overactive imagination."

"Nothing wrong with that. Come on, it's showtime."

Virginia and Socks stepped over just as the hostess handed Byron his press card.

"Hello," Virginia said.

Byron turned and looked at Virginia, then Socks. "Hello, Virginia," he addressed Socks.

"Byron, I'd like you to meet my roommate, Socks McManus."

"Charmed," he oozed.

"Likewise," Socks purred.

"Hey, Mortimer," Virginia greeted him. "You remember Socks."

"Hello," he whispered. He was paler than usual, his skin a ghastly shade of chalk under the low blue lights.

"Shall we all sit together?" Byron asked, drinking up Socks with his eyes.

"Sure," Virginia replied. "Lead the way."

The club was packed, the room buzzing with lively chatter and the sound of clinking glasses, everyone eager to hear the great Rex Royal Quartet. Byron headed for the skinny tables in front, as Virginia knew he would. Those seats were the least comfortable, forcing you to sit thigh-to-thigh with strangers and crane your neck to see the stage. But the tables brought you closest to the musicians, making them the preferred choice for dedicated jazz lovers.

After elbowing a few people out of the way, Byron managed to find four empty seats. Next thing Virginia knew, she was sitting beside Mortimer on one side of the table, and Socks and Byron were sitting across from them. Perfect, Virginia thought. Let the sleuthing commence.

A harried waitress leaned over their table. "What can I get you?"

"Ladies?" Byron queried.

"I'll have a Shirley Temple," Socks ordered.

"Make that two," Virginia chimed in.

"Glenfiddich," Byron stated. "With one ice cube. If you give me more than that, I shall send it back immed-jiately."

"All right," the waitress said, eyeing him dryly. "Glenfiddich, one ice cube. And you?" she asked Mortimer.

"A Bud," he whispered. "No ice."

The waitress rolled her eyes and moved on to the next table.

"One of my favorite albums," Byron commented, fingering the sleeve of Socks' T-shirt.

"Me as well," she said. "I'm in mourning for Betty Brown."

"Tragic, that."

"Did you know her?"

"Never had the pleasure. But I'm a tremendous admirer of her old boyfriend Shinwell Johnson." He tilted his head. "Are you a jazz fan?"

Socks opened her gray eyes wide and said most sincerely, "I'm *learning*."

"Ah." Byron arched an eyebrow, clearly enjoying himself. "Then you must need a teacher."

"Know any good ones?"

He patted her hand. "Oh, I most definitely do."

Virginia put a hand over her mouth to hide her smile. Good old Socks! You could always count on her.

Now for Mortimer.

Virginia leaned in to face him. "How are you doing? We haven't talked since last week. So much has happened since then."

Mortimer's eyes filled with terror. "What do you mean?"

"Betty Brown, of course. Her murder."

"Oh. I thought you meant—" Beads of sweat popped out on his forehead.

"Meant what?"

"Nothing."

Virginia studied him carefully. "Has something happened? Is there anything you need to tell me?"

Mortimer clenched his lips together, eyes fixed desperately on his fingernails.

Virginia leaned closer. She couldn't risk Byron overhearing. "Is it about John Coltrane?"

Mortimer's eyes flew open. "What about him?" he whispered.

"You know."

He shook his head vehemently. "I don't know anything!"

Aha! Virginia thought triumphantly. She was sure Byron was involved with the missing tapes, and it appeared he had gotten Mortimer mixed up as well.

"Tell me what you know," Virginia said, her voice low and urgent. "This is a serious matter."

Sweat trickled down Mortimer's face. "I realize that."

"If you know something—"

The waitress set down a tray on their table. "Two Shirley Temples, one Bud no ice, and one Glenfiddich with one ice cube exactly."

"Thanks," Virginia and Socks said in unison.

Byron grabbed his glass and frowned into it.

"Ice cube the right size?" the waitress deadpanned.

"It will do," he answered coldly.

Virginia fought the urge to stuff her cocktail stirrer up Byron's nose. She glanced at Socks, who remained composed as she plucked the maraschino cherry out of her drink and popped it into her mouth.

When Virginia turned back to Mortimer, he had already fled. She spotted his blue-and-white striped back disappearing up the stairs toward the men's room.

"Does Mortimer have a glandular situation?" Socks asked.

"What do you mean?" Virginia replied.

"I've never seen anyone expel so much sweat."

"I don't know what's wrong with him." She looked at Byron. "You two seem to be getting along well, especially after—"

"My Hot Five record?" He exhaled sharply through his nose. "An abomination. An absolute travesty. I haven't forgiven him, but at least he's working off his debt. Mortimer is useful to me."

"How so?"

"For instance, the other day I purchased an Ornette Coleman box set from J&R Music World, and blessed be but one of the CDs had a small skip. Quite tiny, but my ear is fine-tuned. I phoned Mortimer at midnight, and in the morning he came to my house so he could return the box set for a new one."

"But you live in Manhattan, and Mortimer lives in Weehawken. Why didn't you just stop by the store on the way to work?"

"You're missing the point. Mortimer is indebted to me. He needs to pay it off by any means necessary."

Virginia felt her face redden with anger. She opened her mouth to speak when Socks jumped in. "How marvelous to have such sensitive ears! I'm afraid I can't even distinguish a trumpet from a saxophone."

Byron looked at Socks as if she were edible. "With a little training, I'm sure you'll do fine. If you like, I can direct your listening tonight during the show."

"I'd be ever so grateful," Socks replied, gazing at him coyly. "You can't imagine how distressing it is to labor under such an aural handicap."

"Fear not, my pretty. We'll fix you right up."

Socks and Byron were exchanging gooey smiles when the waitress returned and set down two more Shirley Temples.

"I'm sorry," Virginia said. "We didn't order these."

"Courtesy of Mr. Togasaki," the waitress answered, pointing to the back of the room.

Virginia turned around to look. One of the back tables was full of Japanese guests, including Mr. Togasaki and several bodyguards the size of sumo wrestlers. Mr. Togasaki waved at her, and she waved back. Virginia also noticed Mr. Togasaki's girlfriend, a short Japanese woman with black hair in a ponytail and high-cut bangs, just like June Christy.

"How kind," Socks exclaimed, plucking out the cherry from her new drink.

"Virginia," Byron said, folding his hands on the table and giving her a look of feigned sincerity. "I would be ever so grateful for an introduction to Mr. Togasaki. I'm sure he'll stop by later to speak to you. After all, he is your patron."

"OK," Virginia agreed. "Let's see how it goes."

"And you?" Byron eyed Socks provocatively. "Do you have a patron?"

Socks matched his look. "Virginia is subsidized by Mr. Togasaki, and I'm supported by my ex-husband. Modern and feudal economics, you might say."

"Who pray tell is your ex-husband?"

Socks said his name, and Byron raised an eyebrow. "Wasn't he on the cover of *Forbes* a few weeks ago?"

"Probably," Socks replied, waving a hand in dismissal. "I don't keep up."

"Not afraid of powerful men, I see."

"What's to be afraid of?"

Byron moved his seat back slightly and looked at Socks from head to toe. "Virginia," he declared. "I must scold you for keeping such a charming creature hidden all this time. Who knew you had such a thoroughly enchanting roommate?"

Virginia opened her mouth to reply, but suddenly stopped. There, next to the bar and looking totally out of place, stood that Detective Smith! What on earth was he doing here?

Virginia looked beautiful. So beautiful Robert thought he might melt into a puddle on the floor.

He and Tony arrived just as the doorman announced to the line of waiting guests that the club was at maximum capacity. A flash of Tony's badge convinced him otherwise, and they ended up squeezed into the crowd around the bar.

Luckily Robert could see the stage perfectly. As his glance moved around the club, he spotted Virginia Farrell. She wore a dark-green dress and pearls, her auburn hair swept behind her ears. She's so colorful, Robert thought. Delicate too.

Suddenly Virginia looked up. Her eyes met his, and Robert felt a deep pang as a look of annoyance crossed her face.

She turned her head, and Robert peered closer at her companions. Mortimer Burns had just taken the seat next to her, her roommate sat across the table, with none other than Byron Ffowlkes on her right. What on earth was Virginia doing with him?

Again Robert remembered his feeling that Virginia had lied to him the first time they spoke. She had also wrinkled her nose in distaste when Robert asked if she had told Ffowlkes about the tapes, and now here she was socializing with him. Then again, he was Virginia's boss, so maybe she didn't have a choice . . .

"Here you go," Tony said, handing Robert a Dos Equis. He clinked his beer against Robert's bottle. "Cheers to being off duty."

"Maybe not," Robert replied. "In front by the stage, you see that beautiful redhead? That's Virginia Farrell. And look who's sitting diagonally across from her."

Tony narrowed his eyes. "Mr. Gemstones. Who's the blonde whispering in his ear?"

"Virginia Farrell's roommate. The one who gave her the honey for Betty Brown."

"Ah ha. And the dweeby redhead?"

"Mortimer Burns."

"Aw, jeez. This is our last beer, Boberino. Enjoy it while you can."

The lights dimmed. Three middle-aged Black men in dark suits came down the stairs and walked onto the stage. The audience hushed as one man sat at the piano, another lifted an acoustic bass, and the third picked up a saxophone. The drum kit, set up in the middle of the stage under a golden light, remained empty.

Another five minutes passed, then a man in a white silk djellaba slowly descended the staircase. Completely bald with smooth ebony skin, his lean face was marked with prominent cheekbones, his expression dignified and composed.

At last, the famous Rex Royal.

A few people up front started applauding wildly, and soon the entire audience was clapping and cheering. Royal stepped onto the stage, inclined his head modestly at the crowd, then sat at the drum set.

The saxophonist leaned in and whispered something to Royal. He laughed, revealing bright-white teeth in a mischievous smile. Then he lifted his drumsticks and counted off, "A-one, a-two, a-one, two, three, four," and music burst from the stage.

Robert tried his best to listen closely. To prepare for the gig, he had dug out his lone jazz CD, a grab-bag gift from his New York days. *Kind of Blue*, it was called. When the detective who put it in the grab bag saw Robert unwrap the CD, he rushed over and enthused about the music for a solid fifteen minutes. As a result, Robert never listened to it.

Tonight Robert not only played the CD, he also read the liner notes. To his surprise, the music was enjoyable. More accessible than he imagined, since Robert had always assumed you had to be highly intellectual to appreciate jazz. If pressed, Robert would have to admit that he considered himself intelligent, yet he was completely out of his depth when it came to music.

It quickly became clear that Rex Royal was accessible too. The music was easy to follow, with a fresh, bouncy rhythm. This isn't bad at all, Robert realized. Royal was also a magnetic stage presence, draped in his white djellaba and moving with power and grace.

When the first song was over, Robert looked down at Tony.

"It's all right," Tony said with a shrug.

"But it's not Sinatra," Robert grinned.

Tony put a hand over his heart. "Only Sinatra is Sinatra. And don't you forget it."

As the set continued, Robert half-listened to the music while planning his conversation with Rex Royal.

Robert doubted he'd get much time with Royal tonight, but maybe they could arrange a meeting in the next days. Royal might find it strange that Robert was interested in Shinwell Johnson's murder, but talking about Betty Brown first might ease the way.

A flicker of frustration passed through him. The Betty Brown case was stuck in circumstantial evidence. Now it was a matter of personalities, of getting someone to crack and confess. Shinwell Johnson's murder felt like a relief in comparison—no one expected answers, so there wasn't the same pressure to solve the case. Or find a box of priceless tapes.

After reading the Johnson file twice, Robert found himself totally engrossed. It was a strange puzzle, lost in the past and probably unsolvable. But it was always the difficult things in life that interested Robert, which was probably why he became a detective.

Speaking of difficulties, Robert allowed himself another glance at Virginia Farrell. She was turned toward the stage, her face lit up with rapt attention. He looked at the pearls resting on her collarbone, the set of her lips, her large, expressive eyes, her lovely auburn hair, such an unusual shade . . .

The song concluded, and the audience erupted in applause.

"Thank you all so much," Royal said, wiping sweat off his face and bald head with a hand towel. "Now we got a special treat for you, a tribute to a dear friend of mine. Two friends, actually."

Royal took a long drink from the glass of water at his side, then continued. "Some of you may know that just this week, Betty Brown died in a tragic way. They didn't make 'em sweeter than Betty. Our other dear friend is Betty's old boyfriend, the great trumpeter Shinwell Johnson. I was lucky enough to play with both of them on a song that surprised us all by hittin' the Top 40."

"'Dashiki!'" someone shouted out.

"That's right," Royal called back. "But you supposed to shout that at the end, not before we even start!" The audience laughed, and Royal flashed a thousand-watt smile. "I gotta tell ya, that song's been good to me. Shinwell wrote it, but I punched up a couple things, so he gave me credit as cowriter. I'll tell you, there ain't nothin' like a royalty check, especially when times are lean.

"Now, we're a simple quartet up here, so we need to ask a few friends to help us out. So first, to fill the large shoes of Shinwell Johnson, we'd like to get the talented shoes of Roy Campbell up here."

The audience clapped wildly as a dark-skinned Black man carrying a trumpet climbed onstage. The saxophonist gave him a high five, then stepped offstage so Campbell could have his mike.

Royal beamed. "Our bass player has put down his acoustic and is pickin' up his electric, so we're cool with that. But we need a guitar player. Back in the day, we did this song with my man Sonny Sharrock—"

"Sonny!" an enthusiastic fan yelled out.

"Ain't nobody like Sonny. But he's passed, so we gotta fill his place too. I do believe Mr. George Benson is in the house?"

Finally, Robert thought, a name I recognize. The crowd went wild as Benson climbed onstage, gave Royal a hug, then plugged in his guitar.

"Last but by no ways least, we need a flute. As you know, the original 'Dashiki' had the legendary Sam Rivers, and wouldn't you know Sam's in town recording a new CD. So ladies and gentlemen, I need your help to welcome Mr. Sam Rivers!"

The crowd went wild again as Rivers stepped on stage and embraced Royal in a bear hug. Robert glanced over at Virginia. She and Mortimer Burns were staring at one another, their eyes wide with excitement.

As the musicians found their places and checked the mikes, Royal went on, "Since this is a tribute to Betty, we need to fill in for her too, so at the end y'all got to yell 'Dashiki'! Now, this ain't no Love Supreme. I don't want no low voices, I want you to shout it up to the stars for Betty. Got it? All right then—a-one, a-two, a-one, two, three, four!"

They launched into the song. A few moments later, Robert had a flash of recognition. So this was "Dashiki"! He knew the song well, but he had never thought of it as jazz. It was a great tune, energetic and catchy, and Robert enjoyed watching the musicians, particularly Royal and Rivers.

The last note died down, then most of the audience raised their hands above their heads and shouted, "Dashiki!" Except Robert, because that was not something he would ever do. And not Tony, but only because he considered himself on duty.

Onstage, Rex Royal threw back his head and laughed in delight. When the applause died down, he said, "That's for you, Betty. You too, Shinwell. Y'all rest in peace."

Robert looked over at Virginia. She and her roommate were laughing, leaning in so close their foreheads were practically touching. She looked very, very pretty.

"**H**ow absolutely cathartic!" Socks declared. "Nothing like screaming in public."

"I admire your enthusiasm," Byron drawled.

"And I'm impressed by your restraint," Socks countered.

Because Byron, of course, had not deigned to shout "Dashiki!" Even Mortimer had given it his best shot.

Virginia looked over at Mortimer, but he studiously avoided her gaze. He knows something, Virginia thought excitedly. I'm sure he does.

With all the guest musicians still onstage, the band launched into a raucous version of "Night in Tunisia." Byron leaned toward Socks and started telling her in a low voice about Charlie Parker and Dizzy Gillespie.

The expression on Socks' face! Virginia wished she could frame it. Whenever Virginia talked about jazz, Socks looked nauseous, but now she was gazing at Byron rapturously. She was Bess and George all rolled into one.

Then something most unfortunate happened. Socks, in her effort to be pleasing to Byron, moved an elbow closer to him. This upset one of her Shirley Temples, which splashed onto Byron's immaculate lemon-yellow outfit. He tried to move his chair back, but with everyone packed in so tightly, he had no choice but to endure the unwelcome shower.

Byron's eyes bulged, and his nostrils flared so wide that anyone could see up his nose, if they cared to. But he couldn't get up to leave; he would have disrupted several other tables, and since their party was in front of the stage, he would have disturbed the musicians as well. Roy Campbell was in the middle of a scorching solo, and even Byron knew that jazz was ultimately more important than clothes.

As a result, he had no choice but to sit and soak, the red grenadine from the Shirley Temple combining with the lemon-yellow cloth to form a most fascinating shade. Virginia couldn't look, or at least not often, otherwise she would have burst out laughing. But she was also sorry, because surely this was the end of Socks and Byron's lovefest.

The song lasted a good fifteen minutes, the band giving it their all. When they were done, Rex thanked the musicians one by one, then said good night. The audience was on its feet, applauding wildly and begging for an encore. Rex grabbed the mike again and said, "Sorry folks, I gotta get these youngsters off to bed. I think I tired 'em out!" The musicians filed offstage and headed upstairs to the green room.

The house lights went up, and the club's sound system began playing *Art Pepper Plus Eleven*.

Byron turned to Socks, who was innocently examining her nails. His blue eyes were ice-cold as he bit off the words, "You are a clumsy oaf!"

Socks looked him up and down. "You don't have to get into such a snuff about it! I'm dreadfully sorry, if that helps."

"It does not help. Not one bit."

To make matters worse, Mr. Togasaki and his party were about to pass their table. Byron turned his head and moved his chair slightly, too embarrassed to be introduced in such a sodden state.

Mr. Togasaki stopped at Virginia's chair. She rose, and they exchanged bows. He began telling her about the Stan Kenton bootleg he had purchased just that day, with an incredible version of June Christy singing "Tampico." Virginia told him that her friend John from the Institute of Jazz Studies had tracked down an obscure interview with June Christy's arranger Pete Rugolo.

They would have stood there and talked June Christy all night, if not for the crowd pressing around them and trying to leave.

"Ah! Never enough time to talk," Mr. Togasaki exclaimed in his flawless English. "We can meet for lunch late next week, yes? My secretary will call you to set something up. Meanwhile, I'll make a copy of the bootleg and send it to you."

"Sounds good," Virginia beamed. "I look forward to it."

They bowed again, and Mr. Togasaki moved on, followed by his enormous bodyguards, who were trailed by Mr. Togasaki's June Christy–look-alike girlfriend. Virginia was startled to see that the woman was wearing an exact replica of Christy's dress from the cover of the album *Duet*, an unusual black-and-white design with thick black straps adorned with buckles.

I may be obsessed with June Christy, Virginia mused as she and the woman bowed to each other, but these people are on a whole other level. Never mind, though; they weren't hurting anyone. Mr. Togasaki's wealth allowed him to indulge his whims, which included of course subsidizing Virginia.

She looked back at her table. Byron sulked while Socks struggled not to laugh. As for Mortimer, he looked terrified.

"If you guys don't mind," Virginia said, "I'm going to go upstairs and say hello to Rex. It shouldn't take long."

Socks winked at her, and Mortimer whispered, "Bye, Virginia."

"I'll be back," she told him sternly. "Don't leave without me."

He turned exactly one shade paler.

Virginia worked her way through the crowd and up the staircase. The second-floor hallway was jammed with musicians and well-wishers, talking and laughing excitedly.

And there, standing by the souvenir case, utterly lost with no clue how to proceed, was Detective Robert Smith.

Virginia sighed. He looked so pitiful; she had no choice but to help him. She wriggled through the crowd and positioned herself directly in front of him.

"Hi," she called up.

He looked down. "Oh—hello. How are you?"

"Good. Great show. You want to see Rex?"

"I was hoping to, but—" He waved at the thick crowd.

"Follow me."

Virginia propelled herself through the tight pack of people.

"Excuse me," she called out cheerfully. "Pardon me."

She waved to one of the quartet, greeted a photographer from *Down-Beat*, and accepted a kiss on the cheek from a writer she met via the Jazz Journalists Association. Occasionally she looked back to make sure Detective Smith was still trailing behind her.

Suddenly they were on the threshold of the green room, next in line to see Rex Royal.

"Nice work," Detective Smith said, a smile playing on his lips.

"Just part of being a journalist."

Virginia looked into the green room. Rex was seated on a leopard-skin velvet couch, with a fresh white towel draped around his neck and navy-blue slippers on his feet. He was talking to two men who Virginia recognized as music company executives. His manager and agent were huddled in one corner, and in another corner three attractive middle-aged Black women were filling glasses with champagne.

As the executives left, Virginia stepped in, gesturing for Detective Smith to follow. When Rex saw her, he broke into a big grin.

"My favorite redhead! What you doin', slippin' and slidin' on the back streets?" He looked at Detective Smith, then back at Virginia. "Cop?"

"About Betty Brown," she said.

"You need to speak to me?" Rex asked Detective Smith.

"Yes, sir," he replied. "If you have a few minutes."

"There's all these people waitin' to talk to me, but how 'bout we meet in the diner round the corner? In half an hour, let's say?"

"That's fine. I appreciate it."

"You comin' too, Red?" Rex asked.

Virginia looked at Detective Smith, who nodded. "Sure," she agreed.

"See you then, then."

As Virginia and Robert made their way downstairs, Virginia silently thanked Rex. This would be an excellent chance to continue her sleuthing.

Downstairs the tables were empty, but the bar was still buzzing. Socks was seated on a stool, talking to a short man with thick black hair that stood straight up, defying all laws of gravity.

"Virginia!" Socks called excitedly. "Meet Detective Tony Oliveto. He works with Detective Smith."

"Hello," Virginia greeted him.

"Pleasure," Detective Oliveto answered, eyeing her carefully.

"So, Detective Smith," Socks continued breezily, "we meet again. Did you enjoy the show?"

"I liked it."

"The highlight was definitely 'Dashiki.'"

"Actually," Detective Oliveto said, looking at Socks appreciatively, "the highlight was watchin' you splash a drink on that pompous Englishman. You got a hell of an elbow there."

Socks shrugged. "It comes in handy."

"Where are Byron and Mortimer?" Virginia asked.

"Byron is cowering in the men's room, and Mortimer has been dispatched to Byron's apartment to get a fresh set of unicolored clothes. Once he's back, they're heading over to the Village Vanguard, and we are most definitely not invited."

"That's OK," Virginia said. "Detective Smith and I are meeting Rex Royal in the Washington Square Diner in a little bit. Do you mind waiting?"

Socks lay a hand over her heart. "Anything for Betty Brown."

"I'll keep you company," Tony offered saucily.

"Isn't that sweet. You two run along to the diner, we'll wait right here."

Socks is going to do some sleuthing, Virginia realized. Maybe between the two of them, they could get some information out of these detectives.

The night air was pleasantly balmy as Virginia and Detective Smith stepped out onto Third Street. As they headed toward Sixth Avenue, Virginia suddenly felt shy. Maybe Detective Smith didn't actually want her to come.

"I hope it's all right I'm tagging along," she said tentatively. "Rex suggested it, so . . ."

"It's fine," Detective Smith assured her. "I think he'll be more comfortable with you there. Besides, I'm just gathering background information."

"So it's not an interrogation?" Virginia asked mischievously.

He laughed. "It's not even questioning."

She looked up at him, and the oddest thing happened. It was as if her entire body blinked. Why, she thought, Socks is right. Detective Smith *is* handsome. Virginia had thought so before, but this was the first time she felt it. She looked away to hide her reddening cheeks.

"Watch out!" He put a hand on Virginia's shoulder as a basketball came bouncing out of the court on Sixth Avenue.

A young Hispanic man came running after the ball. *"Lo siento!"*

"No hay problema!" Virginia called back. The boy laughed and went back to the court.

"Are you—?" Detective Smith asked, looking at her curiously.

"My mom's Spanish," Virginia said. "My dad's American, although his parents came over from Ireland. They met when they were both interning at the United Nations."

At Fourth Street, they made a right and walked into the Washington Square Diner. They sat in a booth by the back window, and a waitress came over with menus.

"Black coffee for me," Detective Smith ordered. "What would you like?"

"Tea, please," Virginia said. "And do you have coconut cake?"

"Fresh out of the kitchen," the waitress supplied.

"Ooh, that sounds yummy. I'll take a piece."

"Is there chocolate cake?" Detective Smith asked.

"We just sold the last slice. But the coconut's good, and we have apple and cherry pie. Plus doughnuts, they're out of this world."

"Oh. Well—coconut is fine."

"Coming right up," the waitress said.

Suddenly Virginia felt self-conscious—of her dress, the pearls, and her newly born realization that Detective Smith was quite attractive. She looked down at her hands, suddenly unsure what to say.

Virginia was looking at her hands and staying quiet.

All right, Robert told himself. Conversation. Talk to her. Ask a question.

He cleared his throat. "I know you told me that Rex Royal is a living legend, but I don't know much about him. What's his background?"

Virginia looked up, her eyes bright. "You really want the whole story? In detail?"

"Sure."

And detail he got. Virginia launched into Royal's biography, starting with the Royal family moving to California in the late twenties.

Was it right for Robert to sit there nodding like he was genuinely interested? He was intrigued by Virginia, after all, if not jazz. She could have talked to him about anything, it was just a pleasure to sit and watch her.

"So Rex was born in LA in 1930," Virginia explained eagerly, "and he started playing drums when he was only five. In the forties, he was part of the Central Avenue scene. Can you imagine? A teenager sitting in with Charlie Parker and Dizzy Gillespie at Billy Berg's."

"That's impressive," Robert commented politely.

"Isn't it? Thank you," Virginia said to the waitress, who set down their food and drinks. "In 1954, Rex filled in for Max Roach in Max's quintet with Clifford Brown. He was also a part of The Lighthouse gang, which is when he got close with June Christy and her husband, Bob Cooper."

"That's the woman you're writing a book on."

"Exactly." Virginia paused to sip her coffee, clearly relishing the chance to share her knowledge. "Rex was also friends with saxophonist Eric Dolphy. Rex and Dolphy moved to New York City together at the end of the fifties. New York was full of great jazz musicians back then," she added. "Which is when Rex got to know Coltrane, and sometimes subbed for Elvin Jones in Coltrane's famous quartet."

"It sounds like he knew everyone," Robert remarked.

"Just about. In the mid-sixties, Rex joined the free jazz movement and performed at the October Revolution in 1964. That period was huge for him. He made a couple of seminal avant-garde albums, and during that period he also cowrote 'Dashiki' with Shinwell Johnson."

"So that's the connection," Robert mused.

"Since the late sixties, Rex has led the quartet you saw tonight. They played hard bop this evening, but they're so versatile. They can play anything—Dixieland, swing, cool, bossa nova, avant-garde, fusion." Virginia took a deep breath. "And on top of all that, Rex is a nice person. Very generous."

"Did you interview him for your book?"

"Several times. We spent a few afternoons together, and he gave me access to his archives, which had some great photos." Her voice was warm with gratitude. "We had a lot of fun. Rex also tracked down a few phone numbers for me, people I was having trouble getting in touch with. He loved June Christy and her husband, and he was happy to help out."

"That was kind of him."

Virginia's eyes lit up. "Oh! There he is."

Robert turned around. Still wearing the white djellaba, now with a mink coat draped over his shoulders, Rex Royal strolled into the diner. Several customers approached to shake his hand, while another offered pen and paper for an autograph.

Royal eventually made his way to their booth. The hostess took his fur coat, and he slipped into the seat next to Virginia.

"Sorry I'm a little late," he apologized. "Some guy had a stack of my old albums for me to sign, stuff I hadn't seen in years. So here you are, Red!" He gave Virginia a playful hug. "How you doin'? You're lookin' real pretty tonight."

Virginia rolled her eyes. "Thanks."

"This one I love," Royal said, covering Virginia's hand with his own. "She's takin' care of my girl June. Now, how 'bout you?" he asked Robert. "What's your name?"

"Detective Robert Smith."

"Nice to meet you, Robert. Tell me, how can I help out?"

The waitress came over, but instead of asking Royal what he wanted, she presented him with a large slice of cherry pie with towering mounds of vanilla ice cream and whipped cream, plus an extra-large glass of milk.

"Thanks, doll," Royal said, tossing her a wink.

Robert folded his hands on the table. "I know you were friends with Betty Brown, and I was wondering if you could fill in some gaps. We don't know much about her. It seems she kept mostly to herself."

"That's Betty," Royal replied, digging into his pie. "Or that's how Betty became after Shinwell passed. We was real tight before Skin died, I saw him and Betty most every day. Then after Skin was found dead, Betty moved to Jersey City, so it was never like before. But I kept an eye on her, called her mostly. I didn't want Betty to fade off into nowhere, like so many do."

"OK," Robert said.

"I also gave her money from time to time," Royal continued. "See, when Skin passed, all his 'Dashiki' royalties went to his brother. Betty never saw a penny of it, which didn't seem right to me, what with her being such an important part of the song. So whenever I got a big royalty check—and believe me, some of them checks was big—I always passed somethin' along to Betty.

"The money slowed down after a while, but it never stopped completely. When we landed the car commercial a few years back, everyone got a nice piece of change, and I made sure to pass some along to Betty. That was the last time I saw her, though we did talk on the phone now and again."

Royal took a long sip of milk, then sighed. "I feel bad I didn't see more of her. Hoboken's so close to New York you can practically touch it, but you know how it can be, you get caught up in your life, and I'm travelin' so much. I was plannin' on lookin' Betty up next week when I went to *Jazz Now*, but that ain't happening anymore."

He looked at Robert. "I don't get why anyone would kill her. If it were some kid hard up for money who did it, you wouldn't be talkin' to me, would you? So somethin's up."

"You're right," Robert acknowledged. "It wasn't a random burglary. Tell me, did Betty Brown ever mention anything to you about some old recordings she had? Tapes that belonged to John Coltrane?"

Royal's brow furrowed. "Trane's tapes? I know Betty used to sit for Syeeda way back. Maybe Trane gave her somethin', but nothin' she ever mentioned to me."

"And Shinwell Johnson never mentioned any tapes?"

"Me and Skin talked about a million things. Sure we talked about Trane and his music, but I don't recall him ever sayin' nothin' about no tapes. What are we talkin' about here?"

"Recordings of performances that John Coltrane and Thelonious Monk made at a club called the Five Spot."

Royal's eyes bulged. "You tellin' me Skin had tapes of the Five Spot gig? Believe me, I woulda remembered that! But what does any of this have to do with Betty?"

Robert looked at Virginia. "Maybe you'd like to explain?"

Virginia exhaled loudly. "The thing is, Rex, I interviewed Betty Brown on Tuesday, the day she died. She brought out a box of tapes that Shinwell Johnson stole from Coltrane way back in 1958. I saw the labels, and they were from the Five Spot gig. After Shinwell died, Betty Brown kept them, and she was too ashamed to tell anyone. But because she was sick—did you know she had cancer?"

Royal shook his head no.

"She told me she was dying. And she asked me to help her get the tapes back to the Coltranes and the Monks." Virginia's eyes filled with tears. "Now Betty Brown's dead, and the tapes are missing."

"Aw, Red," Royal said, handing her a napkin. "Don't take it so hard."

"I feel like it's my fault."

"If you didn't steal 'em, it's not on you." Royal pursed his lips. "Poor Betty. I guess that explains it, right? Because otherwise I can't imagine anyone havin' any reason to kill her. And you saw the tapes, Red? You sure they was from the Five Spot?"

"I'm sure."

Royal whistled out slowly. "Damn! I would give my right arm to hear those tapes. And I'm a drummer."

"So this is the first you've heard about them?" Robert asked. "Not a whisper or speculation from other musicians, or John Coltrane himself?"

"Everyone knew Naima made a buncha tapes at the Five Spot, but we all figured they was lost. So, yeah, this is news to me, and everyone else as well." Royal shook his head. "That Shinwell. Don't get me wrong, I loved him like a brother. But Skin had a down on Trane, and it was the oddest thing, 'cause everyone else loved him. Betty always said Skin was mad 'cause Trane didn't want to play with him."

"That's what she told me," Virginia confirmed.

Robert cleared his throat. "Speaking of Shinwell Johnson, I hope you don't mind if I ask a few questions about him. I've been looking into his murder as well, in case it has any relevance to Betty Brown's."

Virginia kept her expression neutral, but her stomach seized up. Stay calm, she told herself. Keep still and don't say a word.

"You sure are thorough," Rex remarked to Detective Smith. "I can admire that in a man. Go ahead, ask me whatever you like."

"I've been reading through the old case file, and I saw your statement. Would you mind going over what happened again?"

"Sure thing." Rex rubbed the back of his neck thoughtfully. "I'll tell you, it was the oddest thing. Skin was on toppa the world. We'd just done *The Mike Douglas Show*, and let me tell you, everyone saw that show. People were comin' up to us on the street, slappin' our backs and sayin' how good we sounded. So everythin' was cool, everythin' was great.

"I met up with Skin a few nights later at Slug's. We had some drinks, sat in with the band. Then at the end of the night, we stood in front of the club. Skin was goin' one way, and I was goin' the other. We hugged and said, 'See you, man.' And that was it. One day Skin was there, and the next, boom, he was gone."

"When did you first realize he was missing?" Robert prompted.

"I guess a day or so after we hung out at Slug's. I called his apartment, and Betty asked me if I knew where he was." Rex tilted his head. "Now, I gotta be frank, that was kinda a tricky question, 'cause Skin had other girls. Betty was his main lady and they lived together, but you know how it goes, some cats are just livin' it that way.

"I told Betty I hadn't seen him, then I called over to my girl, 'cause I knew Skin was steppin' out with her roommate, Christine. My girl hadn't seen Skin at all, and she told me Christine hadn't been around for a few days either."

Robert asked, "Did you tell Betty Brown about that?"

"I called her back and said no one had seen Skin, but I was workin' on findin' him. I figured Skin and Christine were off celebratin' somewhere, and they'd be back soon enough.

"Then that weekend, Skin missed a coupla gigs. Which is when I started thinkin' that somethin' serious was goin' on. Our group was hot, and there we was cancelin' all over town 'cause our main guy was AWOL. All Skin wanted was to make it big, and once he had that fame in his hands, he wasn't likely to drop it."

Rex shook his head slowly. "It went on like that a coupla months, then we got the news about the farmer in Pennsylvania. Broke my heart. Betty's too."

Virginia slowly sipped her tea.

"What do you make of his body showing up in Pennsylvania?" Robert asked.

Rex spread his hands helplessly. "No idea. We all knew folks in Philly, but Skin was nowhere near there. I've thought it over a million times, and it still don't make no sense." He shook his head. "That makes it harder, somehow, not knowin'."

"And no one else has any idea what might have happened?"

"Nope. Skin's death is still a mystery. Same thing with Albert one year later. Trane had passed not long before, and the music couldn't afford to lose any more angels. Hard times, real hard times."

Robert nodded. "I can imagine."

Rex leaned forward. "But I'll tell you, Robert, I'm real glad you've come around askin' these questions. 'Cause I do know somethin' no one else knows. No one official, that is."

Virginia struggled to keep her face neutral. What on earth could Rex know? Surely nothing that would throw suspicion on Betty Brown. Virginia sipped her tea, trying to keep her hand steady.

Rex paused, taking a deep breath. "Like I mentioned, Skin was tight with Christine. She was pretty, blonde with big brown eyes, a real soulful lady. I dug Betty, but I could dig Christine too. I just figured Skin would sort it all out eventually.

"Christine split around the same time as Skin. Me and my girl went over their apartment inch by inch lookin' for some kind of clue, but Christine had cleaned out mosta her stuff, anything with addresses and so forth. We got her parents' number from an old phone bill, but they hadn't heard boo from her either.

"I was sure Christine had gone off with Skin, and let me tell you, I lost a lotta sleep wonderin' what happened to those two. Maybe they was on a spree somewhere, and folks took a dislikin' to seein' a white girl with a Black man. It's possible they killed Skin and took Christine off someplace—anything coulda happened."

Rex leaned closer. "Then about ten years ago, my quartet was playin' in Seattle. This woman came up to me, and damned if it wasn't Christine. Her hair was darker and a whole lot shorter, but she still had them big brown eyes.

"We went out for a drink, and Christine told me she didn't leave with Skin. He had gone to her place after leavin' me at Slug's, and he had some kind of ugly jealous fit, screamin' and cursin' her out. I guess Skin had yelled at Christine before, but this time she got scared. She hightailed it up to Canada to stay with friends, just to get the hell away from him.

"So Christine didn't know nothin' about Skin disappearin'. A few months later, she read in the papers about that farmer finding Skin's body. Christine was too frightened to come forward, specially 'cause she was mentioned in all the stories. Started callin' herself by her middle name, Daisy, and eventually got married and moved to Seattle.

"Christine told me she always felt bad 'cause everyone thought she had somethin' to do with Skin's death. Just for her own peace of mind, she wanted to tell someone the truth. I'd come through Seattle plenty-a times before, but I guess it took her a while to get up the nerve. It was a great relief to see she was still alive, I'll tell you."

Robert asked, "Did Christine have any idea what happened to Shinwell Johnson?"

"Nope. Skin left her apartment that night to go home to Betty. Never saw him again."

"I see."

Rex shook his head sadly. "I'll tell you, hardly a day goes by I don't think of Skin some way somehow. He wasn't no saint, and I sure didn't envy Betty or any of his other girls, but otherwise he was a solid cat. Real funny and quick, and one helluva musician. Never got the respect he deserved, or not until 'Dashiki' came out. At least Skin got a little taste of success before he passed." Rex turned to Virginia. "What do you make-a all this, Red?"

Virginia cleared her throat. "You're right," she said carefully. "It was hard for jazz losing Shinwell Johnson and Albert Ayler within a year of each other."

"Poor Albert," Rex murmured. "Body floatin' in the East River, and still no one knows why or how. They say his old girlfriend was involved, but whatever happened, she kept it to herself."

"Did you ever tell Betty Brown what Christine said?" Detective Smith asked.

"You know, I never did. Anytime I brought up Skin's death, Betty always got real quiet, so I decided to let it be."

Suddenly a curvaceous Black woman in a blue velvet cloak was standing by the table. Virginia recognized her from the champagne ladies in the green room.

"Babe," she purred, her voice honey-smooth. "They're waitin' for us uptown."

Rex flashed his big smile. "Gotta go! Sorry I couldn't give you more information."

"Actually, you were a big help," Detective Smith replied. "I appreciate you taking the time."

"Anythin' for Betty. Skin too."

Rex kissed Virginia's hand, then he and Detective Smith stood and shook. The waitress appeared with Rex's fur coat, gently draping it over his shoulders. He linked arms with his date and strolled out of the diner.

Virginia and Detective Smith watched through the window as Rex and the woman entered the back of a limousine.

"That's Rex," Virginia declared, her voice full of admiration.

"You were right. He's a good man."

Virginia smiled. She was so relieved she was practically giddy; the moment she feared had come, and now it was gone.

Or maybe not.

"You know," Detective Smith said. "I'd like to get a little more background on all this. You mentioned the Institute of Jazz Studies. Would they have information on Shinwell Johnson and Betty Brown?"

Virginia felt the hairs on the back of her neck rise. "Ah—I'm sure they do. I know they do." Think fast! she told herself. "If you want, I could come along and introduce you to my friend John. He works there, and he's a big Shinwell Johnson fan."

"What about tomorrow morning?"

"So soon?"

"If it's not inconvenient for you. I can drive."

She blinked. "That works. I can do some fact-checking for my article on Betty Brown."

And, Virginia thought as she smiled at Detective Smith, I can also keep an eye on you.

Robert was delighted. The evening had gone better than he could have imagined. Seeing Virginia, sitting together in the diner, even making plans for tomorrow.

Speaking to Rex Royal had also proved useful, especially learning more about Christine. Robert didn't necessarily believe Christine was telling the truth, but at least the trail was no longer cold. When the Betty Brown case settled down, maybe Robert could reach out to the police in Seattle and try to find Christine.

Robert and Virginia were walking together on Sixth Avenue, on their way back to the Blue Note. A fat white moon had risen above the city, and the street was even quieter than before. Virginia walked slowly, her expression thoughtful.

Robert cleared his throat. "Are you going back to the Catskills tonight?"

"We're staying in Hoboken."

"Do you and your roommate need a ride?"

She looked up at him. "That would be great. The PATH train can be a little squirrelly this time of night."

"It's no problem."

"Thanks, Detective Smith."

He winced. "You can call me Robert."

"Really?"

"Yes. I'd prefer it."

The Blue Note had mostly cleared out, but about a dozen people were hanging out at the bar. A few musicians stood at one end, and Robert saw Tony sitting with Virginia's roommate at the other. Tony was talking, and Socks was looking at him with a mixture of bewilderment and barely concealed laughter. Which did not bode well.

Sure enough, as Robert and Virginia approached the bar, Robert heard Tony in the middle of one of his sensitive-guy stories.

"See, when fish die, it don't happen so quick. You might think they're dead, and next thing you know, they're floppin' and—"

"Oh, look!" Socks exclaimed, patting Tony's arm. "It's Virginia and Detective Smith. You two came just in time. Tony was telling me how his goldfish died when he was in fourth grade. It's a thoroughly captivating story."

"Damn near broke my heart," Tony said. "You two have a good time talkin' with Mr. Royal?"

"We did," Robert replied. "He's a nice man."

"Helluva drummer too. Especially for an old guy. What is he, like seventy?"

"Seventy-two," Virginia answered promptly. "He was born on October 17, 1930. In Los Angeles."

Tony shook his head. "Jeez, I hope I'm doin' that good at that age."

"Maybe you should take up the drums," Socks suggested. "It might help you forget about your goldfish." She turned to Virginia. "He buried it, you know. There was a funeral, and he served goldfish crackers."

"How appropriate," Virginia commented.

"So," Robert interjected, jumping in to save Tony. "We're going to drive Virginia and Socks back to Hoboken."

Tony shook his head. "I would like nothin' better than to help you escort these two ladies, but I'm gonna stick around and see what's up with Mr. Ffowlkes."

"He's still here?" Virginia asked incredulously.

"Indeed he is," Socks confirmed. "Your fellow redhead just bounded up the stairs with a garment bag."

Virginia looked at the staircase. "I was hoping for a chance to talk with Mortimer . . ."

"He's obeying his master now, you can't get near him. Unless you want to go into the men's room."

"Which I don't."

"We'll be leaving now," Robert told Tony. "You sure you don't want to come?"

"Nah. I'm headin' over to the Village Vanguard. Maybe I'll get lucky and spill a drink on him."

Socks extended her hand. "It's been an enchantingly unique experience, Tony."

"Ditto." He took Socks' hand and kissed her knuckles. "Watch out for that elbow."

"Oh, I shall."

They left Tony at the bar and walked down Third Street to Robert's car. Socks chattered away about goldfish crackers, Curious George, and all kinds of things Robert couldn't exactly follow.

If Robert had to define Socks' character flaw, he would say she lacked gravity. He would even go so far to say she was flippant. Not that Virginia seemed to mind; she laughed at all her roommate's odd comments. But personally Robert found Socks rather off-putting.

"Is this a police car?" she asked as Robert stepped up to a maroon Chevy. "I don't see any divider between the front and back seat. Does it pop up in case you wrangle some criminals?"

"I'm a detective," Robert stated, opening the front door for Virginia. "This car is for investigations, not for transporting perpetrators."

"So disappointing!" Socks sighed dramatically as he opened a back door for her. "I was hoping Charles Manson might have gotten a lift from you."

"Ah—no."

"Pity."

Flippant, Robert thought. Extremely flippant.

As soon as they were all settled in the car, Socks curled up like a cat and fell asleep. A light rain began to fall, turning the traffic lights on Sixth Avenue into sparkling jewels.

"May I ask you something?" Virginia asked softly.

"Sure," Robert said. "Ask me whatever you like."

She stared at him, green eyes solemn. "How was Betty Brown killed?"

Robert hesitated a moment. Virginia was still a suspect, so he probably shouldn't tell her. But if she was the murderer, then she already knew. "Betty Brown was hit on the head. With the crystal vase from the coffee table."

Virginia gave a little gasp, then looked down at her hands.

"It's not as bad as it sounds," Robert went on. "I hope that doesn't sound callous. But Betty Brown was seriously ill, just as you said. According to the coroner, she had a few weeks left at most. I think in a way she was spared a great deal of pain and indignity. And since she was struck from behind, she most likely didn't have time to be scared."

Virginia glanced at him. "Thank you."

"And you know," Robert continued. "I could tell from the recording that you two got along well. She seemed to really enjoy talking about old times."

Virginia smiled. "We did have a lot of fun."

"Plus you eased her mind about the tapes."

"That's true. Although now it's me who's uneasy."

"Hopefully we'll fix that soon." Robert glanced over at Virginia; she looked rather sad. "Tell me about your friend in Hoboken, the one whose apartment you stay at. He's a musician, you said?"

She told him that George was a saxophonist who toured with the Illinois Jacquet Big Band. Apparently George had a Gumby collection, and he let Virginia stay free as long as she dusted his memorabilia.

"He had everything appraised a few months ago," she added. "Turns out it's quite a valuable collection. But it's a small apartment, so the whole place is kind of—"

"Green?" Robert supplied.

She laughed. "Exactly. He even has a life-size blow-up Gumby in his living room. It's a little menacing."

Virginia asked Robert about his apartment, and he told her about his upstairs neighbor who tap-danced to Dolly Parton records. This made her laugh, so he told her about another neighbor's spoiled toy poodle. She giggled at that as well; she was quite pretty when she laughed.

The radio crackled to life. Robert picked up the microphone. "Smith here."

"It's Whiteside from HQ," came the voice over the radio.

"I read you."

"Virginia Farrell checks out. Like you said, she paid cash on the bus to Manhattan, so we couldn't verify that. But Adirondack Trailways confirmed her identity via the ticket stub, and the bus driver remembers she got on board that evening."

"Ah—thanks."

Robert replaced the microphone in its holder. Uh-oh, he thought. He looked over at Virginia. She was glaring at him, her green eyes flashing with anger.

"So I'm a suspect?" she demanded.

Robert looked her straight in the eye. "You were one of the last people to see Betty Brown alive. You also knew about the tapes and understood their value. We had to check your alibi."

"How could you possibly imagine that I killed Betty Brown? I thought the world of her! I would never do such a thing, never, and I resent you for thinking so!"

Her eyes were on fire, her cheeks flushed—she looked very beautiful.

Robert took a deep breath. "Another way to look at it is that your movements are essential to identifying the murderer's time frame."

"Well!" Virginia huffed, crossing her arms. "Still."

There was not much to say after that. Robert knew when to leave a situation alone, particularly an emotional redheaded one.

He turned on the radio to a classic rock station.

"Excuse me," Virginia said coldly. She spun the dial and then—jazz. Exactly what Robert would have avoided.

From the backseat, Socks gave a loud snore.

Friday
August 8, 2003

When Virginia woke up the next morning at George's apartment, she found Socks in the living room, reclining on the couch in her white turban and burgundy silk pajamas.

Slumped like a puppet with its strings cut, Socks was gazing out the window at the lone tree in the backyard. Staring at her blankly was the life-size blow-up Gumby hovering over the couch.

"V," Socks said mournfully. "Ask me what I miss about our house."

"What do you miss about our house?" Virginia asked as she flopped onto the couch.

"Everything. What time can Dr. Bundle pick us up?"

"Two o'clock should work."

"This sleuthing is a tough business."

"Don't I know it." Virginia helped herself to the pot of tea on the coffee table. "So did you get anything out of Detective Oliveto? Or Tony, as you call him."

"Nope. Tight as a clam. But he certainly saw fit to do a little sleuthing of his own."

"Such as?"

"Our goldfish-loving detective asked a great many questions about you."

"The nerve! What did he say?"

"He started by asking how we got to the city, whether we took the bus, how far the bus stop is from our house, and if I can see you getting off the bus from our living room."

Virginia's eyes narrowed.

"I know," Socks said. "He must have thought I was dumb as a watercooler not to see right through him. Our Tony also wanted to know if you ever took a taxi or car service home."

"That must be their theory," Virginia fumed. "Instead of going to Port Authority, I went back to Betty Brown's apartment. I killed her and stole the tapes, then took a car service home. You were asleep so you didn't hear, but last night I had it out with Detective Smith on just this subject."

Socks bit her lip. "To be frank, I heard the whole thing."

"And?"

"You were out of line."

Virginia's mouth dropped open.

"Although I must say," Socks went on hurriedly, "I admired your spunk."

"It just bothered me so much! I would never, ever have hurt Betty Brown."

"But dearest, Detective Smith doesn't know that. He was being perfectly objective. That's his job."

Virginia sighed.

"And honestly," Socks continued, "the first time he called, you tried to avoid seeing him. You even asked him to conduct a police interrogation over the phone! I didn't say anything at the time, but it wasn't your finest hour."

"Oh." Virginia wrinkled her nose. "So maybe it wasn't personal. Maybe he was just doing his job."

"Or maybe," Socks declared, leaning forward, "you like him!"

"Stop."

"You two were getting along fine before he got the call. Laughing, joking—I was starting to blush."

"What about Tony?" Virginia countered. "You were talking to him for a while."

"Listening more than talking. I bet he flushed that goldfish down the toilet without a second thought."

"Agreed."

"Oddly enough, there's something attractive about him. In a different sort of way, of course. But don't change the subject, V. We were talking about you. Dating a cop," Socks pondered. "It's the final taboo."

"I'm not dating him."

"You have plans this morning."

"I'm sleuthing."

"If he's just getting background information, why do you need to be there?"

Virginia hesitated. She desperately wanted to tell Socks that Betty Brown had confided in her about murdering Shinwell Johnson. Virginia had come close to blurting it out several times, but she always stopped herself. She had to keep her word and tell no one.

"I need to go for my article," Virginia replied. "And this way I can introduce him to John. Now tell me, what did you make of Byron?"

"He called me an oaf!" Socks exclaimed. "The clumsy part I admit to, but an oaf!"

"What is an oaf exactly?"

"I don't know. A big troll? Whatever it is, it's not me."

"Certainly not," Virginia chimed in loyally.

"However," Socks said. "I can tell you that Byron is not your man. He's too well-dressed to kill anyone."

"That's absurd."

"On the contrary. He's fastidious about his clothes, and he wouldn't do anything to muss them up."

"You think?"

"I'm not saying Mr. Ffowlkes is uninvolved," Socks went on. "It's clear he has contempt for the human race, and I don't think there's many immoral acts he wouldn't commit. As long as he didn't get dirty in the process."

"Maybe," Virginia said thoughtfully. "But something's definitely up with Mortimer. Last night he practically admitted he's part of this. And if he is, it's because of Byron."

"Your little friend Mortimer is mighty weird."

"He's a good guy, he's just lives in his own world."

"Like someone else I know."

Virginia snorted. "I put on a dress, I wore heels, and I got blisters. If that's the real world, you can keep it."

Socks lifted a very skeptical eyebrow.

"Speaking of Mortimer," Virginia said. "I need to call him." She picked up the receiver of the landline on the side table and rang the magazine.

"*Jazz Now*," Maggie said cheerfully.

"It's Virginia. Can I speak to Mortimer?"

"He called out sick."

Virginia frowned. "Did he say what's wrong?"

"Just that he's terribly ill and not coming in."

"May I speak to Nathan?"

"Sure can."

Then: "Nathan Garrideb here."

"Hey, it's Virginia."

"How's it going? Any luck last night?"

"A little. I think Mortimer is in on it, but I couldn't figure out how."

She told Nathan about the Shirley Temple mishap. He whistled. "Byron's going to send your roommate a dry-cleaning bill. He did that once to a waiter at the Iridium who accidentally spilled water on him."

"Someone should put Byron over their knee and give him a good spanking."

"Don't think the entire staff hasn't wanted to."

"Anyway, Nathan, we're still working on things from our end. I'll let you know if we have a breakthrough. Oh, and I'm going with Detective Smith to the IJS in a little while. He wants some background on Betty Brown."

"Listen, Virginia, if it's at all possible, can you put in a good word for me? I feel like they're going to arrest me any second."

"I'll make a point of it."

"Thanks. How was Rex Royal?"

"Sublime."

"What else? OK, see you."

"Hang in there, Nathan."

Virginia put down the phone.

"What news?" Socks asked.

"Mortimer called out sick, and Nathan says Byron is going to send you his dry-cleaning bill."

"Would it be terribly oafish not to pay?"

"We'll cross that bridge when we come to it."

Socks stood. "Shall I make more tea?"

"Do you even need to ask?"

As Socks banged around in the kitchen, Virginia rang the IJS and asked to be connected with John.

"This is John Upgrove."

"Hey, it's Virginia."

"Hi there! What's up?"

"I have about a billion things to tell you. Listen, do you have any free time this morning?"

John laughed. "Virginia, I'm an archivist. I always have free time."

"I need to bring someone in so you can educate them on Betty Brown and Shinwell Johnson."

"Poor Betty Brown! That's one of your billion things, right?"

"More than you know. I interviewed her right before she died, it's a big mess. Anyhow, we'll be there in about an hour."

"OK. Is it a reporter?"

"A detective," she replied. "He's not so bad, considering. But he doesn't know a thing about jazz, and he wants a crash course."

"No problem. I'll start pulling material together now. We should show him the *Mike Douglas* clip, right?"

"Of course!" Virginia laughed. "Any excuse to see it again. And hey, I saw Rex Royal last night."

"Nice. See you in a bit."

"Thanks, John."

Next she called Mortimer's house. The answering machine came on with a snippet of Coltrane's "Afro Blue," then Mortimer's wife announced, "We can't get to the phone now. Please leave a message at the beep."

"Mortimer, it's Virginia. I called the magazine and they said you're home sick. I'm sorry you're not feeling well, but it's really important that you call me. As soon as possible."

Virginia hung up and looked at Socks, who was setting a fresh pot of tea on the coffee table. "What will you do all morning?"

Socks sighed gloomily. "Drink tea and lie on this couch in abject misery."

"It's not so bad, Socks. And I couldn't have done it without you last night."

"All in the line of duty, my dear. Just hurry back so we can go home."

"OK."

"By the way, did you check the refrigerator?"

"No. Why?"

"George left you a surprise."

Virginia went into the tiny kitchen and pulled open the avocado-colored fridge. On the top shelf was a small white bag labeled VIRGINIA.

She opened it and gasped in delight. The bag was full of chocolates wrapped in foil, little miniatures of Louis Armstrong grinning and holding his trumpet. There was also a note from George:

> To my favorite Gumby-minder: A little something from France, where people take jazz and chocolate seriously. Enjoy!

Virginia unwrapped a piece and popped it into her mouth. Excellent.

Robert and Tony were sitting outside Captain Kelly's office, waiting to be called in for their 9 a.m. meeting.

After a hot shower and a cup of black coffee, Robert was awake and ready to go, whereas Tony looked like he could use a few more hours of sleep. An entire night, actually.

"How late were you out?" Robert asked.

"Very late," Tony yawned. "After the Village Vanguard, that Mortimer dweeb went home, but Mr. Gemstones headed around the corner to a place called Smalls."

"Did you speak to him?"

"Nah." Tony grinned mischievously. "Just sat close enough so he could see me. I wanted to make him nervous."

"And?"

"He kept glarin' at me, so that gave me hope."

"That's a lot of jazz for one evening," Robert commented.

"It wasn't so bad. But there weren't many single ladies there, mostly guys on their own, and a few couples on dates. Not good hunting grounds. Speakin' of women—"

"Yes?"

"That blonde. Mittens?"

"Socks," Robert corrected him.

"She's a whole lotta woman. I'd sure like to get to know her better." Tony rubbed his eyes. "The redhead's pretty too. Seems real smart."

"She is."

"Of course, I would never make a move on her, seein' as you have a thing for her."

Robert looked at him. "Why do you say that?"

"Come on! You can tell Uncle Tony."

"But what exactly did you observe that makes you say that?"

"When you pointed out the redhead to me, you said she was beautiful. I've known you for years, and I've never once heard you call any woman beautiful. Plus the way you were lookin' at her. A little googly-eyed."

"Oh." Robert thought a moment. "Do you think she noticed?"

"Hard to say. Don't get me wrong, I think the redhead's a good choice for you. And she's got an interestin' look. What's her background?"

"Spanish and Irish."

"Ooh, temper!"

"She does seem to get extremely angry with me."

Tony pointed at Robert knowingly. "That's not always a bad thing. At least the redhead feels passionate about you. And she might flip any moment."

"What do you mean, 'flip'?"

"Sometimes it's ladies like that who turn around and tell you they've had a crush on you for ages. Believe me, I know."

Robert had to admit that Tony probably did know. But it seemed rather unlikely that Virginia Farrell was hiding a secret crush.

Captain Kelly's door opened, and the chief of police walked out. "Morning, detectives."

Robert and Tony jumped to their feet. "Good morning, sir," they said in unison.

"Making progress on that murder?"

"We're about to report to Captain Kelly now, sir," Robert said.

"I'd like a result soon. Can't have this town getting a bad reputation."

"Yes, sir."

The chief tipped his hat and walked off.

"Come in," a voice called from inside the office. "I don't have all day."

Captain Kelly was sitting behind his desk lighting a fresh cigar. An athletic man in his fifties, he had a world-weary—or Hoboken-weary—expression stamped on his face. Despite his jaded air, Cap was generally good-natured and easy to talk to.

Tony and Robert sat on the two wooden chairs in front of the desk. "All right, boys," Cap said gruffly. "Give me the rundown."

Robert succinctly outlined the past two days, with Tony adding a comment here and there. Cap listened impassively, taking long, leisurely puffs on his cigar. When they finished, he nodded. "So where does all that leave us?"

"If you ask me," Tony said, "it all comes back to Garrideb." He began ticking points off his fingers. "Knew about the tapes, which gives him a strong motive. Doesn't have an alibi, and admits to bein' in a two-block vicinity of the murder."

"Go on," Cap said.

"Then there's the phone call. The photographer overheard Garrideb calling the victim, and phone records confirm it came from Garrideb's office. Plus that whole business with the Carlo's Bakery bag."

"And so?" Cap asked.

Tony waved a hand. "In a perfect world, it would be this Byron Ffowlkes guy. Robert don't like him, and I don't either. But twelve people who despise him all say they never took their eyes off him for ninety straight minutes. So I vote for Garrideb, and I say we drag him down here for some real questioning."

Cap took another slow drag. "I take it, Detective Smith, that you think otherwise?"

"Things look bad for Garrideb," Robert admitted. "I agree with that. I just wish we had something more concrete."

"That phone call seems pretty solid."

"Only if Joe Pascoe is telling the truth."

Cap raised his eyebrows. "We got ourselves a regular conundrum here, don't we, boys? How about those tapes, any clues?"

"None."

"I gotta say, that worries me. Maybe they got destroyed somehow."

Robert shook his head. "I don't think so. Whoever took the tapes knows their value and won't damage them."

"Even to save their own neck?"

"I strongly doubt it. These people are fanatics; they're devoted to the music and the musicians."

"Except maybe this Ffowlkes."

"He's not like the rest of them."

Cap turned to Tony. "You find anything on him?"

Tony threw up his hands in exasperation. "His last name is misspelled all over Europe. I found a Roger Fowlkes with one F who had a jewelry business in Switzerland, but I still can't confirm it's our guy."

"Seems this Ffowlkes might have some good contacts for unloading the tapes," Cap mused. "They aren't going to show up on the usual black markets for paintings and jewels. The people who'd buy them are a select group, and I myself don't know a damn thing about it."

He looked up at the ceiling and puffed on his cigar. Robert and Tony stayed quiet; they knew better than to interrupt Cap when he was thinking.

"OK," Cap said finally, stubbing out his cigar. "Oliveto, keep digging with Ffowlkes, and also find out what you can about rich jazz collectors. Smith, what about you?"

"I'm doing research at the Institute of Jazz Studies this morning."

"That's OK for now. I also want you to talk to this Joe Pascoe again. Tell him about the tapes, see how he reacts. And I need both of you to keep an eye on Garrideb and Ffowlkes this weekend."

Both Robert and Tony tried to keep their expressions neutral.

Cap laughed. "Don't worry, I'll make sure you get help. But come Monday, we have to make some decisions. Maybe drag all these people down here and see if a real live police station don't shake 'em up. Plus issue a few search warrants. Who knows, maybe the tapes are in that locked office."

Robert and Tony stared at each other.

Cap laughed. "Didn't think of that, did you, boys? I guess that's why I'm the captain." He looked at them. "So what are ya doing still sitting here? Go out and catch a murderer."

"Yes, sir," they mumbled as they stood.

As they walked back to the bullpen, Tony snorted, "Research!"

Robert looked at him. "What's the problem?"

"Redheaded research."

"I would be going with or without her."

"But it just so happens you're goin' with her. Good for you, Boberino. Maybe your luck with women is finally changin'."

Could my luck be turning? Robert asked himself as he organized his papers and prepared to leave. He decided it was too soon to tell.

As Virginia sat on the stoop of 125 Jackson Street waiting for Detective Smith—Robert—to pick her up, she mulled over Socks' comments.

Maybe she had jumped down Robert's throat unnecessarily. After all, any competent detective would have investigated her movements. Virginia was one of the last people to see Betty Brown alive, and that made her a suspect, like it or not.

She was determined to make up for her rudeness, so when Robert pulled up, Virginia got into the passenger seat and chirped "Good morning!"

Robert answered warily, as if bracing for another outburst. But soon they were chatting easily, and he began telling her anecdotes about his fellow police officers. He was rather funny, in a dry sort of way.

At one point, Robert mentioned that he was from Kansas, and a click of understanding went off in Virginia's head. Of course. Nothing about him was East Coast, although apparently he had worked in New York City for many years.

There was a slight traffic jam on the Pulaski Skyway, but they made it to Newark in a half hour. Virginia directed Robert to the Rutgers campus, and soon they were in the elevator of the Dana Library, going up to the fourth floor.

When they stepped out of the elevator, Virginia felt a flare of joy. The Institute of Jazz Studies! Or as she thought of it, heaven on earth.

They walked through the hallway. On their left, construction workers were busy renovating the social work library. On their right was the IJS, with glass display cases built into the walls, showcasing a variety of instruments.

"Ooh!" Virginia stopped to look. "This exhibit just went up, I haven't seen it yet."

She walked slowly in front of the cases. "There's Artie Shaw's clarinet! Sidney Bechet's soprano sax, Papa Jo Jones' high hat—and oh, look!" She pointed to an electric-green trumpet suspended by thin plastic wires. "Miles Davis' trumpet," she said with awe.

Virginia glanced at Robert. He had a strange expression on his face, as if he were confused. Or stifling a laugh.

Never mind, she thought. He doesn't understand.

They opened the thick glass doors and entered the main room, a large rectangular space with a receptionist's desk, several long tables with chairs, and filing cabinets along the back wall. Above the file cabinets were blow-up photos of the greats: Louis Armstrong, Duke Ellington, Benny Goodman, Thelonious Monk, and John Coltrane.

"Hi, Squid," Virginia greeted the bearded young man behind the receptionist's desk. Squid was a graduate student who worked part-time at the IJS while writing his dissertation on pianist Cecil Taylor.

"Hey there," he replied. "What's up?"

"This." She put her knapsack on the counter and pulled out a manila folder. "It fell into my hands the other day."

Squid reached into the folder and pulled out *The Charles Mingus CATalog for Toilet Training Your Cat*. He looked up at Virginia, stunned. "For me?"

"For you."

"How can I ever thank you?"

"No thanks necessary. Use it in good health."

"What was that?" Robert asked as they walked toward the tables.

"A booklet on toilet training cats."

"Oh."

John emerged from the magazine archives. "Good morning," he said cheerfully.

It was always good to see John. He had been working at the IJS for almost two years, and in that time he and Virginia had become fast friends. John had helped her with article research, and now that she was working on the Christy bio, he often supplied her with archival material.

John was in his midthirties, about five-six, cute rather than handsome, with nice features and a slight gap between his teeth. He wore his dirty blond hair in a crew cut, giving him a fifties-retro look that oddly enough suited him.

Virginia enjoyed John's company, and he clearly liked hers. One day after they had been sitting elbow to elbow for hours looking at Shelly Manne's archives, she glanced over at him and thought, Should I have a crush on John?

But no real romantic feelings had ever emerged. He was more like a buddy, a brother. And whether John felt anything for her, Virginia couldn't say. He had never mentioned a girlfriend, but he had also never asked her out.

"John, this is Detective Robert Smith from the Hoboken Police Department."

"Welcome," John greeted him, putting out a hand.

"Nice to meet you," Robert replied as the two men shook.

"Virginia said you wanted to get some background on Betty Brown and Shinwell Johnson?"

"Yes, if that's possible."

"Never fear, you've come to the right place. Let's go back to my office. Although," John said with a grin, "that's a kind word for my workspace."

They left the main room, walking past listening rooms and shelves packed with magazines and books. They turned right, and John opened a door marked IJS PERSONNEL ONLY. Inside was a large room with metal shelves filled with albums arranged by label, as well as two recording studios on the right.

John turned left into his office. One corner of the room had a desk with a computer, while the rest was crowded with stacked boxes of archival material. After opening two gray folding chairs, John sat on his own chair, which was squat with square black cushions.

"Would you like some tea?" He gestured toward a corner of his desk, where an electric teapot sat beside several upside-down mugs on paper towels.

"I'm fine," Robert said.

"Me too," Virginia echoed. "But before we start, I have something for you from France." Virginia dug into her knapsack and handed him two of the Louis Armstrong chocolates. "One to eat, and one to collect."

John smiled broadly. "Ooh!" He put a chocolate on top of his computer, then opened the other and popped it into his mouth. "Yummy," he said as he chewed. "Nothing like European chocolate. So, Robert—may I call you Robert?"

"Sure."

"I've gathered some articles for you." John pointed to a manila folder on his desk. "Also photos. The images can't leave here, but one of our grad students can make copies of any articles you might want."

"That would be great."

"I'm not sure how far back you need me to go. Are you more interested in Betty Brown or Shinwell Johnson?"

"Both," Robert stated. "I'd appreciate whatever you can tell me about the two of them."

"Let's start with Shinwell," John began. "If that's OK."

"Sure," Robert agreed.

"He was born in Brooklyn in 1935, and that's where he grew up. His family was dirt poor and his dad drank." John paused, tapping his pen against the table as if weighing how much detail to share. "Phil Schaap once interviewed Shinwell's brother on WKCR, and he said there were lots of beatings and psychological abuse."

Virginia shuddered.

"Pretty awful stuff," John agreed. "But his dad loved jazz, and apparently he had a hell of a record collection. After Shinwell died, Betty Brown passed his records to Rex Royal, and Rex promised to donate them to us. Have you spoken to Rex, by the way?"

"Last night," Robert replied. "After the show."

"He's a prince," John said. "One of the last of the greats. So Shinwell loved music, and he heard a lot of jazz at a young age. He started playing clarinet when he was eight, then switched to trumpet a few years later. By the time he was a teenager, he was sitting in at clubs in Harlem." John shook his head. "Can you imagine how exciting that was for him?"

Virginia nodded wistfully.

"Anyway. When Shinwell was sixteen," John continued, "he dropped out of school and dedicated himself entirely to music. And not only jazz. You'll see from these articles that he often went to the New York Public Library to listen to classical music and opera." John leaned back, folding his arms. "There's a lot to admire about Shinwell Johnson. He was a self-educated man who pulled himself out of a rough childhood."

Virginia nodded thoughtfully.

"It's just sad," John went on, "because Shinwell never got as big as he could have. Other trumpet players always overshadowed him. Miles naturally, Clifford Brown, Chet Baker, and his great nemesis, Lee Morgan. You've heard of 'The Sidewinder,' of course."

Robert looked blank.

John laughed. "I guess that means Virginia and I will have to sing it for you. You've definitely heard it. 'The Sidewinder' is one of those jazz songs everyone knows, even if they can't remember the name."

"Don't make me sing," Virginia warned.

"Fair enough," John grinned. "Suffice to say it was a popular song. And it made Lee Morgan famous."

"OK," Robert said.

"The thing is, Shinwell always wanted to play with Art Blakey's Jazz Messengers. He sat in pretty often, and when it became clear that Blakey's trumpeter Bill Hardman was ready to leave in 1958, Shinwell thought the spot was his. But Lee Morgan got it instead, and it's clear from these interviews that Shinwell was pretty bitter.

"It was a tough blow, but Shinwell did have some success. From '58 to '63, he had a half dozen records on Blue Note, and he was a sideman on countless others. Unfortunately, Shinwell's records never sold like Lee Morgan's. He was known as a musician's musician—not a big name to the public, but other musicians knew his work and respected him." John looked at Virginia. "Does all that sound right to you?"

"Completely," she affirmed. "Go on."

"Then of course 'Dashiki' came along, and that changed everything. You know 'Dashiki,' of course."

"Yes," Robert answered. "Rex Royal played it last night."

"Sam Rivers sat in," Virginia enthused. "*Sam Rivers.*"

"You lucky dog." John shook his head. "I was stuck here slaving away. So 'Dashiki' was a huge hit. It even got up to number 12 in the Top 40. For an instrumental to hit the Top 40 is unusual enough, but for a jazz song, it's practically unheard of."

"'The Girl from Ipanema' in 1964," Virginia offered. "'Feels So Good' in 1977."

"'Watermelon Man' in 1963," John supplied. "'Mercy, Mercy, Mercy' in 1966. Just a handful, really."

"But I never knew 'Dashiki' was jazz," Robert said. "Isn't it rock, sort of?"

"More like funk. We could argue for hours about what jazz is and isn't, but the fact remains that the Funky Sensations was composed of top-notch jazz musicians. It was Shinwell on trumpet, Rex Royal on drums, Sam Rivers on flute, Ron Carter on electric bass, and Sonny Sharrock on guitar."

"Sonny Sharrock," Virginia said reverentially, putting a hand over her heart.

"A virtuoso guitarist," John explained to Robert. "He really gave 'Dashiki' its sound. The song got a lot of attention, everyone loved it, and right when it was really taking off, Shinwell Johnson disappeared. A few months later, his body was discovered in Pennsylvania. It's odd. As strange as what happened to Albert Ayler."

"What do you make of it?" Robert asked.

John shook his head. "I have no idea. Working here, I'm definitely privy to inside information, but nobody knows what happened to Shinwell Johnson. It seems he ran off with that woman Christine, but from there no one knows."

"Actually," Robert said, "Rex Royal told us last night that Christine had nothing to do with Johnson's disappearance."

He repeated what Rex had said about meeting Christine in Seattle. John raised his eyebrows. "Wow, new information after all these years! So who knows what really happened? I tend to think it was some kind of racial crime. It was the sixties, after all."

"And Betty Brown?" Robert asked. "What can you tell me about her?"

"Not much is known about her. Or it's more that there isn't a lot to know. She was Shinwell's girlfriend, she was part of 'Dashiki,' and that's about it. The only other interesting factoid is that she used to babysit for John Coltrane's stepdaughter."

Virginia and Robert exchanged a glance.

"Did Virginia already tell you that?" John asked.

"Go ahead," Robert prompted. "It's OK to tell him."

Talking about the Five Spot tapes never got easier. It was like giving someone a winning lottery ticket, then snatching it away from them. John's expression reflected this perfectly: wide-eyed disbelief, ecstatic joy, then heartbroken disappointment.

"Oh my God!" he said. "Those tapes have to be found."

"We're working on it," Robert replied.

"I didn't mean to sound rude," John added hurriedly. "It's just that they're a genuine treasure trove. Monk and Coltrane are long gone, and for something like this to turn up!"

"One angle we're working on is that whoever stole the tapes might try to sell them to a rich collector. Something like this won't show up in a pawnshop."

"You're right," John admitted. "That kind of sale would take place deep underground. Whoever has the recordings could get millions of dollars. Literally millions."

"Can you think of any wealthy collectors who might be interested?" Robert asked.

"About a dozen names off the top of my head. If you like, I can write up a list for you. I knew a couple of collectors in England when I was in grad school over there. And then you have Virginia's patron, Toshiro Togasaki."

"Mr. Togasaki would never buy stolen goods!" Virginia said indignantly.

Robert kept quiet. John cleared his throat and said gently, "We'd all like to believe that's true, but it's the Five Spot gig. If I had millions of dollars, I'd definitely be tempted." He reached for the other chocolate. "I see there's more to Betty Brown's murder than meets the eye. I'm afraid I haven't been too useful."

"The list would be a big help," Robert assured him. "And it's always good to have as much information as possible about the personalities involved."

"Speaking of which," John said. "Would you like to see the clip from *The Mike Douglas Show*? I have it cued up in another room."

"OK," Robert agreed as Virginia bobbed her head eagerly.

Upgrove popped the Louis Armstrong chocolate in his mouth and grabbed the file of Shinwell Johnson articles. He stood and motioned for Robert and Virginia to follow him, then led them to a listening room where a small TV was already set up.

"OK," Upgrove said when they were comfortably seated. "Here goes."

He pushed the play button, and Mike Douglas appeared on the screen with thick sideburns and a wide-lapel jacket. Douglas stood in front of the audience and said, "I have a special treat for you, a group that's climbing the charts with their hit song 'Dashiki.' Ladies and gentlemen, please welcome Shinwell Johnson and the Funky Sensations!"

The camera moved to the band. The five men had enormous Afros and wore multicolored dashikis and black leather pants. Betty Brown stood on a circular platform, dressed in a dashiki and black leather miniskirt. Robert couldn't be sure, but he thought he saw a stick of incense burning on Rex Royal's drum set.

As the group launched into the song, Robert could see why the Funky Sensations had made such a strong impression. The musicians played with great energy and were visually striking, five powerful Black men in vibrant dashikis, with multicolored lights swirling around them. Betty Brown was equally captivating, her expression confrontational, her movements sleek and feline. It was sad to reconcile this image with the elderly woman lying facedown on the floor at 1305 Bloomfield Street.

Robert glanced at Virginia. She looked cute in her lilac hoodie, white T-shirt, and jeans. With her knapsack and air of intelligence, she could have passed for a graduate student. Very cute. And she looked so happy, her face glowing as she bounced her head and tapped her foot. She was really in her element.

But hopefully not too much, Robert thought, glancing at Upgrove. When Virginia handed Upgrove the chocolates, Robert felt a stab of jealousy, which he quickly suppressed in the name of duty. But after observing their further interaction, Robert concluded that they were merely good friends, happily joined in their mutual obsession.

After Betty Brown shouted "Dashiki!" Upgrove turned to them and asked, "Want to see it again?"

"Absolutely!" Virginia enthused.

Not that Upgrove was a bad guy. He was pleasant and intelligent, and Robert liked his dry sense of humor. It was just that on the drive over to the IJS, it seemed to Robert that Virginia had—to use Tony's parlance—flipped. She was friendly, she laughed at all his stories, and she didn't make any Wizard of Oz jokes when he mentioned Kansas. After her fury the previous night, it seemed like genuine progress.

But enough of that: Robert was here to do research.

"Dashiki!" Betty Brown cried out, holding her fists above her head. She looked like a wild lioness unleashing a primal roar.

Upgrove stopped the video and ejected the tape. "Johnson disappeared a few days after this show aired. It's hard to believe; he was so full of life, and his career was going great. Apparently Gil Evans wanted to work with him, and that was Shinwell's dream, what with all the great music Gil did with Miles."

"Gil Evans," Robert said. "Wasn't he the piano player on the Miles Davis CD *Kind of Blue*?"

Virginia and Upgrove looked at him with the pity normally reserved for feeble kittens. "That's Bill Evans," Upgrove corrected him. "Bill Evans is a pianist, Gil Evans is an arranger."

"Oh. Did they both work with Miles Davis?"

"Right. But they're two different people."

"Are they related?"

"Ah—no."

Robert grimaced, not daring to look at Virginia. So much for that.

"Here you go." Upgrove handed him the manila folder. "Take a look at these, and let me know if you're interested in getting any copies."

Robert opened the folder. On top was an old issue of *DownBeat* with Shinwell Johnson on the cover: JAZZ'S GREAT UNSOLVED MYSTERY. He went through the articles quickly, making a pile of all those written about Johnson's death.

"All right," Upgrove said as he picked up the pile. "I'll get these copied for you in a jiffy. I'll also write out that list of collectors."

They walked back into the main room, and Upgrove went off with the articles. Robert and Virginia sat at one of the big tables, looking through the photos and marveling at Shinwell Johnson's transformation from his suit-and-tie days in the 1950s to his Afro-and-dashiki look in the 1960s.

"What exactly does your friend John do here?" Robert asked by way of conversation.

"He's an archivist," Virginia explained. "That's why he has all those boxes in his office. He labels and catalogues the materials that people donate. Particularly unmarked tapes." She shuddered. "Nothing worse than tapes with no labels."

Robert bit his lip. "I suppose that's true."

"John's been a big help to me," she went on. "He keeps an eye out for anything related to June Christy, and he's found some great stuff. Speaking of which," Virginia said as Upgrove approached their table. "Did those Pete Rugolo recordings show up?"

Upgrove handed Robert a stack of articles, with a neatly written list of jazz collectors on top. He grinned. "I was saving the best for last. They're arriving on Monday via FedEx."

Virginia clapped her hands. "I'll make sure to be here! What time does FedEx show up?"

"It varies, but they always deliver by noon."

"Excellent." She turned to Robert. "Pete Rugolo was June Christy's arranger for years, and he was also a good friend of hers. These are recordings from a series of interviews he gave to an obscure radio station in the 1970s."

"Great," Robert said with a smile.

"He's also famous for working on the *Birth of the Cool* sessions. With Gil Evans," she added, her eyes twinkling.

Robert blushed. "I see."

"Can I help you guys with anything else?" Upgrove asked.

Robert stood. "I think I've got everything I need." He reached out and shook Upgrove's hand. "I appreciate your help."

"No problem at all. Any friend of Virginia is a friend of mine."

"Bye, John." Virginia stood and gave a little wave. "See you Monday."

Upgrove walked them to the door. "Good luck with those tapes," he said. "If you do find them, I'm happy to help out. Make duplicates, catalog them, whatever."

"Thanks," Robert replied. "I hope we'll need you."

Robert was quiet on the way back to Hoboken, reflecting on the visit to the IJS.

Unfortunately he hadn't really learned anything new. One of the articles might provide a clue, and Tony would certainly be grateful for the list of collectors. Otherwise they were no closer to catching Betty Brown's murderer.

At least Captain Kelly was content to leave things until Monday. That gave Robert all weekend to think through the case, although it looked as if he'd be doing so while trailing Nathan Garrideb.

Virginia's stomach suddenly let out a ferocious growl.

"Sorry," she said, looking at Robert and blushing.

He glanced at his watch. "It's almost noon. Would you—if you want, we can go to the Malibu Diner. Courtesy of the Hoboken Police Department."

"Sure," she answered shyly. "That sounds good."

That wasn't so hard! "What time does your bus leave for upstate?" he asked.

"We're not taking the bus. Socks' friend Dr. Bundle is picking us up at two."

"What kind of doctor is he?"

Virginia looked at Robert. "He's a mailman."

"Oh. That kind of doctor."

"Exactly."

The hostess at the Malibu recognized Robert and quickly seated them in a corner booth. After looking through the enormous menu, Robert ordered the cheeseburger platter, and Virginia asked for a Caesar salad and minestrone soup.

"So," Robert said after the waitress left. "How did you get into all of this?"

"You mean jazz?"

He nodded.

"My uncle was a jazz geek with a huge record collection. He lived in Manhattan in the West Fifties, and one day when we were walking to Central Park, he said hello to a big Black man with sunglasses and a funny hat. As soon as the man was behind us, my uncle stopped and kneeled down in front of me. He said, 'Virginia Farrell, you just saw Thelonious Monk, one of the greatest men to walk this planet. Never, ever forget it.'"

"How old were you?"

"About six. And of course I never forgot. When I was a little older, my uncle and his girlfriend started taking me to jazz clubs, and I loved every minute. Then at NYU, I wrote CD reviews and interviews for the school paper." She shrugged. "I guess I just never stopped. What about you? How did you become a detective?"

Robert hesitated. "You'll laugh."

"Try me."

"Sherlock Holmes. My favorite books. I know them inside out and backward."

"What's not to like? They're wonderful stories." Virginia bit her lip. "Does that make Detective Oliveto your Watson?"

Robert laughed. "I guess so. Jersey-style. But I had an experience sort of equivalent to yours. Did you ever read Truman Capote's book *In Cold Blood*, or see the movie?"

Virginia wrinkled her nose. "The family that got killed by the two drifters?"

"That's right. The Clutters lived in Holcomb, Kansas, a few towns away from where I grew up. My grandparents knew the mother and father well since they went to the same Methodist church."

"Wow."

Robert nodded. "My grandfather was obsessed with the murders. He used to take me on drives past the Clutters' house and talk about the case."

"That's cool," Virginia commented. "In a creepy way."

"I guess that got me interested in murderers, about why people kill and how to catch them. Funny what sticks in your mind from childhood," he mused.

"True." Virginia paused. "Speaking of murders—"

"Yes?"

The waitress came over and set down their food. As soon as she left, Virginia spoke up again.

"Speaking of murders, can we talk about Betty Brown?"

"OK." Robert picked up the ketchup bottle and began shaking it over his fries. "What's on your mind?"

Virginia took a deep breath. On the ride back from the IJS, she had been trying to gather the courage to talk to Robert about Nathan. When Robert suggested lunch, she knew it was her golden opportunity. "It's about Nathan."

Robert stopped shaking the ketchup. "Yes?"

"He told me that you and Detective Oliveto think he murdered Betty Brown. But I'm sure he didn't."

"Why is that?"

"I know Nathan, and he could never, ever murder anyone. He's too moral. Too sane." Virginia's cheeks flushed with emotion. "I know things look bad for him, but I'm begging you—imploring you—please don't arrest Nathan."

Robert was silent.

"If you spent more time with him," she rushed on, "you'd agree with me. Nathan's the type of guy who'd run his car off the road rather than hit a squirrel."

"But isn't it possible," Robert said quietly, "that Nathan got impatient and called Betty Brown right after you left? He went over to her apartment, they had some kind of disagreement, and Nathan lost control. It does happen, even with the nicest people."

"Not Nathan. If he ever got that angry, he'd walk away. Besides, he told me he didn't do it, and I believe him. He's not a liar."

Robert folded his hands together. "I've been a detective a long time now, and I know from experience that people lie. It's only natural; no one wants to go to jail." He thought a moment. "It's amazing how well people can lie, even down to the smallest detail. Then when they're presented with an undeniable piece of evidence, they finally blurt out the real story."

Virginia shook her head firmly. "Nathan isn't lying. And I do have a clue that might help convince you. If you want to hear it."

"I most certainly do."

"The fact is, I've been sleuthing."

"Sleuthing?" Robert's eyebrows arched slightly.

"Strictly on an amateur basis. Although I do have an assistant. We believe Mortimer knows something about the tapes. And whatever he knows comes via Byron Ffowlkes."

"I see. Tell me, what do you think of Ffowlkes?"

Virginia winced. "I don't like him."

"Why?"

"He just—" Makes comments about my height, she thought. "Instinct."

"A gut feeling."

"Exactly."

"But, if I may ask, you were at the Blue Note with him last night?"

Virginia waved dismissively. "Oh, that! Sitting with him was all part of our plan."

"You and your roommate?"

She blushed. "Yes."

"Why do you think Mortimer knows something?"

Virginia told Robert about her conversation with Mortimer and his peculiar behavior. "He's always a bit strange, but this was extreme, even for him. Something's up, but I don't know what."

"I appreciate you telling me," Robert said. "We'll look into it." He paused. "And what about Joe Pascoe?"

"I'm not sure. Although . . ." Well, why not? Robert couldn't arrest her for snooping around someone's bedroom. She told him about their visit to Joe's apartment, leaving out the infamous instrument photos, as well as Socks' accident.

As Virginia spoke, Robert had a most unusual look on his face, something halfway between admiration and incredulity. When she was done, he said, "You've certainly been working hard on this."

"I need to get those tapes back."

"So you don't think Joe Pascoe did it?"

Virginia lifted her hands in exasperation. "I don't know what to think. It would certainly wrap things up neatly if it was Joe. But we didn't find any evidence at his place."

"Did you search the kitchen?"

"No. Why?"

"You've been frank with me, so I'll be frank with you. It's not only the tapes that are missing."

Virginia frowned in confusion. "What else was there to steal?"

"The honey." Robert folded his napkin and pushed his plate over to the right. "The honey you gave Betty Brown is missing."

"Hana's Honey! Are you sure?"

"Definitely. We searched the apartment thoroughly."

"You're saying that the person who took the tapes also took the honey?"

"That's what I think. So if you find the honey, you've probably found the tapes."

"What on earth?" Virginia shook her head. "That's bizarre."

"I know," he agreed. "There are several odd things about this case. Including what happened to Shinwell Johnson."

Virginia stiffened. Shinwell Johnson's murder was the last thing she wanted to talk about.

"But that case is ancient!" she said. "Doesn't it make more sense to just focus on Betty Brown's murder?"

"You never know," Robert countered. "Look what happened with Rex Royal last night. That was a fresh piece of evidence."

"I'm more concerned about the tapes." Virginia shook her head. "I don't get it. If you're stealing a box of million-dollar tapes, why grab a jar of honey as well?"

Robert's eyes lit up. "I know what you mean. It may be the most significant clue of all."

He proceeded to tell Virginia his theory that murderers are either psychological or conditional, and how character flaws play a key role. It could be, he said, that stealing the honey was somehow indicative of the murderer's flaw, whatever that might be. Greed, probably.

When Robert was finished, Virginia remarked, "That makes a lot of sense. But in terms of character flaws, you need to appreciate the collector's mindset. It's possible that whoever stole the tapes won't sell them. Maybe they just want to own them."

"I don't follow."

"If it is greed that motivated this person, it could be a special kind, more about acquiring things than selling them for money." Virginia paused. "I have a theory too, but mine is about jazz enthusiasts. There's the geeks, and there's the collectors."

"Go on."

"Take me. I'm a geek, but I'm not a collector. I'm totally into jazz, the music, the history, the musicians, but I don't collect. I have a decent number of CDs and albums, but I'm not motivated to acquire more."

"OK."

"But a collector is. Those are the guys you see at the Jazz Record Center and Academy Bookstore, going through every single album hoping for a score."

Robert nodded thoughtfully. "I see what you're saying."

She took a sip of water. "Not that there's anything wrong with it. Some of my best friends are collectors. And I would say that most collectors are geeks. But for someone like that, the Five Spot tapes would be the ultimate prize, and they wouldn't necessarily sell them."

"So the tapes may not show up on the jazz black market, such as it is?"

"Maybe not," Virginia replied. "There are even people who would get a thrill out of being the only one to hear the tapes, knowing that others want to and can't. I think Byron's like that."

Robert grimaced. "Him again."

"A prime example of a non-geek collector. Sure, Byron knows a lot about jazz, but his motivation is different. He likes to have power over people, to feel superior because he knows more than they do." She shook her head. "I think that's mighty weird."

"I agree." Robert cleared his throat. "And while we're talking about the murder, there is one little detail I'd like to clear up."

"About Nathan?"

"Something else. At the end of your tape, Betty Brown's final words get cut off. She says, 'Would you like to—?' What was the rest of the sentence?"

Virginia reddened. She remembered Betty Brown's question: "Would you like to promise me somethin' else?" And then Betty Brown's confession about killing Shinwell Johnson.

"Let me—I need to think a moment," Virginia stammered, stalling for time. "What did she say? Yes, now I remember! She asked if I'd like more tea. So yes, it was 'Would you like to have more tea?'"

Robert tilted his head. "That was all?"

"Yep. Just tea."

"OK."

The waitress came over. "Anything else?"

"Do you have the time?" Virginia asked.

"One-thirty."

"Oh!" she exclaimed. "I need to go."

As they walked to the car, Robert was extremely pleased.

Lunch had gone so well! It wasn't exactly a date, but it was the two of them eating together, and that had to count for something. Plus Virginia had been genuinely interested in his theories.

She even brought up the subject again when they got into the car. "Can you always tell from the murder itself what the criminal's character flaw is?"

"Usually," Robert answered, pulling out of the Malibu Diner parking lot and heading downtown. "But sometimes people's motives are deeply hidden."

"How long does it take you to assess someone's flaw?"

"Not long. People tend to reveal themselves pretty quickly."

"So what's mine?"

Robert turned and looked at Virginia in astonishment. She seemed perfectly reasonable. Should he tell her? Robert remembered Virginia's anger last night, as well as the first evening he met her. He didn't want a repeat of that.

"Go ahead," she said. "I'm curious."

Robert took a deep breath and looked her in the eye. "You're naive."

Virginia's eyes flew open, and her cheeks reddened. Uh-oh.

"You're too trusting," he went on quickly. "You don't believe badly of anyone. And you—well, you're not acquainted with basic facts about the world."

Her eyes got bigger, her cheeks redder, and her lips began to quiver. Oh no.

Without daring to look over at Virginia, Robert drove down Willow Street. Her angry, labored breathing filled the car as he stared fixedly ahead at the traffic.

Robert stopped at Fifth Street to let a group of schoolchildren cross. Suddenly Virginia asked sharply, "Would you like to know what your character flaw is?"

He didn't, actually. "Sure. Tell me."

"You judge people too quickly." She raised her eyebrows, folded her arms, and looked out the window.

Robert drove the remaining blocks in shock. A few times he opened his mouth to speak, but nothing came out.

When he pulled in front of 125 Jackson, Virginia unbuckled her seatbelt, hopped out of the car, and slammed the door shut, all without acknowledging Robert's existence. He watched her stalk into the building without so much as a backward glance.

Robert let out a sigh. Tony had said that women could flip, but he hadn't mentioned anything about them flipping back.

Monday
August 11, 2003

When Virginia walked into the kitchen on Monday morning, Socks was sitting at the table with a cup of tea, wearing her usual turban and silk pajamas.

"Good morning," Virginia said as she picked up the kettle. "What's up?"

"I called the psychic on WDST. They told me I'm fifth in line, and I'm supposed to call back at nine-thirty."

"Sounds good."

Virginia made a cup of tea and sat down at the table.

"V," Socks said.

"Yes?"

"You haven't been yourself since you came back to George's on Friday afternoon. And you haven't merely been quiet, you've been brooding."

Virginia twisted her lips.

"As well," Socks continued, "when I asked you about your policeman friend, you didn't want to talk about it. Is that still the case?"

"Yes. No."

"Why don't you tell me what happened? Any more brooding and you'll dissolve into a puddle."

"Oh, it's so dumb," Virginia admitted. "I got mad at him."

"Why?"

"We got along well all morning. He even took me out to lunch at the Malibu Diner, and we had a nice chat. Then he told me his theory that everyone has at least one major character flaw. So I asked him about mine."

"Oh dear. What did he say?"

Virginia stared at Socks, eyes burning. "He said I was *naive*."

Socks gasped. "That's worse than cute."

"I always thought I was the baddest cowgirl on the block."

"Oh honey, you are," Socks assured her. "Just not his block. But if I might interject a comment?"

"Go right ahead."

"If you ask someone to point out your flaws, you're not likely to hear something pleasant."

Virginia frowned. "Are you saying I set myself up?"

"A bit. What happened then?"

"I got mad. Then I told him about his character flaw."

"Which is?"

"He judges people too quickly."

Socks raised an eyebrow. "Well played. What did he say to that?"

"Nothing. Not a word. Then I stormed out of the car in a snuff."

"No goodbye? No thank you for lunch?"

Virginia shook her head miserably.

"Oh dear," Socks commiserated.

"It probably wouldn't matter much," Virginia replied, looking out the window at the meadow, "except I think I can officially say that I have some sort of crush-type thing. On him."

Socks beamed. "That's my girl!"

"Not that it could ever work," Virginia went on hurriedly. "He doesn't know a thing about jazz."

"Glad to hear it."

"But although Robert's not a jazz geek, he is a detective nerd. You should have heard him talk about Sherlock Holmes."

"Common ground. I like it."

"The thing is," Virginia said, warming to her subject, "Robert reminds me of Carson Drew, Nancy Drew's dad. You know, upright and noble. Fights bad guys."

"Nancy would be a horrible stepdaughter. She'd snoop into all your business."

"That's the beauty of Robert: he's Carson Drew, but with no daughter."

Socks stared at her. "You may be onto something. Well! You have a crush. At long last. "

Virginia rolled her eyes and took a sip of tea.

"Robert and Virginia," Socks mused with a faraway look. "Sounds nice. Like a brand of English biscuits."

"Can you stop—"

"Oh! It's nine-thirty. Time to call Madame Flora."

Socks moved to the stool by the phone and dialed. "Hello, I'm on the list for nine-thirty? . . . Margarita," she said, making a face at Virginia. "Yes, I'll hold."

Socks called the psychic once a month, using an alias so no one would recognize her.

"Hello, Madame Flora? It's Margarita . . . Nice to hear your voice again too . . . Just calling for a general checkup . . . Yes . . . Indeed . . . Go right ahead."

Socks stayed quiet while she listened. Then she answered: "I know precisely who you mean, and I'll most certainly tell her . . . You have a nice day as well."

She hung up and sat down at the kitchen table, frowning slightly.

"What did Madame Flora say?" Virginia asked.

"The usual. Health and money excellent, domestic life fine. She sees me getting closer to a man in uniform. That's Dr. Bundle, of course."

"Or Detective Oliveto," Virginia smiled.

"Mr. Goldfish? I think not."

"So all's well."

"Not exactly. Madame Flora told me that a woman I'm fond of is in danger, and I need to warn her."

"She means the murder and our sleuthing."

"What else could it be?" Socks agreed. "Thank goodness you didn't leave anything behind at Betty Brown's! You might have gone back and walked in on—I shudder to think."

"Same here."

"So what's the plan for today, Master Sleuth?"

Virginia pushed away her teacup. "I need to go to the IJS and get some tapes from John. But before that, I'm going to confront Mortimer. Do you know he avoided my calls all weekend? I finally got his wife on the phone, and she told me Mortimer didn't want to talk to me."

"Did she say why?"

"She had no clue, but I could tell she was embarrassed. However, I have a plan."

"Do tell," Socks said.

"There's a secondhand record store in Hoboken called All That Jazz, just a block from *Jazz Now*'s office. Every weekend, the owner goes to flea markets and yard sales looking for records. The new stock is put out on Mondays."

"And?"

"Mortimer is always at the store as soon as it opens on Mondays so he can get first crack at the new albums. My plan is to ambush him there."

Socks' eyes lit up. "Whereupon you'll slowly drip water on his forehead until he reveals the whereabouts of the tapes?"

"Details are sketchy at this point, but yes, something to that effect. If Mortimer confesses, I'm going to march him to the police station and turn him over to Robert."

"And if not?"

"I'll go to the IJS as planned. Afterward I'll come back to Hoboken and stop by the police station for any updates. And maybe while I'm there, I'll—"

"Apologize?" Socks supplied.

"I suppose so. Yes."

"Excellent." Socks paused. "Are you also planning to see Nathan?"

Virginia reddened. "You and I need to agree to disagree about him. He didn't do it."

Socks raised her hands. "Fine. Mortimer Burns is part of my asterisk theory as well. I'm perfectly happy if he's involved instead of Nathan."

Virginia stood. "I better get going. My bus will be here in a half hour."

"Good luck. Don't let the big bad city eat you up."

Virginia laughed. "I won't be in the city, I'll be in New Jersey. All's well in Jersey."

Monday morning at nine sharp, Robert and Tony were sitting at their desks. Two cups of coffee and Tony's partially eaten jelly doughnut sat in front of them. In half an hour, they were scheduled to meet with Captain Kelly.

"Time to play catch up," Tony said. "I spent all weekend trailin' after Mr. Gemstones. I let O'Neal take the morning shift while Gemstones was sleepin', but otherwise it was me."

"Anything turn up?" Robert asked, sipping his coffee.

Tony pulled out a small notebook and flipped it open. "He went to two jazz clubs Friday night, three on Saturday, two on Sunday. Had a different date each night." Tony raised an eyebrow. "Nice lookin' ladies, if I do say so. Each time she stayed over at his place, and each time she left at noon the next day. I assume last night's lady left a bit earlier since he's gotta work today."

"What else?"

"He stopped at a couple of record stores Saturday and Sunday late afternoon and bought a few things. Drank lots of black coffee from fancy shops—no cheap deli stuff for this guy. And he was dressed like a tropical bird the entire damn time. In other words," Tony said, shutting his notebook, "I got nothin'. What about Garrideb?"

"Left the house to buy a paper each morning, took a walk to pick up Chinese food on Saturday, went to a neighborhood restaurant with his girlfriend last night. Otherwise he stayed in."

"More nothin'," Tony muttered. "So what's next?"

Robert rested his chin on his hand. "Let's go over everything from the start."

"OK. Shoot."

"Let's agree that whoever killed Betty Brown knew about the tapes and went to her apartment with the intention of getting them. It's not impossible that someone stumbled upon them, but it's unlikely."

"Alrightee."

"So Virginia Farrell was at Betty Brown's apartment and got a piece of information. She shares this with one other person, Nathan Garrideb, who shares it with no one. He does write it down on a piece of paper, but he takes the paper with him when he leaves his office. And although Virginia Farrell discussed the information with Garrideb in his office, it wasn't possible for anyone else to overhear them."

"I'm with you."

"So," Robert went on, "only Virginia Farrell and Nathan Garrideb knew about the tapes. There is, however, the possibility that Betty Brown told Joe Pascoe about them."

"Which he denied when we requestioned him Friday afternoon," Tony chimed in. "Claimed Betty Brown didn't say a peep about the tapes, and he never asked what was in the shoebox."

"Pascoe could be lying, of course. We can't be sure. What we do know is that Virginia Farrell and Nathan Garrideb were both aware of the tapes."

"Agreed," Tony said.

"Virginia Farrell, however, has a solid alibi. Joe Pascoe's photos prove that Betty Brown was alive after she left, Steve Dooney confirms she was at *Jazz Now* until four, Adirondack Trailways verifies she got on the bus to the Catskills at 4:50."

"That leaves Garrideb. What do you think happened?"

"Garrideb got impatient and decided not to wait. He called Betty Brown, then walked over to her apartment and arrived just after Joe Pascoe left."

"And then?" Tony prompted.

"He asked for the tapes, and Betty Brown said no. Maybe she changed her mind, or she wanted to talk to Virginia Farrell again. Whatever the reason, she was reluctant to hand them over."

"Go on."

"Garrideb panicked. His emotions took over in a powerful way, and he became fixated on getting the tapes. This fixation overrode his morals, and he acted in an uncharacteristic manner."

"In other words," Tony said, taking a large bite of his doughnut, "Garrideb wanted the tapes, so he whacked her over the head."

Robert sighed inwardly. Tony was the anti-Watson: no respect whatsoever. "Yes, you can put it that way."

"Sounds to me like you've come over to the Garrideb camp."

"Once I stopped thinking in terms of personalities and started following a piece of information—yes, I think it was Garrideb. But I still maintain it could have been Pascoe."

"Don't forget the phone call," Tony warned.

"Pascoe could be lying about what he heard. Maybe he figured out about the tapes from Betty Brown's end of the conversation, and now he's using the phone call to implicate Garrideb. And because Garrideb is scared, he denies making the call."

"It's also possible that Pascoe is telling the truth."

"Fair enough. So it's either Garrideb or Pascoe."

"And Ffowlkes?" Tony asked.

"The murderer confided in him, and now Ffowlkes has enlisted Burns in some way. But Ffowlkes definitely didn't murder Betty Brown. Even if Garrideb did tell him about the tapes before going out for a walk, his alibi is airtight. Same with Burns."

"So it's all wrapped up. Cap's gonna be happy."

Robert hesitated. "Except—"

"What?"

He told Tony about Virginia's plea. Tony listened impassively, then said, "Since when did you start takin' advice from suspects?"

"Virginia Farrell isn't a suspect anymore. And I think she might be right. Call it instinct."

"Oh, it's instinct all right. An attractive woman acts all helpless, and your mind gets screwy." Tony circled a finger close to his ear. "Unclear."

"The fact is," Robert said calmly, "certain types of people aren't likely to murder. Virginia has known Garrideb a long time, so she's in a position to make a judgment about him."

Tony rolled his eyes. "Spare me from you and your types! Let me tell you what type Garrideb is: he's the type with all the motive in the world, and absolutely no alibi." He shook his head. "Jeez, I thought you had more sense than that."

"I think Virginia made a valid observation," Robert said calmly. "Despite the fact that the evidence points otherwise."

"Oh, it points all right! Directly to Garrideb." Tony raised an eyebrow. "While we're on the subject of types, what type is the redhead?"

Robert looked straight ahead. "She is in a category all her own."

"Ah ha. I guess your research went pretty well then. You were awful tight-mouthed when you came back on Friday."

"I wouldn't exactly say it went well." Robert filled Tony in on the character-flaw conversation.

Tony shook his head. "Dumb, Boberino. Real dumb. When a lady asks you somethin' like that, you say, 'Your flaw is that you're so beautiful I get dizzy just lookin' at you.'"

Robert winced. "I would never say anything like that."

"Instead you said what you said, and now she's mad at you."

"It's just that sometimes she's so sensible, and other times she's really emotional."

Tony looked at him with pity. "Welcome to the wonderful world of women! They're all like that. And I got news for you: that's the way it's always been, and that's the way it's always gonna be."

"Enough about Virginia Farrell," Robert said briskly. "One other thing bothers me."

"What's that?"

"The honey."

"Aww, that again? I thought we agreed, it's a mishmash thing. It's not relevant."

"But it might be the most important clue of all. We can't just forget about the honey because it doesn't fit in with the rest of our evidence. It troubles me that Garrideb honestly didn't know what we were talking about when we mentioned it."

Tony blew out in frustration. "As far as I'm concerned, Garrideb didn't honestly anything when we talked to him. The guy's a good liar."

"You saw his reaction," Robert countered. "He had no clue what we were referring to. Same with Ffowlkes, and Pascoe too when I mentioned it. All the talk about honey flew right over their heads."

"So what are we gonna tell Cap? 'Sorry, we can't haul in Garrideb 'cause he puts sugar in his tea.' The honey may be relevant, but you gotta show how."

"I know. And at the moment, I can't."

"Your moment is runnin' out." Tony put the last piece of doughnut in his mouth. "It's nine-thirty. Time to go see Cap."

"OK," Robert said, gathering the files on his desk. "Let's go."

At ten minutes to one, Virginia stood in a doorway across the street from 111 River Street, with a perfect view of the building's front door. Knowing what a creature of habit Mortimer was, Virginia felt confident he would be walking out in exactly five minutes.

It had been quite a morning already. When Virginia got on the bus in Little Mountain, Bill the bus driver yelled out, "There she is! What's a nice girl like you doing with the police on her trail? They were asking me all kinds of questions about you."

Virginia turned beet-red as Bill's voice boomed throughout the bus, and several people craned their necks to look at her. Great, Virginia thought as she took her seat. People remembered everything in Little Mountain, and old ladies would soon be clutching their purses at the very sight of her.

Then when Virginia arrived at Port Authority bus station in New York, she had a bit of an identity crisis. She stopped into Duane Reade to get a new notebook, and while standing in line to pay, she glanced at one of the store's mirrors. Virginia saw her entire reflection: a short woman with shoulder-length red hair tucked behind her ears, dressed in a hoodie, T-shirt, jeans, and sneakers, and holding a notebook.

Socks was right! Virginia did look like Harriet the Spy. The realization left her so stunned that the cashier had to call out twice to get her attention.

Suddenly Virginia, who rarely paid attention to such matters, became consumed by thoughts of her appearance. How on earth could she go see Robert looking like this?

It was most disconcerting, and Virginia's bus was halfway to Hoboken before she snapped out of it. I'm a writer, she reminded herself. A journalist. My brain is what matters, not my wardrobe.

And good thing I did wear this, she told herself stoutly as she stood in the doorway staking out Mortimer. I'm comfortable and I'm inconspicuous, and that's exactly what I need to be.

At five to one, Mortimer walked out of the building. Virginia watched as he looked both ways, crossed the street, and headed up River Street.

Good old Mortimer, Virginia thought as she trailed behind him at a safe distance. Talk about a wardrobe! He wore the same thing every day, and he never tried to change himself for anyone. Mortimer was probably the weirdest person Virginia knew, but it didn't matter in the least to his wife, because she loved him just as he was.

Virginia trailed him from the other side of the street, diving into a tailor shop when Mortimer stopped in front of All That Jazz. He peered into the store, then checked his watch. Not yet one o'clock, Virginia thought. He sat on the small stoop in the doorway and stared dreamily into space.

A few minutes later, the door to All About Jazz opened, and Mortimer darted inside. Virginia left the tailor shop and crossed the street. Looking into the window, she could see Mortimer stationed at the bin with the new stock, head down as he methodically flipped through the albums.

Virginia hesitated. She wanted to rush in and grab Mortimer by the collar, but etiquette demanded she give him time to browse through the new records. She stood outside and watched impatiently as he worked his way through the bin.

Mortimer was almost at the end when he pulled out an album. Taking the record out of the cover, he slipped the vinyl from its white sleeve. He held the album aloft, turning it in several directions to examine the grooves in the light. With utmost care, he returned the record to its cover and set it to one side—jackpot! Virginia felt vindicated for waiting.

He flipped through the rest of the bin, then took his find up to the cash register. Virginia waited until Mortimer handed the album to the storeowner, then she came into the shop and walked up behind him.

"Hello, Mortimer."

Mortimer turned to face her. His pale blue eyes widened, looking around wildly for an escape.

Virginia gripped his wrist firmly. "You can run, but you can't hide. It's time to face the music."

"What music?" he whispered.

"*The* music."

"Hey, Virginia," the storeowner said. "Your friend got a real treasure. A mint-condition first pressing of Coltrane's *First Meditations*."

"Great," she commented, tightening her hold.

Mortimer paid, his expression full of dread. The owner put the record in a plastic bag, then Virginia led Mortimer out of the store.

"Let's go to Pier A Park," she said. "We can talk privately there."

"But it's getting late! I should—"

"No," she replied sternly. "Enough with the excuses."

Virginia steered Mortimer toward First Street, and they followed the road down to the park. In a little while, she thought excitedly, I'll have solved the mystery of Betty Brown's death! And hopefully get the tapes back.

They sat on one of the benches facing the center of the park, a large rectangle of grass where a dozen people were eating lunch and relaxing. Virginia turned to face Mortimer, her hand still wrapped around his wrist.

"You've been avoiding me ever since the Rex Royal gig," she said. "I know something's up, and it's got to do with John Coltrane."

Mortimer pursed his lips and looked straight ahead, sweat beading on his forehead.

"Listen," Virginia urged. "You have to tell me what's going on. If you keep sweating so much, you'll die of dehydration."

He gulped.

"I know you didn't kill Betty Brown," she went on. "You were at the listening session when the murder happened. So what's wrong?"

"You're going to hate me," he whispered.

"That's doubtful."

"I did a bad thing."

"Just say it."

"Your Coltrane LP, *Live at the Village Vanguard Again!* I scratched it. And not only did I scratch it, but it happened during Coltrane's solo on 'My Favorite Things.' Your favorite."

Virginia didn't know whether to laugh or cry. "Is that why you've been avoiding me?"

He gulped loudly. "I was scared you'd be mad, and terrified I was going to get a reputation as a record scratcher."

"Mortimer! You know I'm not the kind of person who cares about things like that. In fact, just keep the record."

"I don't want it," he replied. "It's scratched."

She laughed and laid a hand on his shoulder. "Don't you know by now that you and I are friends? No dumb piece of vinyl is ever going to change that."

"I suppose. But not everyone feels that way."

"You mean Byron."

Mortimer nodded feverishly.

"Byron's a sociopath!" Virginia exclaimed. "He totally overreacted when you scratched his Hot Five record, and you don't need to be his personal slave one moment longer. What you did was an accident, but what he's doing to you is a crime."

"That's what my wife says. But what were you talking about before, Virginia? You thought I had something to do with Betty Brown's death?"

"I know you didn't kill her, but— The fact is, Betty Brown had something that belonged to John Coltrane. The person who killed her must have stolen it."

Mortimer's eyes sharpened. "What was it?"

Virginia hesitated. Everyone else had been devastated by the news of the lost tapes, but Mortimer would be suicidal.

"Shoes," she answered, mentally crossing her fingers.

"You're joking! Oh, Virginia—we have to find them."

"I know. That's what I'm trying to do."

"Did you see them? What color were they?"

"Brown," she lied desperately. "Dark brown."

"I bet Coltrane wore them when he played."

"Probably."

"They should go to the Coltrane Cultural Society in Philadelphia. If you find them, I'll write an article about it for my column."

"You'll be the first to know." She sighed. "I'm glad you're not involved in any criminal activities, Mortimer. But this means I need to keep looking for—the shoes."

"Don't let me stop you. What's the plan?"

"I'm going to take the PATH train over to Newark and go to the IJS. Afterward I'll come back here and see the detective in charge of Betty Brown's case."

"Detective Smith?"

Virginia smiled faintly. "Yes. You met him last week, right?"

"He was nice. For a cop."

"Yes, he is," she said thoughtfully. "For a cop."

While Virginia walked Mortimer back to work, they talked about the album he had just bought, which was one of her favorites. As they arrived outside 111 River Street, Mortimer said, "The thing about Coltrane is, he never lets you down."

"Never," Virginia declared.

They smiled at one another.

"Sorry I strong-armed you, Mortimer," she told him.

"And I'm sorry I scratched your record. Good luck with the shoes."

"Thanks. I'll take all the luck I can get."

Robert sat at his desk, chin resting on one hand, staring aimlessly at Tony's wall calendar. The theme was television stars from the sixties, and August's picture featured Sheriff Andy Taylor and Deputy Sheriff Barney Fife. Who looked a bit like Robert and Tony, at least in terms of height.

As usual, the bullpen buzzed with activity. Tony was on the phone and eating his perpetual doughnut, the other detectives were caught up in heated discussions, and traffic noise floated in from the open windows. It was all a blur to Robert, who was aware of only one thing, namely the ticking clock on the wall.

At their meeting that morning, Captain Kelly laid down the law: arrest Nathan Garrideb today, plus get search warrants for Garrideb's house and *Jazz Now*.

Robert convinced Cap to put off the arrest until three o'clock. Cap agreed reluctantly, then warned, "But not a moment later. I need this wrapped up."

After the meeting, Robert filled out the paperwork for the warrants and took a long walk. He headed up Frank Sinatra Drive to the Fourteenth Street Pier. He walked all the way to the end of the pier and spent a few moments at Nathan Garrideb's thinking spot.

Afterward, Robert went down Fourteenth Street and made a left onto Bloomfield to Betty Brown's building. He sat on a stoop across the street and stared at the building a long time. Then he walked over to Washington Street and headed downtown. He even stopped in at Carlo's Bakery and looked at the Oreo cookie cakes.

Robert hoped the walk would bring new insight, but no matter how many times he turned the problem over in his mind, the solution always led back to Nathan Garrideb.

Yet Robert was sure Garrideb wasn't a murderer. These jazz journalists were scholarly types who spent time alone with music and words. People like that were typically harmless; they were caught up in their individual passions, and not particularly interested in the outside world.

Someone like Byron Ffowlkes generally made Robert's job easier. He remembered the Harvard man who murdered his older wife in the nineties. The man had the arrogance of most sociopaths, plus a barely concealed contempt for his fellow humans. Robert could see the type of man

Ffowlkes was, or wasn't, but Ffowlkes definitely didn't murder Betty Brown. A dozen people could attest to that.

"Hey, daydreamer."

Robert looked up. Tony was standing next to his desk, coffee in one hand and doughnut in the other.

"Warrants all sewn up?" Tony asked.

"Yep."

"Still tryin' to work things out?"

"Yep."

"It's a tough one, that's for sure." He took a long sip of coffee. "Well, if you need me, I'll be across the hall at Pedulla's desk."

"What about you?" Robert asked. "Aren't you trying to work it out too?"

"They don't call me Sherlock, do they? Lemme know when you got somethin'."

Tony left the room, and Robert let out a sigh. He looked up at the clock: 2:15.

OK, he thought. You have forty-five minutes. Go back again to square one.

Robert went over the facts meticulously once more. He ended up where he always ended up: Nathan Garrideb. But in his heart, Robert didn't believe it was true.

Something's missing, he thought. Something small.

Absently, he pulled a yellow pad closer and began to doodle. Without realizing it, he wrote VIRGINIA FARRELL.

He stared at the name and bit his lip. What was the point of thinking about Virginia? Everything he did made her so mad.

He tore the sheet of paper off the pad. And then—

Robert leapt out of his seat. "Tony!" he cried out. "Let's go!"

"Where to?" Tony asked.

"*Jazz Now*. Time to arrest Byron Ffowlkes."

When the elevator doors opened on the seventh floor, Robert and Tony leapt out. They turned right and burst through the glass doors into *Jazz Now*'s reception.

Nathan Garrideb was leaning against the counter and talking to Maggie. When he saw the two detectives, he turned gray and took a step back. Robert caught a glimpse of Garrideb's relieved expression as they rushed past him and went down the hallway.

Byron Ffowlkes was standing next to his desk, reading the back of an album cover.

"Greetings, detectives," he said, looking up as they rushed in. "Don't we knock anymore?"

Robert strode over to the desk. Grabbing a yellow pad and a pen, he scrawled JAZZ on the page. Then he tore off the top sheet and lightly shaded a spot on the pad.

As if by magic, the word JAZZ appeared, perfectly clear.

Ffowlkes went pale. He sat down, mouth grim. "Aren't you the clever one."

"Talk," Robert demanded, leaning over the desk and glaring at him. Tony stood close to the door, arms folded and legs spread.

"Since you seem to know so much," Ffowlkes smiled wryly, "it hardly seems necessary."

"A woman has been murdered, and a box of priceless tapes is missing. Talk."

Ffowlkes thought a moment. His color was returning, as was his arrogant demeanor. "When I saw Virginia in the hallway last Tuesday afternoon, I could tell she was extremely excited. Her complexion shows emotion easily." He paused. "Surely you've noticed."

"Go on," Robert prompted.

"I was curious. After Virginia visited Nathan, she passed my office looking even more excited. When Nathan walked by soon afterward appearing just as agitated, I couldn't sit there and twiddle my thumbs."

Robert stared at him coldly.

Ffowlkes waved a hand. "I knew all about Nathan's notes and his hope for a book, so I used an old trick. When I saw what Nathan had written, I could barely believe it."

"Then what?"

"I found Betty Brown's information in Nathan's Rolodex, then I called her using his office phone. I pretended to be Nathan and told her I was coming over to look at the tapes."

"And then?"

"I called an old friend. Whereupon I gave them Betty Brown's address and asked them to pay her a visit." Ffowlkes paused. "They weren't supposed to kill her. That was not even discussed as an option."

Robert slammed his hand down on the desk. "Who?"

"Hello, John," Virginia said as she poked her head into his office.

"Hey!" He looked up from the stack of old letters he was examining and smiled.

"Got anything for me?"

"As a matter of fact, I do." John pointed to a square FedEx package on the corner of his desk.

She jumped for joy. "Oh my God, I'm so excited! How many cassettes are there?"

"I don't know. I figured I'd leave you the pleasure of opening it."

"Like Christmas," Virginia enthused. She set up a gray folding chair next to the desk and brought the box onto her lap. "Thanks, John. I really appreciate this."

"No thanks needed. Just do your best to lift June Christy from the depths of obscurity."

"That's the plan."

"How's everything else?" he asked. "I assume if the tapes had been found, you would have told me."

Virginia's face fell. "There's nothing new to report. I thought things might wrap up earlier today, but it turned out to be a false alarm."

"Too bad. How about that detective, does he have any leads?"

"I don't know. I haven't seen him since Friday."

"He was pretty cool for a policeman."

Virginia gave a little shrug. "I suppose. So where is everybody? I didn't see a soul."

"Mr. Morgenstern took the whole staff to the Dave Brubeck concert in Central Park," John replied. "Squid's driving everyone in his van. They just left."

"Why didn't you go?"

"I have things to catch up on. Plus someone has to hold down the fort in case a stray jazz researcher wanders in."

"Campus is pretty dead too," she remarked. "Even the construction workers next door are gone."

"I like it better when things are nice and quiet. Speaking of which," John said, rising from his seat, "I better leave a note on the reception desk saying to call me back here."

"Can I open up the package?"

"Go ahead. The scissors are in my pencil mug."

John left the room, and Virginia moved over to his seat. She carefully set the stack of letters aside and put the FedEx package in the center of the desk. The scissors were in a Montreal Jazz Festival mug; she took them out and ran the blade across the thick tape.

In her excitement to open the box, Virginia moved the scissors too quickly, and the blade nicked her in the index finger.

"Ouch!" She looked at the cut. Blood. Not a lot, but it was flowing fast.

John's got that Boy Scout spirit, she thought. He must have a first-aid kit or Band Aids.

The desk had three drawers along the right side. Virginia didn't find any Band Aids in the first two drawers, so she pulled open the deep bottom drawer. She rummaged through tea boxes and cookie packages, then moved aside a maroon tin and saw a jar of Hana's Honey.

Virginia frowned. She didn't remember giving this to John. In fact, the only person she had ever given a jar of Hana's Honey was Betty Brown.

Suddenly she remembered Robert's words: if you find the honey, you've probably found the tapes.

Virginia turned and surveyed the small room with its stacks of boxes. They're here, she realized. John's got them, and he's preserving the music by transferring it to CDs. That's why he didn't go see Rex Royal, and that's why he didn't join the rest of the staff at the Brubeck concert.

She stared at the stacks. They looked chaotic, but there had to be a method behind the mess.

John's working on the tapes, Virginia thought, so he needs to keep them accessible. If I were him, I'd put the shoebox in one of the larger boxes, cover it with something inconspicuous, and place a few lighter boxes on top.

She stood up and began rifling through the stacks. When she reached the third stack, a thrill of excitement surged through her. The top boxes were nearly empty. When she opened the next one, she found a pile of *DownBeat* magazines.

Virginia lifted up the magazines and saw a blue plastic bag underneath. She took out the bag and looked inside.

John Coltrane's shoebox.

Virginia drew the box out of the bag. She opened the lid and felt a wave of relief when she saw the tapes. Thank God, they were safe.

Just one little problem. If John had the tapes and the honey, that meant he had murdered Betty Brown. And now Virginia was alone with him in an empty library on an almost deserted campus.

Virginia put the shoebox back in the bag. She covered it with the pile of magazines and restacked the boxes. Then she shut the bottom drawer and sat down again.

Stay calm! she told herself. Don't let him see that you know.

Footsteps. Virginia looked up just as John walked into the room.

"Hey," he said, sitting behind the desk. "Are you OK? Your cheeks are bright red."

"I cut myself." She held up a finger. "Do you have a Band Aid?"

"Always prepared." John reached up to the shelf above his desk and took down a small box. "Shall I?" he asked.

"Go ahead."

Virginia swallowed nervously as John unwrapped the Band Aid and carefully applied it to her finger.

"There!" he announced with a smile. "Good as new."

"Thanks."

"Want me to open it?" John offered. "Since you're injured."

"Sure."

While John wrestled with the FedEx package, Virginia concentrated on taking long, slow breaths.

OK, she thought. In a perfect world, you could get the tapes and leave. In a less perfect but still rather good world, you could slip away without John realizing that you know about the tapes. Then you can call Robert from the lobby.

All Virginia needed to do was get out of the IJS in one piece. Her knapsack and hoodie were on a table in the main room, so she just had to grab them and run out the door.

"Here we go." John set the open package in front of her.

Virginia forced herself to focus. An envelope with John's name lay on top of the tapes. "This is for you," she said, handing him the letter.

He opened the envelope and read quickly. "It's a note from the radio station. You can keep it, just be sure to thank them in the acknowledgments."

"Will do. Well!" she said, trying to sound cheerful. "Guess I better get going."

"Don't you want to hang out a bit? I thought we could listen to one of the tapes together. You know I'm a big Pete Rugolo fan."

"I—I'd love to," Virginia stammered, "but it's been a long day. I need to get back upstate."

"You're not staying in Hoboken tonight?"

"Socks and I have a dentist appointment in Little Mountain tomorrow morning."

John frowned. "The two of you are seeing the dentist together?"

"No." She stood and started repacking the FedEx box. "But Socks is deathly afraid of drills, and she needs someone with her. You know how it is."

"I sure do," John laughed. "Practically every tooth in my mouth has a filling." He started to stand. "I'll walk you to the door."

"That's OK," Virginia replied. "I'll just grab my knapsack and be on my way."

"Call me tomorrow after you've given the tapes a listen."

"I definitely will. Bye!" she called over her shoulder.

As soon as Virginia was out of John's line of sight, she started walking rapidly through the warren of shelves and offices. Go! she told herself. Go, go, go!

Once in the main room, she grabbed her hoodie and, with shaking hands, tucked the FedEx package into her knapsack.

"Virginia."

She looked up. John was standing in front of her, holding a bright-pink portable record player.

Virginia's heart sank as she realized that he was blocking her way to the main exit. It sank further when she understood why John was carrying the record player: he intended to kill her with it.

Robert rushed down the hallway of *Jazz Now*, leaving Ffowlkes in Tony's capable hands.

Suddenly Robert had a horrible thought: he didn't know how to get to the Institute of Jazz Studies! He knew how to drive to Newark of course, but Virginia had directed him when they went to the IJS, and Robert had been so distracted by her that he hardly paid attention.

Before Robert could decide his next move, Mortimer Burns stepped out of the men's room and almost ran into him. Robert grabbed Mortimer by the shoulders. "Do you know how to get to the IJS?" he asked urgently.

"Yes," Mortimer whispered.

"Come with me. It's an emergency."

"I can't go. Byron—"

"Forget him," Robert said sharply. "He's under arrest."

Mortimer's eyes lit up. "Really?"

"Yes. Let's go now, we don't have time to waste."

Once in the car with Mortimer, Robert screeched onto Observer Highway and simultaneously radioed HQ. He told the dispatcher to send officers to *Jazz Now* and to contact Newark for backup at the IJS.

After making the calls, Robert relaxed a bit. Maybe his urgency was overwrought. It was a working day at the library after all, and surely it would be as full as it was on Friday. It wasn't as if Virginia was alone with Upgrove, nor did she suspect him of anything. Robert would meet the Newark officers at the IJS, then they could make the arrest. Upgrove seemed like the type who would go quietly.

Type—what type was Upgrove, after all? Robert could kick himself for being so taken in by him. But it never occurred to Robert that Upgrove was involved, plus Newark seemed so far away from Betty Brown's apartment in Hoboken.

Yet when Robert considered the facts, the timing worked. Ffowlkes called Upgrove at 4:15. After a short conversation, Upgrove left work, retrieved his car, and drove to Hoboken. He arrived in Hoboken around five, then started looking for a parking spot.

Finding parking in Hoboken was notoriously difficult. But what if Upgrove got lucky and found a space close to Betty Brown's apartment?

Maybe he got Joe Pascoe's spot in front of the building. Then he went to Betty Brown's apartment and posed as Nathan Garrideb. But something went wrong, and she wouldn't hand over the tapes. In a blind panic, Upgrove picked up the vase and hit her.

Ffowlkes was probably right. Upgrove hadn't meant to kill Betty Brown, he was simply overcome by greed.

Greed! Yes, that was the clue. Robert remembered Virginia handing over the Louis Armstrong chocolates. Two, she had said, one to eat and one to collect. Upgrove ate the first one immediately, unable to wait. He put aside the second chocolate as if to save it, but then he ate that one too.

He has a sweet tooth, Robert thought, nodding to himself. That's why he took the honey.

But how did Upgrove know Byron Ffowlkes?

"Mortimer," Robert said.

"Yes?"

"Do you know John Upgrove?"

"Is that who we're going to see?"

"Yes. And Virginia too."

"I know John. I go to the Institute pretty frequently for research."

"Decent guy?" Robert asked.

"Yes. Always helpful."

"Do you happen to know if he's friends with Byron Ffowlkes?"

"Friends—no. But they know each other."

"How?"

"I'm not sure," Mortimer said. "But I remember when Byron bought the magazine, I mentioned it to John. He turned pale and said he knew Byron. I asked how, but John didn't say anything more."

"OK."

"I do know John went to graduate school in England, and he was helping some old rich guy archive his jazz collection. John said the man had bootlegs from Coltrane's 1960 European tour with Miles Davis. It was one of the last times Coltrane worked with Miles."

Robert thought a moment. "Did you mention to Virginia or anyone else that John Upgrove knew Ffowlkes?"

"Virginia and I only talk about John Coltrane. I only talk to anybody about John Coltrane."

As they drove over the Pulaski Skyway, Robert took in what Mortimer had said. Ffowlkes must have leverage on Upgrove, most likely something illegal, and as a result Upgrove felt he had to do Ffowlkes' bidding.

If it weren't for the listening session, Ffowlkes probably would have gone to see Betty Brown himself. Or maybe not. Ffowlkes seemed like the type who always got other people to do his dirty work.

"I saw Virginia today," Mortimer said suddenly.

"Really? What time?"

"At one."

"For how long?"

"Maybe forty-five minutes. Then she went to the IJS."

Robert tightened his lips and said nothing.

"Virginia's not in danger, is she?" Mortimer asked quickly.

"I don't think so. I hope not."

Mortimer made an odd scraping noise, as if he were trying to speak.

"You sound like you want to say something," Robert observed.

"Virginia thought I had something to do with Betty Brown's murder."

"Did you?"

Mortimer shook his head vehemently. "No, not at all! I was avoiding Virginia because of something else. I scratched her record. And not any old record, but Coltrane's *Live at the Village Vanguard Again!*"

Robert stayed quiet.

"That's why I was nervous when I spoke to you the other day," Mortimer went on. "I thought that somehow you knew, and I was in trouble."

"Scratching a record," Robert said, "is not a crime."

Mortimer looked at him solemnly. "It is in my world."

"You're off the hook with me. What did Virginia say?"

"She said she would never let a piece of vinyl get in the middle of our friendship. And she told me about the shoes."

"Shoes?"

"John Coltrane's shoes. The ones Betty Brown had that got stolen."

Robert looked at him, puzzled. "You mean the shoebox?"

"With the pair of brown shoes inside. We can't let anything happen to them, Detective! They're a piece of history."

"Right," Robert said slowly. "Of course, the shoes. If all goes well, we might have those back in a little while."

Mortimer glowed. "Really? Can I touch them?"

"Yes," Robert promised. "If we find the shoes, you may touch them."

"That's our exit," Mortimer said, pointing at a sign. "Hurry! Follow those shoes!"

Robert was not in the mood to hear about nonexistent footwear for the rest of the car ride. "Why don't you put on some music?"

"WKCR?"

"Is that jazz?"

Mortimer looked at him as if he were insane. "Of course."

Robert turned on the radio and motioned for Mortimer to flip the dial. Mortimer quickly found his station, and jazz filled the car.

I know this song, Robert thought. He glanced at Mortimer, who was staring at him with a feverish light in his eyes.

"It's Coltrane," Mortimer whispered. "'My Favorite Things.' From the Atlantic album of the same title, catalog number SD-1361. Recorded at the Atlantic Records 56th Street studio in New York between October 21 and 26, 1960. Released March 1961."

"Is that so?" Robert remarked.

"It's a sign. From Coltrane."

"A good sign?"

"The best. We're going to find those shoes."

"**D**on't leave yet." John's voice was calm, almost coaxing. "I want to show you this record player."

Virginia eyed the bright-pink box with the shiny black handle. If I bend down to look at it, she thought, John's going to swing it up and smash me in the face. And if I turn my back on him, he'll hit me over the head, like he did to Betty Brown.

She edged to her left. Whereupon John moved slightly to his left.

After John killed Virginia, then what? He would drag her into one of the empty offices in the construction zone across the hall. When her body was discovered, John would say she left with the Pete Rugolo tapes, and that's the last he saw of her.

Would Robert end up working on the case? And what would Socks wear to Virginia's funeral?

Wait a second! she told herself, shifting a little more to the left, with John again following suit. He's clever, but so are you. Keep your head! Stay calm and make a plan.

Virginia shifted again. Now she was closer to the display windows. She longed to look into the hall and see if anyone else was there, but what was the use? They both knew the floor was empty.

"Actually, I have a stereo," Virginia said, sliding over a little more. "Or rather, Socks does. It's got a nice turntable."

"I know you already have one," John replied smoothly. "It's just that this is really cool. Look closer! It's vintage."

"I might miss my bus," she countered, taking another step. "That would be a shame."

"There are always other buses."

Suddenly Virginia had an idea. One of the oldest tricks in the book, but maybe it would work. She shifted her gaze over John's shoulder and cried out, "Oh, there you are!"

John whirled around to look. Virginia jumped up, her hands darting into the display window to grab Miles Davis' trumpet. She tugged firmly to break the supporting wires, which released the instrument into her hands. With all her might, Virginia swung the trumpet around and hit John on the side of the head.

The blow sent John and the record player crashing to the floor. Virginia hastily set the trumpet on a table, then looked around wildly for a way to prevent John from getting up. She placed three chairs over his prone body, then sat on one and stretched her legs across the other two to hold them down.

Virginia looked at John's head sticking out from under the chairs. His forehead had a thick red welt, and his eyelids were fluttering.

I'll take a moment to catch my breath, she thought, then I'll run over to the wall and pull the fire alarm.

"Virginia."

She looked down at John. "What?" she asked scornfully.

"My head," he moaned. "It hurts."

"Not as bad as Betty Brown's!" Virginia's eyes filled with tears. "How could you do that to her? If only you'd waited! You were the second person I was going to tell."

"I had to have them. I just had to."

"But Betty Brown! 'Dashiki!' We watched *The Mike Douglas Show* clip together so many times."

"I know." John looked tearful as well. "I'm sorry."

Virginia held out a palm. "Don't be sorry. Be careful."

He winced in pain. "It's too late for that now."

"How did you know I knew?"

"When I came back to my office, your face was red and you were acting funny. As soon as you were out the door, I checked the tapes. There was a drop of blood on the top issue of *DownBeat*."

Virginia shook her finger at him. "You were going to kill me with that dumb pink record player!"

"No, not at all! I—I was maybe going to stun you. I wanted to talk to you, I needed to make you see reason."

Virginia heard a noise in the hallway. She looked up and saw Robert, followed by two policemen and Mortimer, all running toward the IJS door.

Was she glad to see them! Although, Virginia thought, looking down at John, I did rather well on my own.

The Newark police agreed to escort John Upgrove to the Hoboken station, and Robert offered to drive Virginia and Mortimer.

Virginia sat in front next to Robert, holding John Coltrane's shoebox firmly on her lap. Mortimer was in the back, leaning over and staring at the box.

No one spoke. Robert was eager to ask Virginia what happened at the IJS, but she was staring out the front window with an unreadable expression.

He decided not to push her. Virginia would be questioned at the station, and it was probably a good idea to let her collect her thoughts.

As Robert focused on the road, his mind wandered back to the scene at the IJS. He knew he would never forget the sight of Virginia sitting trimly on top of the chairs, with John Upgrove pinned underneath. She was truly a courageous woman. Not to mention levelheaded and sensible.

Robert looked over at Virginia. She was crying silently, discreetly wiping away her tears with the back of her hand.

"Here." He passed her a handkerchief.

"Thanks," she sniffed.

"You're upset about John?"

"I thought we were friends!" Virginia burst out. "And that he was a good person. But it turns out John cared more about things than people."

Robert waited for her to continue.

"He wanted to murder me!" she exclaimed. "That record player may not have looked like much, but if he had hit me hard enough . . ." She blew her nose. "John said he just wanted to stun me. But I know the truth. He was ready to kill me."

"But he didn't," Robert said quietly. "You outsmarted him."

Virginia managed a slight smile. "I feel bad about the trumpet. It's a little dented." She gave back the handkerchief. "How did you know to come here?"

Robert told her what he discovered from the pad of paper. Virginia shook her head. "Byron never could keep his hands off other people's property. He has no sense of privacy."

"And a great sense of entitlement," Robert added.

"Where is he now?"

"At the police station. Tony brought him in a while ago."

"I guess Nathan can run the magazine for now." Virginia raised an eyebrow. "I take it he's in the clear?"

"Completely. You were right about him."

"I knew Nathan couldn't kill anyone. But I would have said the same thing about John," she commented sadly.

"He was greedy. That's what did him in."

"I guess I might have seen it if I wasn't so naive."

Robert glanced at her quickly. She was looking back at him and smiling.

"I missed it too," he admitted. "Did you know he had a sweet tooth?"

"Sure," Virginia replied. "That's why I brought him the chocolates."

"Coltrane had a sweet tooth," Mortimer piped up from the back. "His favorite dessert was sweet potato pie."

Virginia turned around to look at Mortimer. "Which is one of the reasons he had so many dental problems."

"As well as blowing on his horn twenty-four hours a day."

Robert looked up at the rearview mirror. "Mortimer was a big help. He's the one who directed me to the IJS. He also told me about your conversation today."

"So Mortimer's off the hook as well?" Virginia asked.

"Absolutely."

"If only John had waited!" she sighed. "He was a big part of my plan to save the tapes. Betty Brown died for nothing."

"Maybe so," Robert said slowly. "But despite everything, I think she died in peace. From everything she said in your interview, it was clear she'd been tortured by those tapes for decades. You were able to ease her mind."

"That's true. And I kept my promise," Virginia said, laying a hand on top of the shoebox. "Now they're safe."

"What tapes?" Mortimer asked.

Robert and Virginia exchanged a glance. Then Robert inclined his head.

"The thing is, Mortimer," Virginia said, turning around to look at him. "I have bad news, and I have good news."

"Tell me," he said urgently.

"The bad news is that there are no shoes."

"No shoes!" Mortimer made a gagging noise. "How can that be? Oh! I wanted to touch them so much!"

"The good news is that the box isn't empty. Would you like to see?"

"What's the point?" he asked huffily. "Detective Smith told me there was a pair of shoes, and now my heart is broken."

Virginia passed him the shoebox. "Just look."

Mortimer sighed in exasperation. "I don't see why—"

"Open it."

Virginia winked at Robert, then stared straight ahead.

Seconds later, a bizarre subhuman noise issued from the backseat. Robert looked into the rearview mirror and saw Mortimer Burns' face radiating bliss. Only in images of saints had Robert ever seen such pure ecstasy.

"Hey, Virginia," Mortimer whispered. "That's some pair of shoes."

She turned around and grinned. "Not bad, right?"

"Definitely not. Although I did want to see the shoes."

"The shoebox might be Coltrane's. But we can't be sure."

"I can," Mortimer supplied.

"How?" Robert asked.

"I know his shoe size." Mortimer turned the box around until he found the number. "It's Coltrane's," he whispered reverently.

"Nice detective work," Robert remarked.

Mortimer clutched the box and closed his eyes. "This is the happiest moment of my life," he declared. "I will never be happier than this, because it's simply not possible."

Robert looked at Virginia. She was biting her lip and trying not to laugh.

He turned back to his driving. They were on the outskirts of Hoboken, a few minutes from the station. How would they ever wrest the shoebox from Mortimer?

Oh well, Robert thought. We'll cross that bridge when we come to it.

The next few hours passed in a blur for Virginia.

When they walked into the police station, they passed the booking desk and saw Byron Ffowlkes. Dressed entirely in fuchsia, he was proclaiming loudly, "Two Fs. One big, one small."

Next to him was a man wearing an expensive suit and the shiniest pair of shoes Virginia had ever seen. Undoubtedly his lawyer.

"What's going to happen to him?" she asked Robert.

"He'll get out of it. His kind always does."

Robert put Virginia in a back room and said someone would be in shortly to take her statement. He asked if she wanted tea, and she nodded eagerly.

A few minutes later, a police officer came in with a cup of tea and two packets of sugar.

"So you're the heroine," the officer said as he handed over the cup. "Rumor has it you caught a murderer with a trumpet."

"Miles Davis' trumpet," Virginia replied with a weak smile.

"Nice work. People like you make our job easy."

Detective Oliveto came in next. At first he was all business, turning on a tape recorder and firing off a series of rapid questions for a good thirty minutes. When they finished, he leaned back in his chair and nodded approvingly.

"You done good," he said. "Nice piece of work, spottin' that jar of honey in Upgrove's desk."

"Thanks. But it was only by chance."

"This whole case has been one accident from start to finish. I'm sure glad to see the backside of it. But I'll tell you, I was convinced it was your buddy Nathan Garrideb."

"I knew it wasn't."

"So I heard," Detective Oliveto grinned.

"What's happening with John?"

"Robert's with him now."

"I wonder if he's confessed."

Detective Oliveto shrugged. "It's not the norm, but I suppose I could go check it out. We can toss you a bone after all you've done."

"I'd appreciate that."

He left the room. Virginia rested her head on her arms. What a long day! It felt like it would never end.

About fifteen minutes later, Detective Oliveto came back with a fresh cup of tea.

"Thanks, Detective," she said as she took the hot cup.

"Call me Tony."

"OK." Virginia took a sip. "What's going on?"

"Your buddy John is singin' like a canary. Turns out he knew Ffowlkes in England. Mr. Upgrove found himself in a little mess with black-market bootlegs, and Ffowlkes got him out of trouble."

Virginia nodded thoughtfully. "I knew John had been in the UK, but I never made the connection."

"Ffowlkes has been blackmailing him ever since, which is why he called Upgrove and told him to get the tapes from Betty Brown. They wanted to make copies for themselves, then sell the originals to a rich collector."

"So that was their plan," she mused.

"Here's another little fact," Tony said. "Ffowlkes ain't even English. He's Welsh. Apparently when he came to America, he thought that would be more impressive."

Virginia shook her head. "One lie after another. And what did John say about Betty Brown?"

Tony shook his head. "Damn shame. I guess Ffowlkes put on some phony American accent when he called her, but when Upgrove showed up, she could tell it wasn't the same person."

"Betty Brown loved music," Virginia said sadly. "She had a good ear."

"Too good, unfortunately. She confronted him, then at one point she turned her back, and that's when he struck her with the vase. Took the tapes, and in some oddball afterthought, helped himself to the honey as well."

Virginia's face fell. "Poor Betty Brown."

"The good news is, you're all done. Plus you've got a visitor."

Socks! Virginia had called her from the IJS, and Socks said Dr. Bundle would drive her to Hoboken at once.

"She your ride home?" Tony asked.

"No. A friend dropped her off."

"If you don't mind hangin' out a bit, maybe we can arrange some transportation for you ladies."

"That would be great," Virginia said with relief. "I don't think I'm up to the bus right now."

"No problem." Tony rose from his seat. "We Hoboken cops aim to please. Come on, let's get you outta here."

He led Virginia into a windowless corridor. Socks, resplendent in an oversized white sun hat and sleeveless floor-length mauve dress, was talking eagerly with Nathan and Mortimer.

"Socks!" Virginia called out.

"There she is!" Socks cried, rising to hug her. "Thank God that evil oaf didn't hurt you!"

"He came pretty close. Hi, Nathan."

"Hey," he said, giving her a hug. "Nice work."

"Did Mortimer call you?"

"Actually, Detective Smith did. He needed me to bring Alice Coltrane's and T. S. Monk's numbers so he could contact them."

"What did they say?" Virginia asked.

"He spoke to Alice Coltrane first. She's in California, but she's going to get a plane out here tomorrow. T. S. Monk is teaching a music class in Harlem this evening, but he's coming as soon as it's over. Detective Smith asked me to wait here for him, which I'm happy to do."

"I'm waiting too," Mortimer said eagerly. "I want to see the tapes again. I need to touch them."

Socks raised an eyebrow at Virginia. "Mortimer has been keeping us entertained with stories about your high jinks this afternoon."

"They took my statement," Mortimer offered. "I told them all about Byron."

"Did you see him?" Virginia asked.

"Only for a moment," Socks replied. "It looks like he'll be spending the night in jail. Fortunately, prison jumpsuits are all one color, so he won't be breaking his fashion code."

"Byron has a bail hearing tomorrow morning," Nathan added. "Judging by his lawyer, he'll be walking out the door."

"Maybe a night in jail will humble him a little," Virginia reflected.

"Doubtful," Socks said. "So, are you finished here? Should we start to think about going home?"

"Actually, Tony offered to find us a ride."

"Did he? Let's see what he comes up with."

They chatted a while longer, Mortimer waxing so enthusiastic about the tapes that Socks was compelled to check his pulse to make sure he wasn't in heart-attack range.

A door opened, and Robert came down the hallway. Suddenly Virginia felt shy, her cheeks reddening slightly.

He kneeled in front of her. "How are you doing?"

"Better," she said softly. "It's nice having my friends here."

"We're pretty much wrapped up. Upgrove and Ffowlkes are in the cells, and another officer is going to speak to T. S. Monk when he gets here."

"Will you give him the tapes?" Virginia asked.

"At the moment they're evidence, but I thought he might want to have a look at them."

"That's mighty organic of you."

Robert smiled. "If you like, Tony and I can take you and Socks home."

"That would be great."

"We'll come get you in about ten minutes."

Robert left. Socks turned to Virginia, her eyes twinkling. She opened her mouth to speak.

Virginia lifted a finger. "Not a word, Socks. Don't utter a single sound."

By the time the car hit Route 17, Virginia was fast asleep.

When she opened her eyes, Robert was just pulling into their driveway. Socks had fallen asleep as well, and for reasons unknown, Tony was now wearing her sun hat.

As they walked into the cozy cabin, Virginia's whole body relaxed. Home at last! She took off her shoes and curled up on one of the purple couches. Socks settled Robert and Tony on the other couch, offering them tea.

Virginia looked at the stereo, then at Socks.

"Very well," Socks relented. "Because you caught a murderer and recovered priceless tapes, you may play whatever you like."

Virginia went over to her CD collection and chose *Something Cool*. Socks, who was standing behind the couch, pointed at Robert and made wild throat-slashing gestures. Virginia knew what Socks was trying to say: Robert would think the music was maudlin and decide Virginia was not for him.

I don't care, she thought defiantly. This is what I like to listen to. She put on the CD, and June Christy's velvety voice filled the room.

"I don't know about the rest of you," Tony said, putting his hands behind his head and stretching out his legs, "but I sure am hungry. You got any decent restaurants up here?"

Socks widened her eyes. "V!" she exclaimed. "It's time for the karaoke diner."

"Oh!" Virginia glanced at Robert hopefully. "It's a wonderful place. But it's about twenty minutes away."

"That's OK," he said, smiling at her. "If that's where you want to go, we'll go there."

"Do you sing karaoke?"

"No."

"Do you like to watch other people sing karaoke?"

"Sure."

"You'll love it."

"Virginia," Socks said. "It's been a long day. Perhaps you'd like to change?"

"Oh, I don't need— Actually," Virginia reconsidered. "That's a good idea. I'll be right back."

She went into her room and examined her closet. Now what? she wondered.

The door opened, and Socks walked in. Without a word, she marched over to the closet and rifled through Virginia's clothes. After a quick search, she pulled out a white peasant blouse that Virginia had forgotten about, along with a long-ignored pair of black satin pants. Socks handed Virginia the clothes, raised her eyebrows, and left the room.

Good old Socks, Virginia thought as she changed. How would I ever manage without her?

A moment later, Socks opened the door again and tossed a pair of dark-green drop earrings onto the bed.

When Virginia emerged from her room, she found Socks and Tony standing in front of the *Dashiki* cover and discussing the musicians' outfits. Robert was sitting on the couch drinking tea, and Virginia sat down next to him. He looked over at her warmly.

"Ready?" he asked.

"Very. I'm hungry." She paused. "What do you think of the music?"

"I like it. She reminds me of Frank Sinatra."

Virginia's eyes lit up. "June Christy was a big admirer of Sinatra and his music. That's an astute comment, Detective Smith."

Robert smiled at her, and Virginia gazed at him thoughtfully. Maybe he wasn't so hopeless after all.

The Toad Demento Diner was a charming one-story building nestled deep in the heart of the Catskills. Virginia explained to Robert that the diner had been opened by hippies in the early seventies. An enterprising Greek couple bought the diner in the nineties and installed a small stage and karaoke machine.

True to his word, Robert wasn't onstage singing. That was something he could never imagine doing, not in his wildest dreams. Instead he watched with amusement as the others took turns with great gusto, occasionally stopping to dig into the spread of food covering their table.

At one point, Robert and Tony were sitting by themselves. Tony was glowing from a heartfelt rendition of "My Way," while Virginia and Socks were on stage belting out an off-key "I Will Survive."

"These ladies sure are a lot of fun," Tony commented, biting into his hamburger. "Think we can sleep at their place tonight?"

"Tony. No."

"Just askin'. Never mind, I gotta be home tomorrow. My cousin in Bloomfield just had twins, I need to pop by the hospital."

"It already is tomorrow," Robert observed.

"Look at you, Mr. Straight-Laced, out all night! This is what I like to see." He eyed Robert proudly. "Nice work with the redhead, by the way. You and her get along gangbusters."

"You think?"

"Uncle Tony knows!"

Virginia and Socks finished their song and dropped into the booth laughing. Virginia looked flushed and happy as she picked up her milkshake and took a long sip.

"We have competition," Socks said. "That couple over there just booted us out. So!" She raised her glass of iced tea. "I propose a toast. To Virginia and me, for avenging Betty Brown's wrongful death."

"You two?" Tony snorted as they all clinked glasses. "Gee, I thought me and Robert might have had somethin' to do with it."

"You were tangential."

"Oh yeah?" Tony retorted. "I didn't see you show up with a pair of handcuffs."

"If I hadn't given Virginia that jar of honey," Socks countered, "we never would have solved the case."

"Don't take so much credit! You didn't give Betty Brown that honey thinkin' it would help catch her murderer."

"Of course not. But it certainly worked out that way."

Tony rolled his eyes. "Ha-na. What kind of name is that?"

"You pronounce it 'Hannah,' like the woman's name. And for your information, it means 'happiness' in Arabic."

"She your boss?"

Socks shrugged. "I work for her on occasion."

"So you draw on stickers for a livin'?"

"Is that all right with you?"

"Just seems like an odd way for an adult to make ends meet."

"At least I don't carry a gun."

"Oh!" Tony clutched his chest. "Your insult has mortally wounded me."

"You don't really need a weapon," Socks went on. "Virginia and I have proven that it's possible to catch a murderer without firearms."

"That's right," Robert joined in. "All you need is a trumpet and a few chairs."

"That's my Virginia," Socks said, patting her hand. "Smart and sensible. But I must admit, I always knew there was something squiffy about that John Upgrove."

"How?" Virginia asked. "You never met him."

"I didn't need to. The fact is, there he was working closely with a woman of subtle beauty, and he didn't once make a move on you."

Virginia rolled her eyes.

"Undone by a jar of honey," Socks pondered. "It's all quite karmic. He's going to come back in his next life as Winnie the Pooh."

Again Robert felt puzzled. Flippant, he thought. Very flippant.

"Maybe he'll come back as a bee and sting you," Tony suggested.

"Or maybe," Socks replied, "he'll—"

But she never finished her sentence, because her hand gesture knocked over a bottle of ketchup, which landed in the middle of Virginia's onion rings.

"You know, Mittens," Tony said, plucking out the ketchup bottle and wiping it off, "you're kinda clumsy. I like that in a lady."

"My name is not Mittens. My name is Socks."

"But that's not your real name. Come on, cough it up. What're you hidin'?"

Socks took a deep breath. "Since you insist on knowing, I'll tell you. My name is Gertrude Griselda McManus."

Tony whistled. "Scottish."

"Through and through." Socks plucked a French fry from Tony's plate. "They called me Gigi at school."

Virginia's eyes lit up. "Like Gigi Gryce."

"Yes," Socks sighed. "I'm afraid so. At home my nickname was Socks. My mother used to make me wear gray socks over my elbows to keep me from hurting myself when I banged into things."

"Where'd you grow up?" Tony asked.

"New Jersey."

"A Jersey girl!" he exclaimed. "Where?"

"Cape May."

"You call that Jersey? That's a country club. You wanna talk about New Jersey, talk about Hoboken."

"I don't, actually, want to talk about New Jersey."

Tony raised an eyebrow. "So do we call you Gigi?"

"Call me Gigi and I'll slit your throat. Socks works just fine." She exhaled in annoyance. "Or it was, until the Clintons came along in the nineties with that damn cat. By then it was too late, I'd run out of names."

"Hey," Tony said eagerly. "That couple finally sat down. Whaddya say we find a duet?"

"You're on."

Alone with Robert, Virginia felt shy. She took a sip of her milkshake and glanced over at him.

He was looking at her. "Everything OK?" he asked. "You've had quite a day."

"I'm fine," she replied. "Still in a bit of shock, but a good night's sleep will cure that."

Robert checked his watch. "I'm afraid we're keeping you out late."

"Oh no!" Virginia protested. "This is exactly what I need. It's such a treat to be here; we only come on special occasions."

The strains of "I Got You Babe" rose up from the stage, and Socks and Tony stepped up to the mikes. Virginia caught Robert's eye, and they both laughed.

"How did Socks' hat get on Tony's head during the ride home?" she asked.

"You were lucky to sleep through it."

"I was fortunate in a lot of ways today," she remarked quietly. "Oh well. It's good to have all the loose ends wrapped up."

"Actually," Robert said, "I still have a question for you. But I'm afraid you'll get angry."

"I won't."

"I've heard that before."

Virginia laughed. "Really. I promise."

"The first night we met, when I asked about your interview with Betty Brown? I felt there was more you weren't telling me."

"You're right," Virginia answered promptly. "I didn't tell you everything."

"Can you tell me now?"

She shook her head no. "Betty Brown confided something to me, and I promised never to tell anyone. I think it's OK for me to say that much."

Robert watched her closely. "This secret. Was it about—"

Virginia held up a hand to stop him. "I swear it has nothing to do with the Five Spot tapes or Betty Brown's murder."

Robert stared at her. "You're right," he said finally. "Don't tell me, and don't tell anyone. You should keep your promise."

"I'm glad you understand."

The waitress came over and set down an assortment of doughnuts on a large plate.

Robert looked at her helplessly. "We didn't order these."

"Your friend asked for them before he started singing," the waitress replied. "Enjoy! They're fresh."

"Ooh!" Virginia picked up a doughnut oozing with chocolate cream. "My favorite. Will you split it with me?"

"I don't eat doughnuts."

"Why? Don't you like them?"

"I love them."

"But you don't eat them?"

"Right."

Virginia cut the doughnut in half and handed a piece to Robert. "If you love them," she stated, "you should eat them."

She watched as Robert stared at the doughnut, then took a tentative bite.

"Good?" she asked.

"Very," he answered.

Virginia picked up her milkshake and looked over at the karaoke stage. Tony was still singing, but Socks was laughing so hard she was practically doubled over.

"Too bad there's no June Christy karaoke," Virginia murmured wistfully.

"Yes, too bad," Robert agreed.

"Her real name was Shirley Luster."

"Really." He bit his lip, trying not to laugh. "Virginia, do you ever think about anything other than jazz?"

She wrinkled her nose. "What else would I think about?"

Now Robert really did laugh. "I don't know," he said. "Diners, for instance. We're sitting in one."

"Diners! Is that what you think about?"

"No. Not particularly."

Robert's smile faded. He took his coffee spoon and started tapping it on the saucer.

"You know, Virginia, if you wanted some time, we could do something together. Go out, or something. Dinner or music. Or dinner and music." He coughed. "Soon. If you want."

"OK," she said casually. "Sounds good."

Virginia turned her head and glanced out the window. Not because there was anything to look at, but because she didn't want Robert to see that she was smiling.

THE END

Afterword

I began this novel in March 2004 and completed it by spring 2006. At that point, I shared the book with several people to get their feedback. One of my readers told a jazz musician they knew about my story, and he responded, "Oh, they found those tapes."

When my friend repeated this to me, I had what was probably the most selfish moment of my entire life. I thought, "Oh no! What's going to happen now with my novel?"

Turns out the musician wasn't referring to the Five Spot tapes, which as of this writing have still not been found. He was talking about one of the two great jazz discoveries of the decade (the other being bassist Henry Grimes in 2002): Larry Appelbaum's unearthing of the 1957 Thelonious Monk–John Coltrane Carnegie Hall concert in the vaults of the Library of Congress.

Ironically, before I started *Dashiki*, I had called Larry in 2003 to ask what kind of tape recorder Naima Coltrane might have used, and what the tapes would look like. Congratulations to Larry for this great discovery, and for bringing such a precious recording to light.

As for what Larry's find meant for *Dashiki*, I debated whether to add the information to the book. Finally, I decided to mention it in this afterword and leave the novel as is. Since Betty Brown told Virginia about the Five Spot tapes a year before the Carnegie Hall recording was found in 2004, I felt that the plot of *Dashiki* still held up.

The good news for readers is that if you would like to listen to some rediscovered Monk–Coltrane recordings, check out *Thelonious Monk Quartet with John Coltrane at Carnegie Hall* (Blue Note, 2005).

I should mention that this is the second edition of *Dashiki*. The plot remains the same as the original, but otherwise I have shortened chapters, broken up long paragraphs, and tightened the language throughout.

The novel received positive feedback in its first incarnation, but it never broke through as I had hoped. Perhaps things will go better this time around. In any case, it was a pleasure to work on *Dashiki* once more.

Acknowledgments

Many people helped me with the first and second editions of this book, in both direct and indirect ways. I'd like to thank:

Perry Robinson. Jazz mentor extraordinaire.

Laurence Donohue-Greene and Andrey Henkin. For encouragement, opportunity, and friendship.

Michael Ricci and the editors at AllAboutJazz.com. For an education in jazz journalism, and for providing an essential forum for jazz musicians and listeners.

Chris May. For enthusiastically reading and reviewing the first edition of this book, as well as permission to use his quote on the back cover. Sadly, Chris passed away in November 2024, so I won't be able to send him a copy of this new edition as planned, but it feels good that he's part of this update.

Flora Sugarman. For reading the second edition, assisting with cultural sensitivity, and pointing out several logical discrepancies.

Henry Chen. For consistently amazing artwork and cover design.

Carol Binkowski. For reading the second edition and providing a lovely cover quote, and for our ongoing conversations about the writing life.

Brian Cassidy and W. Todd Levinson. For their fabulous song "D'sheeki," which provided enormous inspiration. Listen to the song at https://www.reverbnation.com/yearofthetigerflyingcarpetproductions

Uwe Stender, TriadaUS Literary Agency. For his unwavering support of this book and his insightful editorial suggestions for the first edition, which included changing the title from *The Promise* to *Dashiki*.

Michael Fitzgerald. Jazz educator and author of the excellent biography *Rat Race Blues: The Musical Life of Gigi Gryce*, for information on jazz record labels in the sixties.

The late Elvin Jones. The most royal drummer of them all.

Larry Appelbaum. For information on old recording devices, and for proving that truth is indeed stranger than fiction.

The Woodstock Library and its indefatigable staff. For their support, including special orders of Nancy Drew mysteries, and for providing free Internet access and computers for the first drafts of this book. Thanks also to the Phoenicia Library for their computers and support.

The Hoboken Police Department. For graciously answering questions about their procedures and daily life.

The Institute of Jazz Studies at Rutgers University. For providing a (safe!) place for jazz scholars and jazz history.

Will O'Neil. For lending his laptop and giving the first edition of the book a close, enthusiastic reading.

Written Word Media. For sound advice and encouragement.

The Kiwi Brethren. For reading an early draft of the book. Special thanks to Geoff Moore for careful proofreading and reining in the semicolons.

Susanna Yurick. For suggesting I read the Dalziel and Pascoe series.

Hope Tarullo and Kasey Jueds. For overall encouragement about writing and the creative process.

Joy Chute. My beloved writing teacher from Barnard College. She died in 1986, but continues to inspire me today.

Agatha Christie, Sir Arthur Conan Doyle, and "Carolyn Keene". For their wonderful characters and stories, which have provided me with enormous pleasure throughout my life.

Finally, thank you to jazz musicians, jazz journalists, and jazz fans everywhere, for doing your part to keep this wonderful music alive.

Stay in Touch

Thank you so much for taking the time to read my book!

If you enjoyed *Dashiki*, please consider leaving a review on one of the many available platforms, especially Amazon, Goodreads, and BookBub.

You can contact me at florencewetzel@yahoo.com. I'm on Facebook as Florence Wetzel, and Instagram as @florencewetzel108. Feel free to follow my BookBub author page.

If you would like to learn about my new releases, use the following link to join my email list: https://florencewetzel.com/list

Happy reading!

Printed in Great Britain
by Amazon